Get a Room

Casey Dembowski

Get a Room
Red Adept Publishing, LLC
104 Bugenfield Court
Garner, NC 27529
https://RedAdeptPublishing.com/

This is a work of fiction. Names, characters, places, and incidents either are the product of the author's imagination or are used fictitiously, and any resemblance to locales, events, business establishments, or actual persons—living or dead—is entirely coincidental.

For Hailey – Dream big, princess

Chapter 1
Sarah

"I want you out of this house!" Tyler tossed another armful of Sarah's clothes into a box, followed by the stack of books by the bed and the contents of her nightstand drawers.

This wasn't going well. Sarah had known her rejection wouldn't be met with cheers, but still, she hadn't quite expected this meltdown. Tyler was a grown man after all. A successful, well-coiffed doctor to be exact. Men of his stature didn't throw tantrums—and this was definitely a tantrum.

Her stomach roiled, and an uncomfortable feeling worked its way up her spine. "Tyler, would you just stop for a minute?"

The shock from her not-fiancé's reaction was wearing off. The panic she'd felt at his proposal—and the complete shattering of any connection they might have had—were coming to the forefront. Hurt inched across her body and seized her heart in a vise grip. But his reaction was even more proof of why she couldn't marry this man. Clearly, she didn't know him. Tyler rarely got angry, and he'd never flown off the handle like this before. At least not around her. He had a reputation at the hospital for behaving like that, but in the year she'd been with him, she'd never seen evidence to support the rumors.

The closet door swung open, and another pile of clothes went into the container. Sarah wasn't even sure where Tyler had found this box—she'd painstakingly broken down each empty moving box as she'd unpacked weeks ago, and the rest were still stacked in the den, waiting for Tyler to find space for her things among his.

She pushed the thought aside as a more urgent question came to mind: *Where am I going to go?*

"I want you out tonight," he said.

That much was already clear. Perhaps her rejection of his proposal could have been handled with more care. But it had been so shocking. And she hadn't said no—she'd just said, "Not yet." They'd lived together for barely two months and had literally *never* spoken about marriage. Yes, he was thirty-five and successful and set up to settle down, but at twenty-six, she wasn't any of those things. She was building her career and would rather dance the night away with her best friend than play house—something she'd told him more than once. She'd never signed up for marriage.

Tyler was the one who'd kept changing the rules. First, they'd been a fun fling, and who didn't want a fling with the hot doctor who spent his free time helping at a nonprofit for local kids? But then he wanted to be exclusive. She said yes because it wasn't like she was sleeping with anyone else. And yes, they *had* fallen in love, and when he wanted her to move in, she'd acquiesced because she spent most of her nights there anyway and rents in Philadelphia were expensive. Not to mention, working at a nonprofit didn't exactly line her bank account with dollar bills.

"Tyler," she said again, reaching into the growing pile and grabbing her Rothy's shoes—a splurge that had left her eating frozen food for a month. "Can we just talk about this?"

He paused midway through dumping the rest of her shoe rack into the box, and she wondered how exactly he expected her to carry this oversized and overweight dismissal. "Talk about what, Sarah? How you *don't* want to marry me?"

Fine, maybe she should have seen this coming. But she hadn't. Honestly. When she'd gotten home from work that day, she'd expected a sweet, romantic surprise, maybe a dinner. Maybe in Tyler's world, that was what he'd given her. But to Sarah, the ring had looked like a weight she wasn't willing to bear.

"I said, 'Not yet.' That's not 'No.'"

"Might as well have been no." Tyler pulled her Binghamton University duffel bag out of the closet and held it out. "Get your shit out of my house."

"Can you stop acting like an asshole for two seconds?"

"What I don't get…"

Apparently not.

"Is what you think is better out there than me? I'm a freaking surgeon. I open doors for you. I keep you living comfortably instead of in the dumps you can afford with your pittance of a salary." He motioned to himself, running a hand down the length of his body. "It doesn't get better than this. And you are going to regret this moment when you're back to the pathetic life you lived before."

She wanted to vomit. Tyler had said things like this before but in teasing ways, with a soft voice and a kiss to her temple. She'd brushed it off, but now she saw what it was. He'd been constantly gaslighting her into making decisions because he was Dr. Tyler Ackerman and she'd never do better. How had she ever considered herself in love with this egomaniac?

Straightening her back, Sarah stretched to her full height, all five feet, four inches. She still had to look up at Tyler, but cowering before this asshat was not an option. "Those are some strong opinions about someone you wanted to marry ten minutes ago."

She picked up the little black dress he'd shoved into the box and folded it before placing the dress in her duffel. She followed it with her flats before surveying the room. She grabbed her Fitbit off the dresser, followed by her iPad and slippers. With each item she put in the bag, she felt him bristle, a reaction that only made her move slowly.

"You're right," he practically growled.

A brute. Tyler was a brute, just like everyone at the hospital had said. *Wow.*

"I'm glad you said no. Marrying you would've been the biggest mistake of my life. So thanks, I guess." He shoved past her and clomped out of the room.

She listened to him make his way through the house to the kitchen, fish his keys out of the tray on the counter, slip his coat on, and grumble at his phone, which was pinging the obnoxious chimes he'd set as a page from work.

"I have to go to the hospital," he shouted. "When I get back, I want you and your shit gone."

She glanced at half her life thrown carelessly into a box. What a night. The clothes could wait. Tyler would be at the hospital for a few hours at least. The only upside was that she hadn't unpacked completely—a fact which, two months in, should have spoken volumes. At least that would make getting out of here easier, assuming she could muscle everything into her car.

Sarah walked through the house, taking it in, letting it go. Every inch of her ached from the shock of the last hour. Her head throbbed. She wrapped her arms around herself in lieu of curling into a ball. Their life hadn't been perfect, and she'd never considered it permanent, but she wasn't ready to say goodbye.

Then you should've said yes. She shook that thought from her mind. Accepting a marriage proposal from someone she didn't want to marry was even worse than turning him down. At least she'd been honest.

Candles still burned in the dining room, and there were flowers and rose petals everywhere. Gourmet meals waited, hidden beneath silver covers. *Only Tyler.* He would have to clean up the evidence of his proposal gone wrong later—a small but heartening consolation.

She took a sip of the champagne and nibbled at the bread in the middle of the table. It was time to get her shit together. She needed to organize the mess he'd made of her things and then get her hands on some hair dye and somehow fit her life into her Jetta. But first, champagne and this five-star meal.

She pulled the lid off her plate, her stomach grumbling at the scent of perfectly seasoned steak—a food choice that would not fit into her new budget—and topped off her flute. "Happy fucking birthday, Sarah."

Chapter 2

Brian

"This was an awful idea." Brian fingered the polka-dot curtains—big colorful dots, not tame, muted ones. There wasn't a single shade of gray in this whole apartment. He clearly hadn't been thinking straight when he decided to move to Philadelphia and stay with his younger sister. His parents' place hadn't been that bad. Who didn't like sleeping with the threat of being squashed by a treadmill every night?

Too late now. He stripped the bed of the totally not-gender-neutral yellow set that his sister had picked for her guest room and pulled his own navy-blue sheets from his suitcase. Maybe if he unpacked, he would feel more at home in this Technicolor nightmare. He tossed all the pillows off the bed and tugged on his sheets. That was a start. He chucked two pillows at the headboard and followed them onto the bed.

"Oh, I love you," he mumbled against the mattress. It was so plush and bouncy and not the futon he'd been stuck with at his parents' house.

"Am I interrupting?"

He rolled over and sat back against the headboard. "What's up?"

"I just washed those." His sister, Jess, leaned against the doorjamb, her arms crossed, looking, aggrieved, at the yellow sheets bunched into a ball next to his bed. "Special. For you."

Brian was afraid to ask his next question. "What color was on here before I arrived?"

"Lilac." She pointed to the curtains. "Like that one in the corner."

"I know what lilac is, Jess."

"I would never have guessed, with your arsenal of navy."

He rolled his eyes. "There's nothing wrong with blue."

"You're right," Jess said, stepping into the room, dragging a heap of light blue, which she tossed onto the bed unceremoniously. "Here's your comforter. Robin's egg. In case you were wondering about the shade."

"I totally was." Brian cracked a grin. "Thanks for having me, sis."

It was a warmer welcome than he'd gotten at home. His parents were not sad and lonely empty nesters. He'd never seen two people so poorly hide their annoyance at their child's return home, as if it was his fault the company he worked for had folded and a thousand people were applying for the same positions he wanted.

She waved away his thanks. "Between your whining and Mom's nagging, having you move in was my best option."

He glared at her. "I was not whining."

"Oh, Jess," she mimicked, "they turned my room into a fitness center. They don't want me here. Corey is trying to offer me a job. I have to get out of Fairford before I'm stuck here forever."

Okay, so maybe he'd whined a little bit. But it had been warranted. He'd spent the summer in his hometown, a place he actively avoided whenever possible. And in that short time, one of his old high school friends had offered him a position at his company in Fairford. It was a good gig, but there was no way Brian could permanently return home. He couldn't live in that small town in the middle of nowhere with residents who clung to their hang-ups and secrets. He couldn't be whoever he'd been at seventeen for the rest of his life. And that was all Fairford offered him.

"Well, thank you," he said. "I appreciate it, whatever your reasons."

Jess nodded before stepping around his boxes and pulling open the curtains. Light flooded into the small room. He squinted against the onslaught, seeing all the dust and dander she'd put into the air. Great. He'd have to dig out his allergy meds. Technically, he wasn't allergic to cats or dust any more than an average person, according to his doctor. They simply exacerbated his seasonal allergies, which he had three out of four seasons. He'd gotten tested back when he had health insurance and a girlfriend with a cat she loved more than him.

"I have one rule, big brother," Jess said, turning away from the window, which had a view of the building next door and a similar curtained window.

"And what's that?" He grimaced, not liking where this was going.

"No wallowing. It's been almost a year since the breakup." Her tone softened for a moment, but when he looked again, her hands were on her hips, and her lips were a thin line of disapproval. "I won't have you bitching at me every time *Talented* comes in the mail."

Right, because his sister was the only person in the world who still got print magazines on subscription. Even ones filled with articles written by his ex. Talk about the shock of his life—he'd gone to peruse an article about the Lumineers at the coffee cart one morning and had seen Hannah Abbott-Thorne under the headline in *Talented*. It was like a kick to the groin. After losing his job at the beginning of May and still being unemployed on the Fourth of July, he'd had no choice but to get out of the city to save his sanity—and his checking account. But as his sister had put it, she shouldn't have to suffer because he couldn't keep a girlfriend. As if he had a choice in the matter. His options had literally been to either marry Hannah when he wasn't ready or watch her marry another guy. *Rock, meet hard place.*

"Got it, no wallowing," Brian said.

"Good. Then I think we'll get along just fine. I ordered Chinese food—you still like General Tso's, right?" It wasn't actually a question, and she turned away before he even had a chance to reply. Fortunately, his Chinese food preferences hadn't changed much since high school.

Jess stopped in the doorway, and Brian waited for her inevitable exit line. Instead, she bent down and scooped up a gray ball of fur. The cat's yellow eyes fixed on him, and it hissed. His sister nuzzled her nose into its fur, murmuring words he couldn't make out.

She glanced up at him with an evil glint in her eye. "If you're mean to my cat, your ass will be on the curb so fast you won't know how you got there."

He stood up and pulled the comforter flat against the mattress. Resisting the urge to tuck it in, he followed her out into the living room. "I would never dream of being mean to Hades."

"That's not his name."

"Right, Lucifer."

"Wrong side of heaven." She glared at him, and he laughed in an attempt to walk back his teasing. His sister was almost as serious about her cat as his ex-girlfriend had been about hers.

He reached out a hand and scratched the furball's head. "As long as Chuck stays out of my room, we'll be all good. Won't we, boy?"

They sat down to dinner a few minutes later. His sister chattered on about her job—she worked in accounting for a major multinational company—and their parents and her friends. He half listened, his mind scrolling through the list of things he needed to do. *Unpack, get a part-time job, buy a nice-fitting suit, interview for a full-time job, figure out my next move—move back to New York? Stay here in Philly? Go somewhere completely new?*

Less logistical and much more immediate needs came next. First, get drunk and not wallow about his current predicament. Second, get laid—it had been far too long. Third, buy noise-canceling headphones to avoid overhearing his sister's "escapades," as she called them. And fourth, install a lock on his bedroom door. See number two for the reason.

"Do you want the last egg roll?" Jess asked, pulling him out of his head.

"And deprive you of breakfast tomorrow? No, but I'll take these." He picked up the bag of egg noodles and a packet of duck sauce.

"So gross."

"Thank you for dinner." He fished out a ten from the meager collection of bills in his wallet. "Will this cover it?"

A banging sounded on the front door. They looked at each other, but neither of them was expecting a guest, it seemed. Jess shrugged and walked over to the door. A smile grew on her face as she peeked through the peephole. She flung open the door, and a young woman stormed in. She brought with her a chemical scent and too many bags. Her eyes were red and puffy. Her hair was brunette on top and pink on the bottom. She jumped into Jess's arms with a "Harrumph" and hung on for dear life.

Brian eyed the woman and the bags and the shock on his sister's face. Whatever this was, he did not like it. Not one bit.

They turned to him after another moment, Jess's eyes wide and her friend's narrowed in a glare. He sat back and crossed his arms, inspecting her from top to bottom. Nothing about this woman seemed different from the last time he'd seen her, two years ago at Christmas—except maybe her hair. It had been bright neon blue on the bottom then.

Jess turned a too-bright smile on him, and her next words dripped with wary sarcasm. "Bri, you know Sarah."

He grimaced at them, unable to bring himself to smile. He dug his fingernails into his arms to keep from saying something snide. As if he could forget the perpetual thorn in his side that was his sister's best friend.

Sarah's eyes narrowed to slits, and her hand went to her hip. "Are you going to sit there like a turd or get the rest of my things, *Bri*?"

Chapter 3
Sarah

Jess stared at her as if she'd lost her mind. Maybe she had. Just a little. But she couldn't help it. Tyler had kicked her to the curb, her life was in shambles, it was her birthday, and she needed pink hair, dammit.

"It's just some wax," Sarah said, pulling her hair over her shoulder and then pushing it back. It was stiff and still reeked. "It'll wash out."

The color had been an impulse. She'd always kept some brightness in her hair—highlights, lowlights, ombré—but for the last few months, she'd just been brunette. Tyler liked it that way. He'd commented more than once on how much he liked her natural color. The first time, it had felt like a genuine compliment. After that, she knew it was a hint. So she'd tried not dying it, and everyone seemed to love it. Approval had poured in from all sides. But honestly, how boring. Her hair was something she could play with—blue here, purple there, a few scary months as a bleached blonde. It was hair. It grew out.

Jess touched the pink strands, her nose wrinkling at the smell or the texture or both. "What brand did you use? Your poor hair."

"The options for pink hair wax are very limited at the local drugstore." Sarah shrugged in an attempt to further hide the fact that it was most definitely not *just* wax. It was wax after the drugstore hair dye had done something unmentionable to her threads. "I'm planning on cutting it anyway."

"You hated having short hair. Don't cut it. Let's..."

"Why don't you dye it the colors of the rainbow?" Brian stood in the doorway, with her things crowding his feet. "You can be Rainbow Fashionista Barbie."

Ugh. Brian.

Somewhere in the recesses of her mind, she'd known that Jess had offered her spare room to her brother for the foreseeable future. The information had grated on her. She still thought of the room as hers after less than two months out of the apartment, and Brian was the last person she wanted taking it over—he would not appreciate her style. And it annoyed her even more that she'd forgotten all about the fact that he would be here. As if being homeless wasn't bad enough, she had to compete with her mortal enemy for a bed that was rightfully hers or fork out money she didn't have for a hotel. Because she was not sleeping on the couch on her birthday.

"Up to speed on our Barbies, are we?" Sarah said. He flushed, and she grinned. She turned back to Jess, running her fingers through her hair. "Not a bad idea, though... Jess?"

Jess shook her head, auburn hair flying across her face at her vehemence. "You know the rules."

Right. One color at a time. Unique but professional. And much healthier for her hair—something she'd learned the hard way after doing too many colors too soon and having her hair start to fall out.

Across the room, the door to the bedroom—her bedroom—slammed. Irritation bubbled under the surface. Brian could be such a dick sometimes... no, *all* the time. And she didn't even know why. All those years ago, he'd taken one look at her ripped jeans and off-the-shoulder band tee and then the blue highlights in his sister's hair, and that was it. His easy smile disappeared, his shoulders set, and dislike radiated off him every time they ran into each other. Which had been often in those early days since they'd all gone to the same college. Jess's parents loved Sarah, which made Brian's distaste all the weirder.

Sarah picked up Chuck and cuddled him close. She rubbed her cheeks against his and scratched behind his ears. The cat purred loudly and licked at her fingers. At least someone missed her. She glanced at the couch—a love seat really. No way was she sleeping there. She would have that bed. Somehow. He couldn't stay in there forever.

"Stop brainstorming ways to piss off my brother," Jess said, picking up their wineglasses.

"But it's, like, one of my best skills."

True fact. From the moment they'd met, one of her goals in life had been to be a perpetual thorn in Brian's side. It was just so much fun, watching his face scrunch up as he got worked up over absolutely nothing. His hands would ball into fists, and he'd turn tail and run to his room, where he'd hide out, grumbling into his gaming headset about girls.

"That's what worries me." Her friend eyed the door as if it might explode off the hinges.

"Come on... this is what we do. He makes snarky comments, and I reply in kind. I look forward to it every Christmas."

"I know you do. That's the problem." Jess rolled her eyes. "How long are you staying?"

Sarah steadied herself before responding. Jess didn't yet understand the extent of her exodus from Tyler's. Or just how big her ask was. "Tyler proposed to me tonight, and I said no, and then he totally freaked out and kicked me to the curb. I'm going to need to be back here indefinitely. Please. Please. Please."

She watched her best friend process the information. Jess's eyes went wide and then narrow and then wide again before settling back on Sarah. "Wow. Did you even breathe in there?"

"Yes." Sarah smiled. "After 'curb.'"

"Right. Okay, well, yes, of course you can stay here. But I only have the one guest room, and I told Brian he could stay as long as he wanted, and I'm not picking between you. And before you suggest it, I love you, but you aren't sleeping with me." Jess placed a hand on her shoulder. "I'm sorry about Tyler, and on your birthday? Birthday proposals are *so* not romantic."

"I know, right? Like, way to make my day all about him."

"Was it a good proposal at least?"

Sarah thought back on the night. "It was very Tyler. Fancy dinner, rose petals, cool jazz."

"So, no."

Sarah grinned. Her bestie was the best. "Yeah, not really. You know me. I'd want to be at Penn's Landing or at the Art Museum after we raced up the Rocky Steps, with my friends and hand-painted signs and glitter bombs."

"Which I would've told him if he'd asked my permission."

"Men."

Jess clasped her hand over Sarah's. "Are you okay? For real?"

Sarah glanced down at her pink strands—what a disaster—and gave her bestie a wan smile. "No, but I will be."

The door to her bedroom—the guest room, she supposed, but she couldn't think of it that way—opened again, and Brian walked out, towel and toiletries in hand. He didn't even turn to look at the two women. Sarah winked at Jess and jumped to her feet as soon as the bathroom door closed. She tugged her Binghamton duffel bag along after her. Jess didn't stop her, but Sarah could feel her exasperation all the way across the apartment.

Rookie move, Bri. Rookie move.

Chapter 4

Brian

Brian walked into the hallway, still towel clad. He felt much better after washing off the sweat that had come from lugging not only his stuff but most of Sarah's—after his sister's imploring look—up a flight of stairs. At least Jess lived in a two-story row house. It could have been worse. His first apartment in New York had been a four-story walk-up with narrow hallways, which had made moving a challenge—and with four guys in one space, there'd been a lot of boxes and furniture going in and out.

The women were nowhere to be found, though music played behind Jess's mostly closed door. At least now they were whispering in private. Maybe that meant he could sneak in some television time since the only TV in the apartment was in the living room. His eyes narrowed as he turned toward his room. The door was open. He'd definitely closed it. If Chuck was on his bed...

No. Freakin'. Way. He stopped dead in the doorway, squinting against the brightness and the monster sitting on his bed. A monster in Sarah's clothing.

He'd known one hundred percent that his sister would let her wayward best friend stay. There'd been a spot for her under the Hawkins Christmas tree every year from the time Sarah was a college freshman until she met that boyfriend of hers. Brian's parents bought her presents—nicer and more on-brand than the ones they bought him. He'd known she would still be here when he got out of the shower, but he hadn't expected her to take up residence in *his* bedroom. Well... he at least thought she'd ask first. But this was totally

Sarah and exactly why he'd never gotten along with her, starting that first Christmas break when she and Jess had outvoted him on everything—from music choices on the ride home to Christmas pie options to his spot on the couch.

"What are you doing?" he asked, gripping the towel around his waist tighter, anger boiling under the surface. She sat there in pajama bottoms and a tank top, painting her toenails, a gross green face mask on her skin. Some emo-ass music played in the background—not Wilderness Weekend, thank God—and she'd changed the sheets back to that noxious yellow.

She looked up at him innocently. "Giving myself a much-deserved pedicure."

He turned toward the chair where he'd left his suitcase open but found it covered in bras. *What the hell?* "Where are my things?"

Because it wasn't just his suitcase. Everything he'd unpacked and set up was gone, and it was like her bags had exploded around the room. There were more bras on top of the dresser, underwear on the floor, and a red pair of pointy ballet flats piled on top of sneakers at the foot of the bed.

"In the living room," she said, not looking up. Her lips pursed as she played with her pinky toe before putting the brush to it—bright pink to match her hair.

"This is my bedroom, Sarah. I don't care what you did to screw up your life, but I'm not sleeping on the couch because you ran off another guy."

She rolled her eyes. "You don't even know what you're talking about. Another guy. And you're one to talk if the stories are true."

His eye twitched. "Regardless, I'm not giving up rights to the bedroom."

"And I'm not moving, so hop in." She patted the spot next to her and raked an invasive gaze across his bare chest then lower. After a skeptical look, her eyes returned to his face. Her lips were set in a small smile. "Or get out."

He clenched his fists so hard his fingernails dug into his palms. The thought of sharing a bed with her was appalling, but to win the round—no, he couldn't even consider it. The guest bed was a full. He barely fit in it alone. All the toxic fumes from her hair and her nails and whatever the hell she had on her face might kill him in his sleep.

He scanned the room again but couldn't find his clothes. Flashbacks to high school pranks circled his mind. He cast a look behind him, spotting the clothes he'd pulled out of his bag on the coffee table. "I'm going to get dressed, but we're not done talking about this."

"Whatever you say, *Bri*." She smiled. "Nice boxers by the way. R2-D2 is my favorite *Star Trek* character."

"*Star Wars*," he corrected automatically before storming out into the living room.

After getting dressed in the bathroom, which barely allowed him to get a leg into his jeans, he returned to the living room. His sheets were balled up on the couch, the comforter in a heap on the floor. It was time to set up the PlayStation and break out *Call of Duty* or lose his sanity. Chuck lay on the far end of the couch, stretched out to his full length. His claws dug into the soft material of his sheets, and Brian chafed.

"Move over," he said, plopping down next to the cat.

Chuck glared, his golden eyes boring into him. The cat hissed and curled back against the arm of the couch. Brian went to pet him, hoping a scratch behind the ears would win the feline over, but withdrew as a clawed paw came at his hand. The cat eyed him distrustfully before curling back up on the couch.

"I know exactly how you feel, Chuck."

BRIAN THREW HIS CONTROLLER onto the couch, giving the screen the finger. He should have set up the Wii. He was in serious need of some *Mario Kart* therapy. The cat leaped back, his claws sinking into the fabric. At least it would match all the other scratch marks in this place.

"Stand down, Chuck. That was nowhere near you."

Another hiss. Great. He was going to be clawed to death in his sleep.

The door to his sister's room opened, and she stepped out, bleary-eyed and yawning. "Why are you still awake? It's, like, three in the morning."

"Can't exactly sleep on this thing." He motioned to the couch with a grimace. "I'm either going to get leg cramps from being curled up all night or the worst bout of pins and needles ever. Which do you think is worse?"

She smiled through her sleepiness. "Pins and needles. Do you want my bed? I fit on the couch."

Yes was practically out of his mouth, but he wouldn't kick his sister out of her own bed in her own apartment. He wasn't that much of an asshole. "I'll probably just camp out on the floor. Make a fort or something. Got any extra pillows?"

"No, but..." Jess grinned and pulled open the hall closet. After shuffling a few things around, she pulled out a sleeping bag. "This should help. We can pick up an air mattress or something next week."

He could not afford to waste money on an air mattress. And neither could his sister. She'd refused rent money, though he planned to sneak her cash where he could. He'd given her a ten for dinner, and she'd thrust it back at him, so he waited till she'd gone to bed then stuck it in her purse. He knew this place kept her tightly budgeted without a paying roommate, and now there were three of them using the water and the electricity and eating the food.

Brian pushed the coffee table out of the way and spread out the comforter and both his sheets before setting the sleeping bag on top of them. He slid in, pulled his pillows down from the couch, and turned back to his sister. "This is great. Thanks."

"Of course," she said, crossing to the bathroom. "I should've thought of it sooner."

When she came out, Brian was tucked in, scrolling through his phone. She stopped at the arm of the couch and leaned into it. "Is this what you expected when you left the city?"

He laughed, and nostalgia for his first years in Manhattan washed over him. "Actually, it's kind of the same. I think this spot on the floor is bigger than the space I had back when I had all those roommates."

She smiled. "That apartment smelled awful."

"No worse than Sarah's hair."

His sister shook her head. "I really wasn't expecting... Well, I'm sure we'll figure something out."

His phone pinged, and he glanced down at the message. There were too many typos and a lot of emojis. He rolled his eyes and pocketed his phone. His friend was offering up his couch for a quarter of his exorbitant rent.

"I'm getting my room back," Brian said.

"Was it really so bad back at home?"

"You mean, is it worth living in a small space with the bane of my existence?"

Jess rolled her eyes. "Yes. That."

"It is." And that was the truth. "I'm sure I'll find a job soon."

He was not sure of that at all. It had been months with no takers. And with experience as a full-stack engineer, he should have been an easy hire. The issue was that so much of his experience was off the books. He'd only been with the start-up for two years before they folded. That didn't open a lot of doors. At least not in New York

City. Everyone needed someone proficient in all aspects of IT, so his options for places to look—Philly, Chicago, St. Louis, Kansas City, Denver—were endless. But he hadn't lived outside the tristate area ever, and his whole life was within a few hundred miles of the city. He wasn't sure he could walk away from that for a life in Indianapolis, flying home once a year maybe.

"I know you'll find a job, big brother." Her words came out on a yawn.

"Good night, Jess."

She crossed to her room, giving him a wave. "Good night."

He turned back to his phone and navigated to his last text from Corey—his friend from home who, at twenty-eight, ran his own company, had an elementary-school-aged daughter, and had just reconnected with the love of his life. He could take the job offer. It would use many of his skills, and it was a sure thing. But at what cost? Brian couldn't imagine a life in Fairford after his years away. Small-town life had never been for him. And he certainly wasn't ready to "find a nice girl and settle down," like his mom had not so subtly hinted at all summer. Hell, he hadn't even kissed anyone in the last eleven months.

He closed his eyes and allowed himself to go back to last year. He pictured Hannah standing in a white dress outside his apartment door, a giant diamond on her left ring finger, giving him back the concert tickets he'd paid triple the price for in a clumsy attempt to show her he loved her. Only a few days before that she'd asked him to be the one to marry her. Brian had briefly considered it, but when she'd proposed they get married for purely practical, need-based reasons, he'd shut her down harshly and lost her in the process. Not his finest moment, but there was nothing quite so demeaning as being proposed to for health insurance. It had seemed a doomed start to a marriage based on an already faltering relationship. And Hannah had known it too. Hence her marrying someone else less than a week after she'd walked out of his apartment for the last time. But that wasn't the whole story—the guy was her friend from college, and they'd had a long-standing marriage pact that said friend decided to initiate, and Hannah had decided to accept after Brian's refusal. Knowing all of that, however, didn't make the breakup any easier. Because no matter the truth, it certainly looked like something uncouth had transpired.

He remembered the letter she'd given him that day, as eloquent as everything Hannah wrote.

Dear Brian, I know what you must be thinking. I'd be thinking it too. You may never believe me, but I swear that I wasn't cheating on you. Whatever you hear in the next days and weeks and months, it's a lie. Will and I had a pact...

And then later toward the end, she'd written, *You deserve to be loved by someone who loves all the things about you. Who understands everything that you are. I was never going to be that person for you, and you couldn't be that person for me.*

He rolled over and grabbed his controller from the couch. One more game, and then maybe he'd be able to sleep.

Chapter 5

Sarah

Sarah watched the ceiling fan spin and spin and spin. She'd been up for twenty minutes but hadn't shaken the disappointment that coursed through her whenever her mind caught up to her current situation. And with that feeling came a healthy dose of worry. Tyler was a major donor for the nonprofit she worked for. Many of the kids Sophie's Wish Factory helped were his patients. She and Tyler had met at last year's donors' gala, when the DJ went off script and made everyone dance with someone they hadn't brought. Sarah braved asking the cute doctor everyone talked about to dance. The rest had apparently been a long series of miscommunications.

Tyler wouldn't pull his donation—of that, she was certain—but that didn't mean he had to give her the credit for obtaining it. This year's confirmation paperwork hadn't officially gone out yet, and all he had to do was change the name on the *development officer* line. By exchanging one name for another, he could make reaching her donation numbers exponentially harder. Her donor list was long, but adding Tyler to it last year had helped a lot. Now that was most likely gone.

But that was a worry for tomorrow, when she would have to own up to the mess she'd made and let her boss know that her relationship with Tyler had ended—assuming he hadn't already sent that particular email. At the moment, she had to figure out how to keep Brian from taking back the bedroom unless she planned to lie in bed all day, every day, for the rest of time. Throwing her underwear and bras around the room had seemed like a good plan, but after a night in this freezing apartment—how quickly she'd forgotten how low Jess kept the thermostat—she had no doubt that Brian would touch anything if it meant he got the bed. She needed a plan B.

Sarah glanced at her phone. It was 7:02. Jess had to still be sleeping because Sarah's text to her had gone unanswered. The living room was quiet.

She tiptoed to the door and opened it a smidge, praying it didn't squeak. No television or voices. Good. She inched closer.

Brian was passed out on the floor with Chuck curled up behind his back. A game controller sat on the floor between the couch and Brian's head.

That could work.

She crept over to the couch. Chuck eyed her but only stretched out along the length of Brian's back. She petted the cat's head, willing him to stay put. *Don't wake up. Don't wake up.* If she went over the back and carefully lay down on the couch, she could grab the controller and not wake the beast. But it was risky. With one misstep, she would fall on him. And Sarah wasn't known for her gracefulness.

Brian rolled onto his back, and she held her breath, but he didn't stir further. His too-long hair fell into his eyes, and sleep softened his features. Gone were the hard lines of the night before. She tried to imagine a time when she'd seen him look so content awake. Oh, he'd be a charmer. She'd die before ever saying it out loud, but with his green eyes and toned body—which she'd seen in all its glory the previous night and now again as he stretched an arm behind him—he was handsome. He wasn't that lanky college boy she'd first met. There were muscles on those arms, and if she squinted, she could detect an ab. Maybe two. And he manscaped, a trait she found increasingly sexy the older she got.

"Brian," she whispered, but he didn't stir.

She was going to have to risk going over the back. Moving as slowly and silently as she could, Sarah threw a leg over the back of the couch. She hoisted herself onto the edge and then paused as Chuck's ears perked. His eyes followed her every move. His tail swished—not a good sign.

"It's okay, Chuck," she whispered, praying the cat wouldn't take off or freak out.

With one last deep breath, Sarah dropped onto the couch cushions. Her feet came dangerously close to Brian's groin, and she quickly tucked them up and then flopped down. For a second, she watched him sleep. She couldn't say why, exactly, but seeing him like this almost made him seem likeable. Pulling her eyes away from him, she reached down to grab the controller.

She knew a second before Brian rolled over again that it was too much commotion for Chuck. He wasn't exactly skittish, but with two new additions to the apartment, he'd done plenty of hissing the day before. Brian's arm came around so that he was practically cradling the controller.

Dammit.

Chuck shot to his feet, claws out, as Brian's back bumped him.

"Chuck, no," she whispered vehemently and reached out as if she could stop the feline. The sudden shift knocked her off balance, and before she could right herself, she fell off the couch and onto Brian.

He groaned at the same time she did, and his eyes popped open. He blinked several times before settling his unfocused gaze on her, confusion coloring his expression. "What's going on?"

"Hi," she said, pulling the controller out from under her back and tossing it onto the couch. "Nice sleeping bag."

He glanced at it, his brow furrowed, but the distraction didn't last. His attention was all on her. "Seriously, how did you get"—he glanced between the couch and the makeshift bed—"there?"

Crap. She hadn't planned on being caught. This was totally fine. She just needed to lean into the situation. She glanced from his bare chest to her tank top, an idea forming. It could work.

Sarah leaned in closer and—*damn*, he smelled good. "Whatever do you mean, *lover*?"

His eyes about fell out of his head. "As if."

"I mean, when we said we'd never speak about it again, I didn't think that meant before we were even unentangled." She chanced putting a hand on his arm.

"Are you drunk?"

She pulled her phone out of her pants pocket, keeping it turned away from him, and sighed. "At least we'll forever have these photos to remember it by."

"We did not sleep together last night—or ever—and you'd better not have taken photos that imply otherwise," he said, reaching for her phone.

She shrugged, even though a small part of her was miffed that he thought she'd actually do that. Not even he deserved to be black-mailed that way. "Maybe I did, maybe I didn't. Give up any claim on my bedroom, and it won't matter."

"You're insane."

"Not at all. That room has been mine for three years. Two hours in it doesn't make it yours." She pretended to scroll through some photos. "And if your sister sees these photos, well, it won't be your apartment at all."

He rolled his eyes. "Jess wouldn't care if I slept with you. She'd probably say it was about time and could we please stop being idiots now."

That sounded like Jess, but Sarah knew better. She stuffed her phone back into her pocket. "Your sister made every single one of us promise to never even look at you in college. I have to swear on my sorority letters before I'm allowed to stay with you at Christmas *every year*. I think she'd do plenty to keep this"—she motioned between them—"from happening. Even kick her big brother to the curb."

His eyes darkened, and she almost thought he was going to agree to her terms, but then he grinned. "It sounds like she'd be more pissed at you than at me."

Sarah swatted away his hand as he grabbed her waist. "Are you willing to risk homelessness on that?"

Without warning, Brian lunged and pinned her arms to the ground. He slung a leg over her, and she gasped at the intimacy and the shock of not-hate that shot through her. *Yes, body, he's attractive. Now, stop it.* There were plenty of men in Philadelphia. She did not need to go after the one sleeping on her living room floor. Not to mention, *ew*, it was Brian.

He smiled wickedly. "Are you?"

"What in the world is going on out here?" They both turned at Jess's voice. "Sarah...?"

He was on top, but of course, Jess would question *her* as if Sarah had put them in this situation. Okay, so she kind of had, but still...

Brian met her gaze in a challenge without moving from his perch on her lap. "So, what's it going to be?"

Oh, the game was totally on. She freed one of her hands and cupped his cheek. "Are you going to tell her, or should I?"

"Tell me what?" Jess's voice was loud and panicky. This might have been a step too far, but there was no going back now.

Brian shoved her hand off his face and shifted into a sitting position next to her. "Nothing, Jess," he said, his tone not quite normal, as he pulled the sleeping bag around him.

"The two of you rolling around on the floor is not nothing."

Sarah cleared her throat. She really hadn't thought this one through. "It's nothing, Jessie. I was just trying to steal his controller."

"Is that some weird euphemism? Because first off, gross, and—"

Sarah pointed at the game controller on the couch. "For leverage for the bedroom."

"Oh." Jess looked between them again.

Sarah saw her friend's moment of disbelief and shifted a bit farther away from Brian.

"Can't you guys, like, switch weeks or something? It doesn't have to be a thing," Jess said.

Brian looked right at Sarah, a question in his gaze. She gave the tiniest shake of her head. His shoulders relaxed a fraction, and he turned to his sister with a placating expression. "You're right. I'm sure we can figure something out. But for now, Sarah can have the bedroom." He sounded physically pained saying those words, and Sarah gave him credit for keeping his expression neutral. "In the meantime, I'll pick up that air mattress we talked about last night."

"With what money?" Jess asked, her voice back to normal but still hesitant. Her eyes swung wildly between Sarah and Brian as if taking in their significant lack of clothes and the situation she'd just seen.

Sarah straightened. Her best friend actually thought she'd sleep with her brother in the living room on the floor. Gross. Not to mention, Sarah had been broken up with Tyler for, like, two minutes. And what kind of birthday present would that be? Filled-out chest or not, this was still Brian, owner of R2-D2 boxer shorts.

"I'll ask Mom," Brian said. "Mom and Dad don't want me back, so I'm sure she'll buy us whatever we need until *Sarah* finds other lodging."

Sarah bristled but didn't say anything. He'd walked back the situation and given her the bedroom—for the day at least. She stood up and smiled at the interloper. "Always the gentleman, Bri."

He offered her his own smile, his eyes spewing all sorts of curses at her. "Well, I try, ma'am."

Chapter 6

Brian

"All right, man, well…" The manager—Brian couldn't believe this *kid* was a manager—looked down at his application again. "We'll call you if anything pops up."

The blow off? Seriously? Brian was so overqualified for this job that it had hurt filling out the application. The pittance of a pay he would get at this job was not worth the hassle of working under Doogie Howser. He'd rather starve or mooch off his parents.

If he could get the word out, he could start fixing computers again, but he wasn't good at marketing or writing or design, and neither was Jess. But a flyer should be easy enough. Sarah could probably help with that—if he remembered correctly, she did outreach and communications as part of her job. But there was no way she would help him without putting him through hell.

His mind shifted to that morning and her warm body underneath him. Blood rushed through him. She'd been so soft. And she smelled flowery despite the undertone of something chemical. And then he gave in to her blackmail that wasn't even blackmail—it was complete self-sabotage, and she walked right into it, and he'd let her win because his stupid penis couldn't handle itself. It had been like a high schooler watching Skinemax for the first time down there.

Fuck. He needed to pull himself together. Sarah was the last person he needed to be attracted to. No. He *wasn't* attracted to her. It was morning, for fuck's sake.

He pulled the door of the store open and walked into the warm September afternoon, glancing around, trying to get a sense of his surroundings. There were plenty of options for work, but he couldn't see himself folding shirts or making burritos. He couldn't see himself selling iPads either, but his options were limited. He needed a job. He'd been working since he was fourteen—mowing lawns, running the tractor down at Mr. Langen's, working one scary summer at the local ice cream shop. In college, he'd done everything from campus safety—seriously, yellow jacket and all—to catering to sitting at the help desk in the computer lab until all hours of the night. After staying home and wading through the application process for the past four months, he felt antsy.

He glanced up at the store in front of him and grimaced—Starbucks. He'd worked at a Starbucks until he was hired at the start-up. It was where he'd scored a date with his ex by flirting over the espresso beans. Where he'd spent many a shift wondering why he ever thought working in food service was a good idea. Brian wasn't exactly the king of sociability. And the smell. He'd burned all the clothes he'd worn there after failing to get the stench of stale coffee out of them. Had it really come to this?

A quick peek at his phone showed no new emails, no job pings, no callbacks.

Damn. He was going to have to work at Starbucks.

Again.

"SO, WE'LL SEE YOU THIS weekend."

Brian shook his new boss's hand. "I appreciate the opportunity."

And he did. He'd applied for a barista role, and this woman, Tasha, had seen his experience and boosted him up to a shift supervisor. Which meant better pay, slightly less time on the floor, and no kid telling him how to work the bar. All in all, this was as good as it was going to get. Unfortunately, getting a job in Philadelphia was most likely going to rob him of the rest of his unemployment benefits. But if he was at Starbucks long enough, he'd get insurance, and hopefully, the tips would be enough to supplement his paycheck. He'd done it once—he could do it again.

Tasha motioned to the bar. "You want a drink before you go?"

He wanted a scone, but he'd settle for a coffee. Every little bit helped. He didn't have too many bills, given his lack of a car or a home, and—fortunately—he had no student loans to speak of thanks to his parents' support and a scholarship.

"Caramel macchiato?" he asked.

"Sure. Get back there."

He laughed and followed her behind the counter. "Testing my skills?"

"Something like that." She handed him an apron and called the guy on the bar off.

"What will you have, boss?"

Tasha grinned. "Bone-dry breve cappuccino?"

In barista language, that was a challenge. Half-and-half did not like to foam. Two minutes later, he handed Tasha the driest, foamiest cappuccino ever made at a Starbucks.

She weighed it, her expression shifting from skeptical to impressed. "Wow. Can you start today?"

He shook his head—he was going to savor these last few days of freedom—and sipped his caramel macchiato. "I'll see you this weekend."

He was barely out the door before his phone pinged. But no, he hadn't Murphy's Lawed himself into a job interview. At least, not the one he wanted. Instead, it was a message from his friend back home.

Heard you moved to Philly. Let me know if you change your mind.

He couldn't do this here and now. Before he could pocket his phone, it pinged again. He really needed to put it back on silent. He unlocked it, expecting more from Corey, but found a missive from his mother.

> *Talked to Jess.*
> *Venmoed you money.*
> *Give some to your sister.*
> *She never lets us help.*
> *Love you.*

Brian opened his app and stared at the amount of money she'd sent—three grand. That would make things easier. He could splurge a little on that air mattress and buy a comforter that didn't look like it belonged in a baby's room.

Thanks, Mom, he typed.

A thumbs-up emoji followed shortly after. Seriously. His mother.

Let us know if you need more. See you at Thanksgiving, honey.

Ouch. Thanksgiving was in three months. His parents were really owning this empty-nester thing. Next, she'd be telling him they were wintering in Tampa. He leaned back against the wall and laughed at the absurdity of his life. He hadn't laughed this hard in months, and his ribs hurt from the effort.

When his phone pinged again, he could only imagine what his mom had to add. He swiped at his eyes and focused on the message. Not his mom, but Corey again. *We'd seriously love to have you at Scott and Johnson.*

He shot off a quick thumbs-up of his own. Corey was trying to do him a solid, and Brian knew he should be grateful. He should be walking the halls of that immaculate building instead of drinking his first free coffee as a Starbucks employee. But not yet. He had some savings left, a part-time gig, and a safety net from his mom. He could give Philly two more months, maybe even three, and if nothing cropped up—and if Fairford would still have him—he'd fold.

Chapter 7

Sarah

Her hairdresser, Charli, was laughing at her. Full-on bent-over chuckling. "Girl, what did you use? Dollar-store hair dye? At least the wax washed out easily enough, but…"

She lifted Sarah's hair, looking at the limp, discolored strands. They were orange—not golden or even rust—thanks to the quick-and-dirty blond she'd attempted. Color didn't show in her hair unless she went light first, but she'd never tried dying it at home. It might have worked eventually, but in the middle of the process, one of her friends at the hospital told her Tyler's surgery had finished. Time was up—she'd thrown on the wax over the dye job and hoped for the best.

"Yeah, yeah," she said, glaring at the woman who had done her hair since Sarah moved to Philadelphia three years ago. "Lesson learned. I had a minor mental breakdown after my boyfriend proposed and then kicked me out of the house when I said no."

"That'll do it." Charli ran her fingers through Sarah's hair. "What do you want to do?"

"What are my options?"

"Well, we can go all in, bleach it, pink it, whatever. Or we could dye you back to natural. Either way, I'd wait until next week."

Next week. She really didn't want Jess to see what she'd done. There'd be that look of concern and disappointment that Sarah couldn't bear. Not to mention, her boss didn't mind her crazy hair colors, but there'd be comments on orange. This color didn't look intentional—it looked like the rash decision it had been. And she wanted to ease her boss into her breakup with Tyler, not have it completely obvious the second she walked into the office.

"What are my options today?"

Charli fluffed Sarah's hair. "We can cut it short and get rid of the color. Or we could keep it long and hide some of the color, but the ends would still be there. We do have some of those coloring conditioners around. The teens always want them for homecoming and then Halloween. We could cover the ends with that..."

That was an interesting option. At least then she wouldn't have to pour on the perfume to hide the oddly masculine smell of hair wax. But what color? "All right, have your way with me."

Charli stilled in her examination. "Last time you said that, you cried for a week and your roommate yelled at me."

Sarah laughed. Jess had totally done that. "Fine. Keep it on the long side. I want to be able to pull it back."

"Color? Or are you gonna ride this melted-Creamsicle orange out?"

"I don't know yet," Sarah said. "But let's make it something fierce."

SARAH DROPPED THE BAGS by the door and waltzed over to her best friend, who was lounging on the couch, reading a copy of *Talented*, Chuck in her lap. She handed Jess a Starbucks cup and did a little spin, letting her perfectly blown-out, minimally red hair fall over her shoulder.

"Hello, fabulous," Jess said, her eyes wide. "I don't think I've ever seen you in red before."

"Nope! First time, and it's super temporary, but I kind of love it." She fell onto the couch next to Jess and pulled her in for a hug before pulling out her phone and snapping a selfie. "Hashtag twins!"

"Hashtag how-much-coffee-have-you-had?"

Sarah laughed. "I'm just in a good mood. My hair was salvage-able, and it's still tuggable, which is honestly what I hated most about short hair, and I—"

"Really? Today of all days?"

Sarah eyed her. "It's just a little hair pulling. It's not like I'm, like, all into torture porn or something. Jeez."

"I caught you in a compromising position with my brother this morning. And I can't think about your sex preferences while that possibility is still in my head."

"There was no possibility." Sarah pulled Chuck onto her lap and stroked his back. He went pliant under her hands, and she scratched the spot behind his ears she knew he loved. "I was trying to steal his game controller, and he caught me. End of story."

"Right." Jess sounded doubtful but didn't push the issue. Instead, she leaned her head on Sarah's shoulder. "Is there something for me in those bags? I miss shopping sprees."

"Trust me, your bank account thanks you for knowing how to budget. Mine, on the other hand—well, I might have to take up in-termittent fasting until my next paycheck. And then my only food will be lemon water with honey or whatever the latest fad is." Sarah skipped back toward the door and picked up two small bags. "But yes, two things for you actually."

Jess grinned. "You do love me."

"More than you know."

Buying things for Jess was always a highlight. She loved getting gifts. Big, small, real, gag—it didn't matter. The fact that someone thought of her enough to get her something always brought the biggest smile to Jess's face. Jess was the ultimate gift giver. You'd never find her handing out a gift card, and if she did, it always came with a note about the specific need that card fulfilled. But it was more than physical gifts—Jess gave of herself so freely, housing her and Brian indefinitely and doing a million other small things for Sarah over the years. As if simply being Sarah's friend wasn't gift enough.

Sarah smiled as her bestie opened the first bag with closed eyes, her lips pursed as she tried to imagine what it might be. When her fingers hit the fabric, Jess grinned and opened her eyes, pulling out the pink sweatshirt she'd had her eye on for weeks.

"Oh my god, Sarah! You shouldn't have! This is too much."

"No take backs."

Jess squeezed it to her chest and rubbed her face in the material. "It's so soft and snuggly. I love it."

"Good." Sarah waited while Jess pulled the book out of the second bag and read the back cover, her eyes widening. "Now you'll let me pay you rent."

"No. I can't pick between the two of you. I'm not taking money from you or Brian until we have a better plan." Jess placed the book—a historical romance she'd been talking about for weeks—next to her on the couch. "And if you're thinking of moving back in permanently, that's a whole different conversation."

"Understood, but I can still pay rent."

"Or you could save what you might spend on rent so you are in a better position to make a decision on your next steps…"

"My financial situation is not your problem."

"Fine." Jess snapped the tag off the sweater and slipped it over her head. "You can buy the groceries—and before you say that's not enough of an expense, you're forgetting that Brian eats *a lot*."

"That I do!" Brian stood in the doorway with a ridiculous grin and a brown paper bag that smelled of grease. "I brought cheesesteaks!"

Sarah looked at Jess, wide-eyed. Brian was in a good mood. Sarah wasn't sure she'd ever seen him anything more than indifferent. He waved the bag around, wafting the amazing mix of meat and cheese and grease into the apartment.

"Pat's or Geno's?" she asked, standing up. Chuck protested being displaced by sauntering over to Brian and zigzagging between his legs—apparently all was forgiven from that morning.

Brian glanced down at him. "You want some steak, boy?"

"Pat's or Geno's?" Sarah asked again, her stomach rumbling.

"Pat's," he said as if there was no other option. And, true, there wasn't. "And before you ask, I got a bunch of different options."

"That tells me absolutely nothing."

"Do you want a cheesesteak or not?" he asked, unrolling one that looked like the most amazing thing she'd never seen. Onions hung out of it, and Cheez Whiz oozed down the sides.

"I'll take that." Sarah held out her hands, half expecting him to take a bite and refuse to hand it over. But he shrugged and passed it along.

"Sis?"

"Did you get one with provolone?"

He shuffled through a few options before handing Jess a sandwich. "And the rest are for me."

Sarah sat down at the table, accepting the plate that Jess slid her way. It had been several hours since she'd eaten that granola bar for breakfast, and her stomach grumbled painfully as the sandwich invaded her senses. She could taste the fake cheese and the steak and the grease. Oh, the grease. She pulled the cheesesteak apart, picking up one half. Brian had already inhaled half of his. Maybe he really could eat three cheesesteaks.

"Thank you," she said, cheering him with her sandwich.

His eyebrows arched, and she supposed she deserved that. But it was nice of him to bring food for all of them. He hadn't even hesitated when offering it up.

"Nice hair," he said around a bite of food.

"So, did you get a job?" Jess asked, dropping a glass of water in front of each of them before plopping down between them. Sarah wondered if it was intentional. Maybe Jess really thought she'd interrupted something that morning.

"Yeah, and Mom gave us three grand."

Jess shook her head. "Of course she did. So, where's the air mattress?"

Brian shrugged. "I went to Target, but nothing there had good reviews, and I couldn't pick. And then I started doing research and got hungry."

"Wait." Sarah grinned. "You would rather sleep on the floor again than buy an air mattress with bad reviews?"

"Yes. I don't want to have to buy one twice."

"But..." She rolled her eyes. This was not worth the argument, no matter how easy it was to stomp on that button.

"Sarah has a car," Jess said, picking at the sandwich with a fork. "If you need to go to the mall."

She shot Jess a glare. *What the hell?* The last thing she wanted to do was sit in a car with Brian for thirty minutes or more. And the traffic out of the city was always bad. It was the worst possible scenario.

"Really?" Brian asked, looking between them incredulously. If he noticed Sarah's shift in attitude, he didn't let on, and his mood didn't seem to dampen either.

Jess shrugged and glared back at Sarah. "Well, you gave her the bedroom, so it seems the least she can do."

Seriously? He gave *me the bedroom?* Sarah had no illusions that he wasn't plotting how to get back into that bedroom after her attempt at blackmail. And he wondered why Jess—who was clearly still perturbed by this morning's events—would want them to spend time together.

"Sure," Sarah said with a shrug, hoping her face wasn't as red as her hair. "I can take you to the mall one night."

"Really?" he asked again, his eyebrow arched.

"As long as you're willing to drive my car with me in it. I hate driving in this city."

"And yet you are the only one of us with a car," Jess said with a laugh.

"Well, I wasn't going to leave her in Missouri. Betty's my baby." Sarah turned to Brian. He needed to understand her love for her car. She was like Dean freakin' Winchester when it came to Betty, and she would take a machete to his head if he messed with her Baby. "Betty is old and crotchety, but I love her. You will be nice to her and not break her. I barely have collision insurance, and my deductible is more than I make in a week."

"Betty?" he asked.

"Yes."

He chewed for a moment before turning back to her. "But if you don't like driving, and you take public transportation to work, can't I just take your car during the day?"

"No one but Jess drives Betty without me."

"But..."

Sarah shot him a look so intense that he dropped his sandwich. "Do you want an air mattress with good reviews or not?"

Brian either laughed or choked—she couldn't tell through her fury glasses. "How's Wednesday?"

"Are you going to complain about your back and the cold floor until then? Because I can go tomorrow. Hell, we can go right now."

"I'll be fine until Wednesday. I need to..."

"Do research. Right." She turned to her best friend and silently begged her to come.

Without Jess, Sarah was not going to survive this trip. Nope. Brian was going to end up in a ditch somewhere off the highway, and Sarah couldn't go to jail as she'd already learned that orange was not her color.

"Jess, are you coming? We could make a night of it. Shopping, dinner, movie..."

"I have a date on Wednesday." Jess kept her eyes on her plate and played with a stringy, melted piece of cheese. "You two go and have fun. And don't wait up."

"Jessica!"

Brian's distress was almost worth finding out she'd agreed to a shopping day when Jess couldn't come along. And Sarah couldn't do Tuesday. They had a food tasting for the fundraiser that night.

But Jess's comment raised the question of who Jess was dating. Sarah hadn't heard anything on the dating front since that last guy ghosted her—which was unusual. She glanced at her friend, who was still picking at her food. *A secret lover?*

"Ooo," Sarah said, taking a piece of steak doused in American cheese off Brian's plate. "You'll have to give me all the details later." She turned to Brian. "You sister's sexcapades are always the steamiest."

Jess covered her face and groaned. "Sarah!"

Chapter 8
Sarah

Mondays were for team meetings and bitching and too many pots of coffee. They were not for driving to the suburbs before lunch. Especially considering the weekend she'd had. Cedar Crest Hospital was literally the last place she wanted to be. But Leigh had been buried in paperwork, and Maggie had insisted the tickets and donor confirmation paperwork be dropped off that morning. Maybe Tyler wouldn't be on call, or maybe he'd be trapped in an hours-long surgery, and she could slip in and out without incident.

All unlikely. Doc Ack—the name Tyler went by with all the kids, due to his last name being Ackerman—was famous for being in every day. Even on his days off, he stopped in to say hi to his kids. If they had to be in the hospital long-term, it was the least he could do. The act was sweet in theory but obnoxious in practice. He pestered other doctors—or so she heard—and sometimes got pulled into other cases when he "only planned to stop in for twenty minutes." It made being his girlfriend intolerable sometimes. But she couldn't complain—these were her kids too.

Many of the children were critically ill, but not all of them. Sophie's Wish Factory was local, so the wishes were smaller than those of other bigger charities, but they included a broader range of participants—kids sick with cancer, dealing with cystic fibrosis, receiving in-house treatment for depression, or even suffering a broken leg and having to miss an entire soccer season. Sophie's Wish Factory gave wishes in every shape and size. Celebrity visits were big, but baseball games, trips to Sesame Place, runs up the Rocky Steps…. Whatever they wanted within a one-hundred-mile radius was theirs.

Sarah glanced both ways before stepping off the elevator, though it was unlikely that Tyler would be in this part of the hospital. She stepped into the hallway and turned toward the desk where a nurse—Susan—sat filing paperwork.

"Hey, Sarah," she said, glancing up when Sarah dropped the stack of envelopes onto the ledge. "Those the tickets for the fundraiser?"

"Yes, and a few papers we need signed by some recurring donors." Sarah smiled at the woman. She knew Susan fairly well, given that the woman had only started a few months ago. Susan had jumped on the opportunity to attend the fundraiser gala. "Okay if I drop these in the mailboxes?"

"Of course." Susan paused and then handed Sarah a sticky note with Tyler's familiar handwriting on it.

Great. Hopefully, it had been subtly worded. Hospital gossip was the worst kind.

Sarah took it and paused—how had he known she'd be here today? And the note was obviously written for her to see here and now: *I'll be needing a second ticket to the gala.* He'd signed it with his doctor-scrawl signature, as if every nurse in this hospital didn't recognize his handwriting.

"Thanks, Susan."

Susan frowned and then glanced around the space before leaning toward her. "You're better off."

Sarah could only nod. In less than two days, Tyler had flipped the narrative on their breakup. She wondered what these people thought. But most of them weren't her friends. They were friendly and supportive of Sophie's Wish Factory, but it didn't matter what they thought unless it detracted from their donations, and Tyler wouldn't let that happen, because then Tessa wouldn't get to attend a fashion show, and Dean wouldn't get to go to Sesame Place, and

that visit from a certain celebrity would be off the table. They weren't
the high-profile hospital within city limits—Cedar Crest was small
and prestigious but in the suburbs. It was where Sophie had taken
her last breath and where the doctors had treated her and her mother—Sophie's Wish Factory founder and Sarah's boss, Maggie—like
family. All those years of grief were turned into all these years of hope
and charity, and one marriage proposal gone wrong would not derail
them. Sarah wouldn't allow it.

"Sare." Tyler's voice was stony and rigid. He stood in the doorway to what she knew to be an unoccupied office.

Except, as she stepped closer, she knew that it was most certainly
his office. The scent of his favorite coffee—cinnamon—wafted out
the door, and she could see three of his favorite shirts still in the dry-
cleaning bag hanging off a bookcase, along with a photo of him with
the governor. *All our interrupted lunches in the cafeteria, and he's had
a fucking office the whole time?*

She resisted the urge to throttle him and followed him in, taking
in even more proof that the space was his—diplomas and pictures
and his Penn gym bag. "Nice office."

"Thanks," he said, not offering more. "Maggie said you had something for me to sign."

Maggie would not have told Tyler that. She didn't talk to Tyler,
because she had Sarah on the inside and he was an ass. And Leigh
handled paperwork delivery. Sarah came for kid visits midweek. The
fact that Leigh had been covered in stacks of papers that morning
now seemed intentional.

"You *asked* Maggie to send me here?"

"I might have suggested I wanted to see your face this morning."
He sat down in the chair behind his desk and glanced up at her lazily.
"What did you do to your hair by the way? Red?"

She flushed and shoved the form with his name on it onto the
desk. "Just sign so we can be done here."

"Of course." He scribbled a few things, folded it, and handed it back to her. "And my tickets."

"Right." She shoved the papers back in her bag and pulled out the envelope with the extra tickets. She noted the numbers, scribbling them on the back of his form before dropping them in front of him. They fluttered onto his desk. He didn't move to grab them. "Don't forget to give us the name of your guest."

"Oh, certainly. Monique Miller."

What the hell? Her heart sped up—that would bring press, and press was good. But he was bringing a freaking model to her event... in front of her coworkers, who she hadn't told about their breakup yet.

"I didn't realize you two were acquainted," she said. That would have been nice to know, considering that Tessa wanted to be in a fashion show.

"Reacquainted now." His lips curved up. "I'd forgotten how... fond of her I was."

Gross. "Does she know you were proposing to me minutes before you climbed into her bed?"

He shrugged. "Monique doesn't really care about the particulars."

Grosser. She stepped back toward the door, ready to be done. He'd made her come all the way to the hospital so he could gloat that he was sleeping with a supermodel less than forty-eight hours after she'd left and shove all her inadequacies in her face. He had to prove everything he'd said Saturday night—that he was better than she was and opened doors she'd never be able to walk through on her own. Well, at least she could walk out of this one. And slam it.

She moved as quickly as was unnoticeable to the doctor's lounge then closed the door behind her. A few residents were sprawled on the couches, but it was otherwise empty. She took a few deep breaths. The young doctors didn't even turn her way.

Monique fucking Miller. How can I compete with that? She didn't even have a date lined up, let alone one who was model worthy.

Sarah pulled the stack of paperwork back out of her bag, with Tyler's folded sheet on top. He'd done more than sign it, but she hadn't been able to tell what. She unfolded it. Her eyes narrowed to slits, and she let out a hiss that caught the attention of the doctors, but she didn't care. Tyler had shifted the credit for garnering his donation to Leigh. Sarah had worried this might happen, but she'd hoped he wouldn't do it—that he'd respect the boundaries between personal and professional. Had it been another donor, it might not have mattered in the grand scheme of things. But Tyler was one of her biggest donors. And while the Sophie's Wish Factory fundraising staff didn't make commission, they did have quotas. The more points you had at the end of the year, the more big-name donors Maggie transferred to your list. The bigger your donor list, the easier it was to do the job.

She crumpled the paper. Sarah hadn't considered that he'd bring a date to the gala. They'd spent the last year dazzling everyone at events. So, while their breakup might have been noticed if they both went solo, it was absolutely going to be noticed when he showed up with a model on his arm. She couldn't look like a sad ex-girlfriend at the gala. She needed everything to go as planned. It was the biggest event of the year.

But who the hell was she supposed to bring? Sarah didn't have connections like Tyler did. She didn't have guy friends who could pose as something else. Tyler knew everyone in her life. So basically, she was royally screwed.

SARAH PLOWED INTO THE apartment, dropping her purse on the bench by the door and kicking her shoes off. She struggled out of her jacket and hung it on the hook.

"You okay there, Red?"

Brian. *Couldn't he be out doing something productive with his life? No, you refused to let him use your car, Sarah.*

He was sprawled out on the couch, Chuck at his feet, playing a video game. She could hear the unmistakable music of *Super Mario Brothers* coming from the television. A bag of Twizzlers sat on the coffee table next to a Mountain Dew and a bottle of Claritin. Name brand. Because of course he would buy the name brand when he was unemployed.

"Brian, not now, please."

His gaze met hers, and she thought she detected actual concern there, but then he blinked, and the moment passed. He turned back to his game with a frown.

Whatever. She didn't have time for his emotional needs. She'd already taken a half day after Tyler's throwdown. Maggie had frowned at her screen and then looked over the monitor at Sarah until her stare burned a hole through her newly red hair. After a succinct modified version of their breakup, Sarah had asked for the afternoon off, and Maggie, with a disapproving *I told you so* look, sent her out into the afternoon. But Sarah hadn't accounted for Brian being home. At least she had the bedroom. She'd close that door, turn up the music, and dance it out.

She walked past him and pushed open the door to her room, prepared for anything. He couldn't have given up that easily. But the room looked the same—sloppily made bed, curtains pulled back, clothes no longer touching every surface but still strewn across the furniture. Except that the window she'd opened was closed and the ceiling fan that she'd left spinning was off.

And then the smell hit her. She stepped back and coughed. The musky and overpowering scent of Axe body spray wafted toward her. She coughed again as if the aerosol was still in the air, choking her. Maybe it was. She sneezed and backed up a few steps.

"What did you do?" she hissed, whirling around to face Brian, who was bent over his controller, laughing.

"I don't... know... what... you mean," he said between laughs. "Is something wrong?"

"Yes! It smells like a gaggle of eighth-grade boys got ready for their first dance in my bedroom!"

"How weird," he said, turning back to his game. "Hope you can sleep in there tonight."

She huffed and stormed back into the bedroom. What a complete dick. In lieu of slamming the door, she shoved open the window and turned the fan back on. Jess was going to be pissed when the smell made its way into the rest of the apartment. It would permeate everything. By the next morning, they would all smell like pubescent boy.

She pulled the sheets off her bed along with any clothes that were out in the open—anything that could be washed. This was not how she wanted to spend her afternoon. She wanted to mope and dance and alternate between looking up potential dates on Tinder and adding things she couldn't afford to her Amazon wish list—window-shopping that her mother could access. But no—instead, she had to wash her whole life and de-scent her bedroom.

Maybe this game they were playing wasn't worth it. They could alternate, or he could have the room, or—no. That room was hers. She'd lived in it for almost three years. The decor was still hers—she'd bought that bedframe and that mattress. The desk—hers. The lamp—hers. The room belonged to Sarah even if Brian had beaten her to it by a few hours. *Hours*—not even days or weeks.

The washing machine sprang to life, loud as always. She hoped he wouldn't be able to hear his stupid game and the noise would give him a headache. She hoped Chuck would crawl into his lap—the cat hated the washing machine almost as much as the vacuum—and give Brian a sneezing fit. *Allergic to cats, my ass.* The man hadn't sneezed once in two days.

She stomped across the kitchen and dragged a chair through the front door and out into the hall. Sarah stared up at the hatch to the attic and then down at the staircase to the first floor. This was a safety hazard waiting to happen. But it had to be done. That smell was never going to leave the apartment otherwise.

"What are you doing?"

"I need to get the fans from the attic."

His eyes followed the same path hers had a moment before. "This can't be up to code."

"Well, we don't really go in there. But some jackass doused my bedroom in Axe body spray."

"If you don't go in there, how did the fans end up in the attic?" he asked, his tone half-sarcastic, half-annoyed.

She shrugged. "The landlord put them up there for us when he installed the ceiling fans last year and updated the thermostat."

"And how did he get in there?"

"A ladder."

He stared at her incredulously. "A ladder by the staircase."

"I think it might have been *on* the staircase."

"So, you just..." He motioned toward the attic.

Sarah nodded with a grimace. "Push the cover over and pull yourself in."

"Fuck me."

She snorted. "Not even in your wildest dreams."

"Do you want my help?" he asked, all annoyance now.

"Not really."

"Fine." He clomped back toward the apartment. "Don't die trying to get up there. Jess would be pissed if her home became a crime scene."

Shit. She hadn't thought that retort through. Her options were limited now. She could go ask Brian to help, attempt to get into the attic with her own sad upper body strength, or buy a fan. Or sit in her stripped bedroom, surrounded by boy smell. The ceiling fan would help air out the room, but it wouldn't be enough.

Why today? Couldn't he have given me one more day?

Screw it. She dragged the chair back into the kitchen, noticing the first hints of Axe in the air outside her room. Jess was going to be so mad.

"Move over." Sarah plopped down on the couch next to Brian and picked up the second controller. Her room was going to be unoccupiable for at least an hour. Why suffer when she could play *Super Mario*? "You'd better have more candy. Twizzlers taste like ass."

Brian navigated back to the start menu without a word and switched to a two-player game. He motioned toward the shopping bag. "Help yourself."

She pulled the bag onto her lap. Two bottles of Axe rolled around as she searched for the supposed candy. "Were you even trying to hide the evidence?"

"Nope."

She dug past the body sprays and another bag of Twizzlers to find apple rings—her favorite candy. One she particularly remembered him never eating when he ate every other candy in the house. "Apples of gumminess?"

He nodded. "Have at it."

She popped open the bag, trying not to think about the fact that he'd bought her favorite candy while also purchasing sprays of mass stench. "Do you want one?"

He popped a Twizzler into his mouth. "I'm good."

Chapter 9

Brian

"How's that shoulder?"

Brian shifted his eyes to Sarah. The question sounded sincere, but she was busy swiping at her phone. It was all she'd done since getting home Monday afternoon.

He focused back on the road. "It's fine. My triceps, on the other hand..."

His candor worked, and she quirked a smile. "Someone's been slacking at the gym."

Brain laughed. "Yeah, that's totally it and not the fact that the house is a fucking design disaster."

"It's your own fault."

He had to give her that. His devious plan had totally backfired. The second she'd opened the door to her bedroom, the noxious scent had coated the house. Which royally pissed off his sister and didn't even win him the bedroom. All it had done was make him smell like Axe, which he'd known was a horrible scent since he was twelve. His arms ached like he'd spent hours at the gym instead of twenty minutes pulling himself into a hole in the ceiling to get a fan to help blow the scent out. And the dust up there—despite his daily dose of allergy meds, he'd been sneezing for two days. It didn't help that Chuck had decided he liked Brian. He was constantly tucked under his feet or sleeping on his pillow. That freaking cat was going to be the death of him.

"How's that thumb?" he asked a few minutes later, after she'd returned to her incessant swiping and his phone had told him to go straight for several miles.

"What?"

He glanced over at her, noting that yes, she was still swiping through men at an insane rate. "How can you even tell if you like them that fast?"

She glared at him. "I'm not looking to like them. I'm looking for a guy hot enough to bring to the gala so that I don't look like a complete fool when Tyler brings a model as his date."

"I think that makes him look like an ass more than it makes you look like a fool. He's clearly overcompensating."

"How is screwing a model overcompensating?" she asked, shaking her head. "Reads more to me like he won."

Apparently, he'd missed the part where her ex was screwing the model and not just bringing her to the event. But then Jess and Sarah were always whispering in the kitchen or huddled in her bedroom.

"If he's already sleeping with someone, I don't think he's worth this effort on your part," Brian said.

Her head whipped up, and he realized too late that maybe this wasn't the best conversation for an enclosed space. Particularly if he only had half the story. "You're not a girl. And I'm not taking revenge-dating advice from someone who didn't even put up a fight when his girlfriend dumped him and married another man three days later."

Touché.

They didn't talk for a while after that. Clearly, his sage words weren't going over well, and they still had the entire ride back to get through. But at least she'd given him control of the radio. Her car—Betty, as she insisted he call it—was older, but it had all the amenities. Whenever she'd gotten this car, it had been loaded at the time. Though they were sure to hear a Wilderness Weekend song at least once an hour, he stopped on an alternative rock station and let it play. It was better than the crappy pop that had been playing when he got into the car. He honestly wasn't even sure why Wilderness Weekend still bothered him. Hannah and he had been a freaking mess, and she was happily married now. And when Brian wasn't wallowing, he was happy for her. He'd known before Hannah's failed fake proposal that he was never going to marry her. He'd spent almost every month of that relationship knowing he wasn't a good match for her. They'd clashed where they needed to mesh and settled where they should have soared. But he'd kept texting, and she'd kept coming back. Until she hadn't.

"So," he asked hesitantly as they exited the highway and pulled into the mall parking lot. "Are we shopping or eating first?"

"Shopping," she said, shoving her phone into her purse. "I need to try on dresses, and I can't do that after eating Shake Shack."

"We're at the mall with all these restaurants, and you want Shake Shack, which you can eat anytime at home?"

She rolled her eyes. "Jonesing for Cheesecake Factory? No… CPK."

He laughed. "Anything that is not fast food."

He waited, watching the fight brew in her. But then she nodded and pushed open her car door. "Fine, but you're paying. This haircut took up my food budget for the week."

"I thought you said you were buying a dress."

"I am."

"ARE YOU DONE YET?"

Sarah leaned back against the opposite shelf, her eyes darting from him to her watch and back. Brian glanced behind him.

"It's been ten minutes, and five of those we spent walking through the store," he said.

"You know you already picked a mattress before we got here."

True. He'd done a lot of research and had decided on a standard-sized self-inflating one. If he also didn't need clothes for work, he would have just bought it online. But he couldn't stand the thought of his favorite jeans smelling like coffee. He'd lost his favorite shirt that way the first time around. He still mourned the loss—nothing had fit him as well since.

"I can meet you at the restaurant."

She stared at him, her mouth slightly open. "You have to come dress shopping with me."

"What?" He grabbed his choice of mattress off the shelf and turned to leave the aisle. Her flats dragging across the floor told him that she was following.

"Why?" he asked once they were at checkout.

"Because I'm going to think every dress looks awful."

"You want *my* opinion?"

"It's the only one available to me, so yes." She sighed. "Just be honest but nice. Like, if it doesn't look good, that's fine."

"I have a sister, remember."

"I once heard you tell your sister she looked like a hooker."

"Well, she probably did." He paused and met her gaze. God, she looked weary. For someone sleeping on an actual mattress, she didn't seem to be getting much sleep. *Right, so maybe that's not something to say aloud.* "Okay, I get it. Honest but nice."

She pulled a face and started walking toward the main section of the mall. He trailed her, not liking the disbelief that had marred her expression.

"I can be nice," he said, coming up next to her.

She gave him side-eye. "I hope so, because if not, I will cry, and every woman in a hundred-foot radius will glare at you until your balls shrivel up."

"Noted."

Seven dresses later, his patience was wearing thin. Every dress looked great on her. He didn't even have to be nice. Honest was enough. But she'd found something wrong with each dress despite what he said. It didn't help that the sales lady clearly thought he was the boyfriend or some facsimile of one. The sales assistant winked at him with each dress even though he'd told her he was not the boyfriend and Sarah had backed it up emphatically. Fortunately, after helping Sarah into this final dress, the woman had wandered off to help another customer. Sarah had yet to emerge. He'd learned that she had to look at the dress from every angle before she considered showing him. One dress hadn't even made it out of the dressing room.

The sales lady flitted by with an armful of dresses. Apparently, this wasn't just a Sarah thing. "This is the one, boyfriend."

"I'm not..." The words died on his lips as Sarah stepped out of the dressing room.

His eyes widened as he took her in. The dress was dark red, matching the subtle red in her hair. His eyes traveled from the slope of her shoulders, touched only by the thinnest of fabrics, to the valley between the swell of her breasts and then to the curve of her waist.

"What do you think?" Her voice was hesitant, nervous even. She spun around, and his eyes landed on the expanse of her back and the roundness of her ass, where no underwear lines could be seen. "Too much?"

He shook his head as all the blood in him rushed to his bottom half. He crossed his legs. He'd never seen so much of her before. Never wanted to. But *holy shit*. "That's the dress."

She flushed and met his eyes through the mirror. "Really?"

"Told you!" The sales lady peeked her head around the wall before disappearing again. "Brian?" Sarah asked, her eyes not leaving his.

"Really. No one will be paying attention to Monique Miller if you're in that dress—especially not your ex."

She flushed and stepped back toward the dressing room. "Perfect. Can you unzip me?"

He stood, urging his nether regions to calm the fuck down. He'd seen girls in dresses before and worked more than one out of them as well. His fingers trembled as he slid the zipper down, revealing her braless back and the edge of a G-string.

"Eyes up here, perv."

His head shot up, and he caught her swallowing a smile, her cheeks flushed in the mirror. He released her, stepped back, and then closed the door behind him. He needed a minute—more than a minute. Hell, he needed a cold shower.

"I'm going to head to the Gap."

"Oh, right. Okay. Should I meet you at the Cheesecake Factory?"

He could not sit through a whole meal with her. All he saw was that black lacy fabric sitting on her tailbone and the length of her spine, and—*god*, how hot would it be to have it arched against him as he...

Stop. "Actually, you were right." His voice cracked, and he cleared his throat. "Shake Shack sounds good."

Her head popped out the door, and he could just make out the strap of her bra back on her shoulder. It was black and lacy like the underwear she wore. "But now I want cheesecake. It's, like, the last dessert I get to eat if I want to wear this dress in two weeks."

"I can pick up cheesecake to go," he said too quickly. "We can bring some home for Jess too."

"But that bread..."

"I can pick up bread as well."

She stepped out of the dressing room, back in her normal nonrevealing street clothes. The woman who had just brought him to his knees wasn't there anymore. It was just Sarah in skinny jeans and a summer sweater.

"Are you in a rush or something? I really kind of want to go sit and eat now. I mean, you were right—we're here, so why not make a night of it?"

Because I just saw parts of your body better left hidden? "I just remembered that one of my shows premieres tonight."

She nodded as if this was a perfectly acceptable reason but then cut a glance at him. "But we don't have cable."

Crap. He was out of excuses. "Right. It's on a streaming service."

"Weren't you home all day?"

Damn it all to hell. "It's just a thing I do with some friends back in New York. But it's fine. Why don't you get us a table while I shop?"

Chapter 10

Sarah

“So, what did you get?” Sarah asked as Brian dropped into a chair.

His twenty minutes had been more like thirty, and she'd already ordered for them and devoured half the bread. It had been just long enough for her to shake off the strange feeling she'd had since the dress shop, when he'd clearly checked her out. It hadn't even been subtle. And then he'd been all weird, letting his fingers linger on her zipper and trying to renege on dinner.

“Two pairs of pants and a few button-downs that I won't mind sacrificing to the coffee gods,” he said with a shrug.

“Boring.”

He buttered a piece of bread, not paying her any attention. At least that seemed back to normal. Maybe she'd imagined his gaze in the mirror. “I picked up some lounge pants and a sweater for Jess.”

“Oh, let me see.”

Brian pulled a navy sweater with white dots out of the bag. It had dolman sleeves and was completely Jess. That was sweet. She wondered if her brothers would be like that... if they knew she existed. Her father hadn't exactly left a forwarding when he left Sarah and her mom to start a new family in a new city.

“I stopped at Loft.”

Sarah blinked. That was above and beyond. Tyler would more likely go into Victoria's Secret than Loft. “*You* went into Loft.”

“Yeah.” He shrugged as if it was nothing. As if knowing the exact shirt his sister would love wasn't a thing. It was totally a thing. “I know she loves it there, and I saw this on the mannequin, and it was so Jess."

"Nice job, big brother."

"Thanks." He pulled something else out of the bag and tossed it onto the table. "I got you these."

Sarah looked down at the big fuzzy socks. They weren't a snazzy sweater, but she wasn't his little sister. And the two of them weren't exactly on gift-exchanging terms. In fact, the last gift she'd gotten him had been glow-in-the-dark condoms with a note that said, *In case you can't find it in the dark.* He hadn't appreciated them. The socks were adorned with little unicorns in winter hats and pajamas. She ran a finger over them with a smile. He'd gone to another store to get these. No wonder he was late.

"All you've done for the last five days is complain about how cold it is in the apartment." Brian gave her a crooked smile. "And as someone sleeping on the floor, I concur. I thought these might help." He pulled out a second pair that were more manly but still ridiculous.

"Are those Yodas in Christmas hats?" she asked.

"Yup."

"They'll match those boxers of yours nicely."

He flushed and stuffed both pairs of socks back in the bag with Jess's sweater. "Yes, and the unicorns will match those hideous pants of yours."

She smirked—they were hideous and pink and covered in unicorns, but Jess had gotten them for her last Christmas. "You know, it almost seems like you like me."

His reaction was so subtle she might have missed it if she wasn't watching him. He froze, his shoulders straightening, before he fixed her with a look that she suspected was meant to be alluring but coming from him was just weird. Because Brian.

"Maybe that's what I want you to think." He worried at his lip. "You know, butter you up before my next plan of attack."

The waiter dropped off their food. She stared at her enormous chicken dish, her stomach growling. This was practically three meals' worth of food. Fabulous.

She pointed at him with her fork. "A pair of fuzzy socks and a dinner will not get you into my bedroom."

He grinned, and his green eyes danced with amusement. "And pray tell, what will?"

"Ew. Put those eyes away." She threw a piece of bread at him.

He caught it with a laugh and popped it into his mouth. Neither of them said anything after that as they dove into their meals. Brian seemed happy with the burrito the size of his head, eating it with a fork and knife.

"So..." he said after half the burrito was gone. She braced herself for more banter, but it didn't come. "Who do you think my sister is dating?"

That was unexpected. She'd been wondering the exact same thing since Jess had dropped the "Don't wait up" line the other night. To her knowledge, Jess wasn't dating anyone—which would normally mean that Jess wasn't dating anyone. Because Jess liked to talk guys—likes, dislikes, penis sizes, positions, how talented their tongues were. Sometimes, after hearing Jess talk about a guy, Sarah couldn't look at him for days.

"I don't know. I mean, her last relationship ended in the spring," she said.

She thought back to the summer. They hadn't been living together, but they still talked all the time, so much so that Tyler commented on it. And there hadn't been many guys. Yeah, she'd had her rebound sex, but then it had been a pretty quiet summer.

"There was this one guy she went out with a few times, but he was a total Herpes."

Brian choked on his soda, his eyes glossing over. "You have to be kidding me."

She grimaced. She'd forgotten that Brian's ex-girlfriend's best friend ran the podcast that had coined the term *Herpes*, referring to clingy dates who didn't know when to cut their losses. Brian—though technically mentioned as a nameless boyfriend—had been a frequent topic in the early episodes, including one titled "Is Bigger Always Better?" that hadn't been exactly flattering to his sexual prowess. And then a few months back, there'd been the special edition about Brian's ex-girlfriend and the marriage pact she'd made with her friend and how their marriage of convenience had turned into true love.

Sarah didn't often feel bad for Brian, but after that episode, she had. It didn't help anything to know that the person who dumped you was with their true love.

"Sorry. We love *Bitching about Boyfriends*," she said.

She and Jess had even submitted stories for inclusion in recent episodes, which was the show's new format. Sarah was planning on sending in one about the birthday proposal gone wrong once she wrapped her head around all the ridiculousness. But she wasn't going to tell Brian that.

"I didn't think..."

"It's fine. Just caught me off guard." He took a sip of his soda and watched her order several pieces of cheesecake to go—not adding one in for himself, she noted. Once the waiter was gone, he pulled her attention back to the subject. "So, Jess dated a clingy guy?"

"*Dated* isn't really the right term."

He cringed. "Too much info."

"Well, anyway, he ended up wanting something serious. Like, he was moving or something and asked her to do long distance after, like, two dates and to go to his sister's wedding in six months. But other than that, I don't know of anyone she's dated or is dating."

"I thought you two told each other everything."

"We do. But there's this interloper in the apartment right now." She frowned at him. "She's not exactly going to talk about her sex life at the dinner table anymore."

"Ah!" He covered his ears.

"Oh, grow up. Your sister is a hot babe, and she knows her way around the male anatomy."

"I'm going to vomit if you don't stop."

Sarah giggled. It was too easy. "I'll see what I can find out, but I wouldn't worry about it. She probably picked up some guy on Tinder that she doesn't feel the need to tell me about because he's a hump and dump." She shrugged, though she could see the red rising on Brian's neck even in this dim lighting. "She gets bitchy if she doesn't get her sex on."

Brian dropped his head down onto his arms folded on the table. "Please, no more talk of my sister's sex life."

"Fine." She smiled at him innocently. "We'll talk about yours. Oh, wait."

"Real funny."

The waiter approached with two bags—one of cheesecake and one of leftovers—and the check. Brian handed him his credit card and watched him until he was out of earshot. Then he held up her keys. "Any more stores before we head out?"

She shook her head, surprisingly sad to see the evening end but knowing she couldn't spend more money. Not to mention she'd reached her Brian limit for the day. "I'm good. Better to quit before we start to get on each other's nerves, don't you think?"

He rolled his eyes but nodded. "Sounds about right."

Chapter 11

Brian

Brian sprawled out on the couch, his eyes half-lidded as the latest movie in the *Star Wars* universe opened. There was no crawl, but a backstory flashed across the screen. He let his arm dangle off the couch and fall onto the fluffball that was Chuck. This cat loved him. Chuck had sat on the floor in front of the couch or hung out on the back of it all day, seeking ear scratches. Brian had shooed him away over and over but had finally given up halfway into his first movie of the day. He almost suspected Sarah was catnipping the couch—it would be her right after the Axe debacle—but Chuck was too calm for that. Brian still had the scars from the time his ex-girlfriend left the catnip out in the open.

Tomorrow, he would be employed—not gainfully, but it was a start. So, with his sister on yet another date and Sarah out for the day, he was taking full advantage of the empty apartment. Except, he kind of missed them. The two women worked all week, and with no friends in the area and no job, Brian had spent an inordinate amount of time on this couch with Chuck. His sister was still being cagey. In fact, if he hadn't been sleeping on her living room floor, he might have suspected she never came home last night. But he'd heard her stumble in late and then back out early that morning. It seemed a lot of effort for sleeping with a guy. But what did he know about the female psyche?

Sarah had disappeared midmorning. She said she'd be home by dinner, but there'd been no sign of her, and eventually, he'd ordered a pizza from the place they all liked a few blocks over. He'd thought about moving all her stuff out and taking over the room. It would be easy. But what was the endgame? As soon as he was out of the apartment, she'd move back in. No, he needed to find a way for her to give up the room. Taking it by force wasn't going to work.

He'd sat on the couch for most of the day, minus the awful run he'd taken after he'd completed a few reps of push-ups, crunches, and burpees. Running was not his thing, but with no gym membership and no weights except the three-pounders he'd found in his sister's closet, he decided it was the best option. But *holy hell*, running sucked, and not just because his arms felt like they wanted to fall off. Why did people like that torture? He'd ended up stopping at the coffee shop a few miles away and walking back slowly. At least his favorite techy podcast had a new episode. He pretty much hadn't moved since then except to open the door for the pizza-delivery guy.

The front door opened, bringing in a blast of warm air, but he didn't bother to move. It was one of two people, and both always announced themselves—Jess with a warm welcome and Sarah with a quip. Every. Single. Time.

"Well, that's a sight."

"Red," he said, not looking up at her. "You're late for dinner."

"I know. Sorry. My phone died."

He glanced up at her and did a double take. "You're not red."

"Nope."

He sat up as she plopped down onto the couch next to him. And he couldn't stop staring. Her hair, which had been various shades of any color of the rainbow since he'd known her, fell in long warm-brown waves that perfectly framed her face. It was lighter than her natural color but rich, like a dark cinnamon. He wanted to reach out and touch it, letting his fingers tangle in the tresses. He turned back to the television, leaving Sarah and her hair in the periphery.

"What am I going to call you now?"

"My name." She laughed. "Or, I guess, Chestnut."

"That makes you sound like a horse."

She chucked a pillow at him. It missed, and Chuck went skidding across the floor.

He laughed. "How did you miss?"

"Shut up."

"You're literally sitting right next to me."

"Maybe I missed on purpose," she said.

"Poor Chuck begs to differ."

She scooped Chuck up from his hiding spot under the coffee table and snuggled him. "Sorry, Chucky Wucky. Auntie Sarah didn't mean to scare you. Uncle Brian's just a big ole jerk."

A shiver went down his spine. He was no one's uncle, and it had better stay that way.

She eyed him, letting the cat free. Chuck didn't go far, only curled up next to her. "Did you eat yet?"

He nodded. "There's pizza in the kitchen."

"Thank God. I'm starving."

He watched the movie, the sound of her tinkering in the kitchen reaching him. He took a breath. It was harder than he expected to forget her curves and the softness of her skin. But he had to. He had to forget the hair and the dress and the way her lips curved when she teased him. Sarah was off-limits and a very, very bad idea. No matter what he'd said to Sarah about the supposed photos she'd taken of the two of them entangled in the living room, Jess *had* told him to stay away from her friends. She'd made that rule eons ago, but honestly, complying had been easy because he'd never been into any of her friends, and they'd certainly never approached him. While he didn't believe Sarah's supposed pictures would get him kicked to the curb, the sight of them might make Jess punch him in the arm and threaten his life if he hurt her best friend.

The friend in question walked in and fell back onto the couch, a piece of cold pizza in one hand. Her eyes rolled back in her head in ecstasy. He looked away.

"Oooo!" she exclaimed, her voice oozing with excitement. He chanced a glance at her. Her eyes were fixed on the television, a smile brightening her face. A strand of hair was stuck to her cheek, and he resisted the urge to push it back behind her ear. "Is this the one with my two favorite Chrises or sexy Benedict Cumberbatch?"

He glared at her. "This is not *Star Trek*."

She pointed at the screen. "The *Enterprise* is right there."

"That's the *Millennium Falcon*."

"Oh, who is that hottie? I don't remember him."

"Han Solo."

"Favorite Chris number one's dad?"

The door opened again, and Brian had never been so glad to get out of a conversation. Jess entered, holding a case of beer. She held it up like a trophy.

"Who's ready to get wasted?"

He declined to say that the three of them couldn't get wasted on twelve beers and inched farther away from Sarah. At least her awful knowledge of *Star Wars* had stopped the blood rush to his nether regions. He took in his sister with a frown. She looked frazzled, sad even, and she'd never been a big drinker.

"Bad date?" he asked.

"I wasn't on a date," she said, dropping the case onto the kitchen table. "Had to take a friend to the airport."

"What friend?" Sarah asked, her tone incredulous. She met his eye quickly—confirming his suspicions that she still knew nothing—before turning back to Jess.

"Not anyone you know."

Brian watched the two of them. Sarah clearly didn't buy it, and he didn't either. As far as he knew, Jess didn't have friends that Sarah didn't know as well. At least not of the female persuasion. But Jess wasn't having it. She moved into the kitchen, and he heard the fridge open and shut. A moment later, she plopped down between Brian and Sarah, a cold piece of pizza in one hand, a beer in the other. Sarah toasted her with her own slice. Weird. These two were so weird.

"So, what are we watching?"

"*Star Trek*."

Brian fell back against the couch in defeat and groaned. "*Star Wars*."

APPARENTLY, HIS SISTER *could* get wasted on four beers. And Sarah wasn't far behind her. Brian sipped his, cringing against the taste—light and cheap. The women had quickly grown bored of *Solo*, and he couldn't blame them—it wasn't the best in the franchise by any measure. Now they were watching *Star Trek*, the first one that set up the Kelvin timeline. He wasn't sure either of their eyes had left the screen since Chris Pine showed up. Which suited him just fine. Now that he would have an income, it was time to tackle the second part of his to-do list—get laid. Tinder wasn't his preferred way to meet women, but he couldn't deny that it was effective.

He opened the app and quickly passed on the first few women. He'd updated his profile a few nights ago but hadn't spent any time looking through prospects. Part of him was afraid Sarah would show up in his matches, based on all the swiping she'd done lately. And things were already awkward enough.

"Oh, she's pretty." Sarah grabbed his phone. He reached for it, but she held it away from him, showing Jess.

He groaned. Why had he thought perusing Tinder would be a good idea with these two drunken meddlers next to him? He glanced back at the women. "Don't," he said. But it was too late. She'd already swiped right on the blonde in pigtails and a Harley Quinn-style outfit.

"What? She was cute," Jess said.

"And her ass," Sarah added, eyeing the next woman.

Brian rolled his eyes. "I like a little surprise. I mean, you can practically see everything in her profile picture."

"This is Tinder not eHarmony," Sarah said, "and you need a fuck and duck more than anyone I know."

"Look!" Jess exclaimed. "It's a match."

Crap. "Can I have my phone back?"

They bent over the screen, shielding it from him. Jess oohed, and Sarah aahed. He rubbed his forehead and prayed they weren't matching him with every single person on the app.

"Can I at least see who you are trying to hook me up with?"

Sarah held up the phone. The woman in the photo was good-looking. Her black hair fell in thick, straight strands down her back, and her dark skin glowed with a late-summer tan. She wore a shirt with a picture of Darth Vader and the words Who's Your Daddy? He leaned in closer. She was cute... and familiar. Too familiar. He swapped the Vader shirt for a green apron, imagining her face with her hair pulled back and black-rimmed glasses.

"I think this is a Super Like," his sister said, her finger hovering over the screen.

Oh no. He lunged for his phone.

"Wait!" But it was too late. Jess's finger hit the button. He cradled his head in his hands and let out another groan. These two were going to be the death of him.

"What? She's freaking adorable," Sarah said. "She even has on one of those stupid shirts you always wear."

He glanced at them and rubbed his forehead. It was fine. Totally fine. "Yeah, she's adorable. She's also technically my boss."

He didn't know what he expected them to say or do, but fall into a fit of giggles wasn't it. He glared at them, the drunken idiots, and then laughed. He'd somehow have to explain his drunk sister and her best friend stealing his Tinder. And on his first day.

He pulled the phone from Sarah's hand with a shake of his head. "Okay, out, both of you."

Sarah frowned and pointed at the television. "But he's about to be in his underwear."

"This is my bedroom, and I want to go to bed," he said firmly. "One of us has to work in the morning."

Jess hiccupped. "Give him the bed. I want to see Chris number one in his underwear."

Sarah harumphed. "Give him your bed!"

"Have at it, big brother." Jess motioned toward her room.

No. There was no way he could sleep if they were out here ogling half-naked men. "Out of my bedroom."

Jess snorted but stood up, taking the last beer with her. "Wow, it's like living back at home."

Sarah jumped from the couch, taking a handful of popcorn with her. "You might want to silence your phone." She giggled, happy and tipsy and ridiculous. "I think you are going to have quite the night on Tinder."

"Yeah, thanks for that."

The door to Jess's bedroom opened, and she shoved the inflated air mattress out into the room. Her eyes were bright and her cheeks pink. She smiled at him sleepily. "Here's your bed, big bro."

He looked between his two drunken roommates giggling on either side of the apartment, his whole life sandwiched between them. What had he gotten himself into?

Chapter 12

Brian

Life in a major city never really stopped. Even on the bus before sunrise, there'd been other people. Some looked like they were coming home. Others, like Brian, were going in. A little girl slept on her mother's knee as the bus bumped along, and her brother zoned in on his Nintendo Switch. He could have walked—it was only a mile and change, nothing really. But he'd known he would be on his feet all day.

And six hours in, he was glad to be pulled off the floor to count the deposit from the night before. There weren't true lulls in coffee consumption in a city. There were lines and customers, and he really should have picked one of the million Starbucks not directly in the heart of the city. He'd passed at least one on his way to work. Surely, it was quieter. *Too late now.*

He glanced over his shoulder at Tasha, exactly as he'd been doing all day. As assistant store manager, she'd spent the day getting him up to speed on all the changes since he'd last stepped behind the bar. Tasha hadn't said anything about the Tinder debacle from the night before or even alluded to it. Her mood had been level all day despite the chaos. She was funny and friendly. She asked questions, filled in blanks, and generally seemed like someone he would enjoy working with daily. And yes, her cuteness extended well past her online persona. In another life, maybe he would have asked her out if she'd contacted him on the app. But he'd already met one ex-girlfriend behind the counter, and he wasn't looking to make it two.

"Good job today, Supe."

Brian tucked the money into the plastic envelope and sealed it. He could feel her eyes on his back and knew she wasn't calling him Supe as in supervisor. But maybe there was a chance...

"Thanks. It's kind of like riding a bike."

"Totally. And you're *super* likeable, so you'll have no issues with the staff."

"Right." He shifted in his seat so he faced her. Her shit-eating grin at least proved she wasn't offended. "I can explain."

"If you must," she said with a shrug. "Just know that I don't date coworkers. Ever." Her eyes bored into him on that last part.

He scratched at his temple. "My sister did it."

She eyed him, the ends of her mouth quirking up. "What?"

"My sister and her best friend stole my phone and Super Liked you."

"For them or for you? Because I have no problem dating coworker's sister's best friend."

He laughed, a little sad he didn't have someone to offer her in exchange. "For me. They are of the opinion that I need to get laid."

"Don't we all?"

Her grin and snark were contagious. He smiled and leaned back against the desk. In another situation, he could like her beyond the confines of these walls. "Anyway, I'm sorry for any awkwardness. I tried to stop them, but they were on a mission."

She snorted. "It's all good. I mean, it's kind of weird that your sister was picking out your Tinder hookup, but whatever."

"She was drunk."

"Still weird." She laughed and hopped down off the stepladder she'd been sitting on. "All right, Supe. I'm going to bring this over to the bank. Think you can handle the floor until I'm back?"

Great. He had a nickname. "Of course. Take your time."

SOMETHING ABOUT THE ebb and flow of a day behind the espresso bar always soothed him. There'd been a lot he hadn't liked about the barista gig the first time around—the early hours, the permanent smell of old espresso, the never-ending lines. But any day he got to stand behind the bar was a good day. He liked challenging his coworkers to foam wars and mixing flavors, with sometimes horrifying and sometimes delicious results. Some people loved the register. The conversation, the regulars, the human contact. But what Brian liked best was handing out that drink before the regular got to the front of the line—knowing that the quality and efficacy of his work could make a person's day—which made the position of shift supervisor not quite as appealing. Much of his day would be divvying out breaks, opening and closing registers, handling the problem customers—and there were always problem customers. It wasn't as simple as getting to man the espresso bar.

He drizzled caramel and mocha onto his cappuccino in a crosshatch. He hadn't lost his touch. This drink was bone dry, the foam fluffy and airy. The sweet toppings would offset the bitterness of the espresso, and it would be euphoria inducing. Anticipation sizzled through him at the heady scent. And then the taste hit him, bringing back a cascade of memories of his ex, Hannah. Their first kiss, up against the back shelving on her last day as a barista. Their first time, months later, with him reeking of stale coffee and her of rock concert. Caramel licks off her neck. Naked mornings when he wore nothing but his apron.

"Brian!"

He blinked away the memories. It had been a while since he'd thought about the beginning. There wasn't really a reason to—by the end, he and Hannah hadn't been those people in a long time.

"Earth to Brian!"

He blinked again and focused on the woman in front of him—auburn hair in a ponytail, eyes bright with amusement, and a smirk too much like his own. Jess. His gaze shifted and landed on Sarah, who was glued to her phone again.

"What are you two doing here?" he asked, pulling their order stickers from the machine. He looked at the orders twice. A caramel macchiato and then... a triple-grande nonfat, no foam, one pump vanilla, one pump caramel, one pump toffee, one pump mocha latte.

"We wanted to support you on your first day," Jess said, watching him aerate the milk.

"I just wanted free food," Sarah said. "But you look very cute in your apron, Bri."

He ignored that. "Free food?" he asked, handing his sister her drink. He started the never-ending pumps in Sarah's latte.

"Yeah. With everything that happened last weekend, I never got to take Sarah out for her birthday dinner. So we had lunch and did some window-shopping."

Sarah held up a bag. "Shopping."

"I thought you had no budget until you got paid again."

She smiled. "I got paid on Friday."

He placed her latte down on the counter in front of her. "And now you can't eat until next payday?"

"I can eat lightly. And yes, I will be expecting you to bring me Starbucks at home and at work." She pointed in the direction of city hall. "It's a few blocks that way."

"You realize I have to pay for drinks, right?" he asked, taking a survey of the floor. There was finally a small lull, just a group of teens ordering Frappuccinos. He hated making those things. The guy on the cash register—Kevan—would need his break in another ten minutes.

"And how are we doing over here, Supe?"

Tasha's voice caught him off guard, and he fumbled the drink he'd been making. Muttering, he started another ristretto shot. Jess and Sarah were trying not to laugh and failing miserably.

He glared at them before turning to Tasha. "Fine, fine." He waved a hand at Sarah and Jess. "These are the Super Likers."

"Oh. Why, hello." She mock tipped a hat and turned a discerning eye on them. She pointed to Jess and then Sarah. "Sister and sister's best friend?"

"Yup." Jess nodded, taking a sip of her drink. "We are so sorry."

Tasha waved them away. "Supe explained."

They exchanged a look at the nickname but didn't say anything. He could see them having a silent conversation. Jess's eyes went wide, and Sarah's narrowed. She crossed her arms, holding her coffee like a shield. *Interesting.*

"They came to support me on my first day."

"Yes," Sarah said, sipping her drink. Her shoulders lifted in pleasure as what must have been a too-sweet taste hit her lips. "We needed to see his barista prowess in person, and I must admit, he did not disappoint. Every one of my taste buds is turned on."

Tasha grinned and leaned in close, whispering in his ear, "So weird."

He bumped her with his hip, keeping his hands steady on the cup this time. "You have no idea."

The girls left shortly afterward and just in time. A postlunch rush hit, and he didn't move from the bar for twenty minutes. Tasha, bless her soul, took over the cold bar, and together, they managed it well. Once the line was manageable, Brian leaned back against the counter and watched her shake a passion tea.

She winked and tossed him what was quickly becoming her trademark grin. "What's going on with you and your sister's best friend?"

"With Sarah?" he asked, trying to hold her gaze. "We're mortal enemies."

"Mortal enemies don't usually give each other tongue orgasms."

Kevan glanced over from the cash registers at the words *tongue* and *orgasms*, his eyes wide and his ears red. Brian motioned for her to lower her voice, and Tasha just laughed.

"There's nothing going on. Seriously, we've spent the last week arguing over who gets to sleep in my sister's guest room."

She wiggled her eyebrows. "Seems to me you should just share."

"It's a full."

"Even better. I don't think she'd mind a snuggle."

There was no way. Even if he'd softened to her a bit over the last few days, Sarah was doing no such thing. In fact, she went out of her way to annoy him. Though she had worn the fuzzy socks... No. He would not even entertain this possibility.

He shook his head. "You're totally reading the situation wrong."

She smirked, pouring milk into a blender. "There are many things I've been wrong about, Supe, but this is not one of them."

He turned back to the bar and prayed that this was in fact one of them. Otherwise, his life was about to get immensely complicated—and that was the last thing he needed.

Chapter 13

Sarah

Sarah's phone pinged, and she glanced down, already knowing what it was going to be. Dating sites to ferret out someone to bring to the gala had been an awful idea. She'd had more than a week of dick pics and *hey, sweet thang* messages. Seriously, she wanted to drown her phone in the toilet. The one date she had gone on—well, he'd been blatantly trying to get her drunk and kept flipping the key-card to his hotel room. The room that was above the bar they were in. Jess had come through with a fake emergency to get her out of there after twenty minutes.

The event was in four days. Jess already had plans for the night—a bachelorette party for one of their sorority sisters—and Sarah knew better than to ask her to back out of that. Jess would do it, but she'd been looking forward to a girls' night out for a while. Between both their limited budgets, nights on the town were few and far between. It was much cheaper to order takeout and visit the liquor store than to sit at the bar—fewer obnoxious drunk guys whining about whatever sporting event was on too.

But staying home meant they were stuck with Brian, who—outside of work—went nowhere and knew no one. Well, no one except Tasha. That friendship didn't seem to be getting him out of the house yet. It was, however, improving his mood. He'd even stopped trying to take back the bedroom, which was weird. And annoying. He constantly kicked them out of the living room even though it had the only television, and he slept practically naked despite the frigid temperatures in the room. Keeping the apartment on the chilly side wasn't only a Jess thing—it was a Hawkins thing. Their parents' house was toasty warm in the winters and sweater-weather cold in the summer.

Brian also often walked around in boxer briefs or mesh shorts. No shirt. His chest assaulted her at every turn. She didn't want to see his muscles and chest hair and that happy trail leading to what she had discerned was not a small treasure. Sarah didn't want those dimples to appear every time he got a text from his coworker or saw her in those damn fuzzy socks. Sarah couldn't *not* wear them—they were the most comfortable thing she owned. But every time she wore them, he smiled like she'd given him a freaking award.

"Sarah?"

She jumped back to reality, uncurling her fingers from around her phone. Her boss, Maggie, stood at her desk, a clipboard in her hand. Sarah knew what that meant. And she didn't have an answer.

"Hey, Maggie. What's up?"

"Finishing up the seating chart... I moved Tyler and Monique"—Maggie rolled her eyes, loyal friend that she was—"to table six with some other minor celebrities. But are you still bringing someone? I need to firm up all the details."

"Yes," Sarah said without hesitation.

There was no way she could show up alone when Tyler was bringing a model. It was unacceptable. Too many people who knew her would be there—too many people whose money the charity depended on. He was making enough of a statement. She couldn't let it stand.

Maggie wrote something on the chart. "Okay, good."

Sarah laughed. Maggie had been mum on the subject since Sarah spilled the beans about the breakup, but now she wore a smirk that said she wanted to bury Tyler for his ridiculousness.

"I don't care if he's a bronze partner." She looked around the room, but Leigh was downstairs, getting her afternoon coffee. Coffee was something Sarah couldn't afford until her next paycheck. And Brian was off today. "In this case… make him pay."

Sarah flushed. "I'll try my best, Mags."

"Come on." Maggie motioned for her to get up, and Sarah obliged hesitantly.

"Yes?"

"Coffee. My treat. You can tell me about your prospects."

Sarah groaned. "They're slim."

"Well, then, you can tell me about your dress, because it'd better be a showstopper."

She flushed, thinking of Brian's reaction to her dress. Warmth spread through her, and her spine straightened as if his fingers were on her again. She shook off the feeling and pulled up the photo on her phone.

"Woozah." Maggie grabbed the phone from her hand and started zooming in on various parts of the dress.

Sarah held back a chuckle. She supposed it was a good thing to have a boss who unabashedly zoomed in on her décolletage.

"Post this picture," Maggie said. "You'll get a date."

"I did. That's the problem." She took her phone back and shoved it into her pocket. "It's like every horny guy in Philadelphia saw that picture and is propositioning me."

"I could ask my nephew."

Sarah shook her head too quickly, a blush burning her cheeks. That had *bad idea* written all over it. Maggie's nephew Jace was hot and charitable and good with kids and totally and completely off-limits. She really was in desperate times if Maggie was offering him up.

"No, no. I'll find someone."

"All right, but just say the word, and I'll move his seat next to yours on the chart."

SARAH LAY FLAT ON HER back, arms at her sides, eyes closed. She breathed in and then out. But her mind wouldn't settle.

"This is supposed to be calming," Jess muttered from the same position next to her. "I can hear your racing thoughts from here."

Sarah's leg twitched, and she willed it to be still. Usually, Savasana was one of the best parts of class. She loved the stretching and the motions, but when did she ever get to just lie down and clear her mind? Never. Not when she'd lived with Tyler, who went from one hundred miles an hour to crashed and back to one hundred miles an hour in a flash. And definitely not now, in her old room, which still smelled faintly of boys' body spray. Her mind spun as quickly as the fan each night, going from worry for her job—now that she'd lost credit for Tyler's donation—to worry for her heart as she scoured the internet for a fake date to worry for Jess, who was keeping something from her.

She breathed deeply, forcing her shoulders from her ears. Everything would be fine. Maggie loved her and would never let her go. Sarah would find a date even if she had to call in a ringer. Jess was fine—her quiet was because her brother was in town, the secretiveness because he was sleeping on the floor and would see any guy she brought home. These were not real fears. This was her mom's nagging and her father's absence and every family member who asked her when she was coming home to settle down as if she was playing a game, not building a life.

"You're not breathing," Jess said through her teeth.

Sarah let out a breath and rolled onto her side, bringing her knees to her chest. Her eyes fluttered open, and she took in the rest of the class, calm and breathing and letting the energy of the flow move through them. This was why she preferred Zumba. Dancing it out always worked better than stretching.

The instructor called the class back a moment later, and the stillness of the moment broke. Jess stared at her from her mat, her eyes thoughtful.

"What?" Sarah hissed, sitting up and crossing her legs along with the rest of the class.

No answer came as the instructor ended the class with a "namaste" and a farewell. Sarah stood and started folding her mat, but Jess didn't offer anything beyond another glance. It wasn't an encouraging glance. Last time Sarah had seen it, she had been forced into a double date with a guy who wore a pocket protector.

They walked the few blocks back toward the apartment, stopping for takeout at their favorite hole-in-the-wall taco shop. Jess rambled about her day. Whatever she'd been about to say at yoga didn't come up. Maybe the idea hadn't made sense... whatever it had been. Her best friend had as many good ideas as bad.

"So, I can't believe I'm even going to suggest this, but I have an idea," Jess said, stopping on their front stoop, barring entry.

Sarah frowned. "Can't we talk about it inside, over these delicious tacos and street corn?"

"Just..." Jess held up a hand and fretted at her bottom lip. Her pause was longer than normal, and Sarah could see the internal debate she was having. Jess's eyes met hers with a mix of weariness and resolve. "What if you take Brian to the gala?"

What the what? "You want me to go on a date with your brother."

"A fake date," Jess clarified. "A one-night-only engagement that doesn't end up with the two of you horizontal."

"Brian doesn't even like me. Why would he volunteer to spend a whole evening with me—in a tux no less."

Jess keyed into the building but not before rolling her eyes so hard it looked like it hurt. "You had a fine time at the mall."

Exactly. That's the problem.

"And he brings you coffee whenever you ask. Coffee, I remind you, that he has to pay for and walk across the city to deliver."

Sarah crossed her arms. "He brings you coffee just as often."

"No, I stop at his store every morning, and he uses his comp drink on me. It's not the same."

"Okay, so we're getting along better." She tried to keep the defensiveness out of her voice but failed. "I thought you'd be happy about that."

"I am. What I'm saying is that I bet he'd help you out with Tyler if you asked him. You two might even have fun together. Better than bringing some random guy who could totally ruin everything. It's not like I can call and rescue you at the gala."

This was true.

"And honestly, if anyone could use a night out, it's Brian."

"Fair point. But how does bringing *him* help with the Tyler situation?"

"Don't act like my brother isn't good-looking. You and I both know he is. And don't say his personality negates it."

Sarah snapped her mouth shut. Sometimes her bestie knew her too well.

"You two have an energy that could easily be confused for sexual tension." She gave Sarah a pointed look. "Trust me."

She flushed. Wondering what Brian's sudden nice streak was about and having nightly dreams about his hands on her bare skin was one thing. His sister picking up on sexual tension was a completely other thing. And it was far from okay. So freaking far.

"And you would be okay with us going to the gala together?"

Jess shrugged. "You both say nothing is going on between the two of you, so yeah, fake date my brother all you want."

Sarah shook her head, warning signs flashing in her mind. "He's probably working."

"He's opening on Saturday, so he'd be free." Jess stopped at the door to the apartment and offered a grin. "Did I mention he can ballroom dance?"

"He can *what*?"

"Shush," she said, pushing open the door. She scanned the small space. Brian wasn't in immediate range. "He learned in high school."

"How did I not know this? Was it to impress a girl? Please tell me it didn't work."

"It was for the school play."

"Oh my god, are there pictures? Please tell me there are pictures."

"Hey, Bri!" Jess said too brightly.

Sarah turned in his direction and stopped in her tracks. Her yoga bag fell off her shoulder. She knew she was staring, but she couldn't not. He leaned against the doorjamb of the bathroom in loose-fitting pajama pants—plain gray ones, none of his usual *Star Wars* art—and a towel around his neck. His hair was too long and bedraggled. He had more than a day's worth of scruff, and *holy hell*, his chest. True, she'd been seeing it for days, but not like this, with those Vs on full display and a neatly trimmed happy trail. *Good God.* He was like every fantasy she had about hot guys appearing half-naked in her apartment.

"Hey," he said, not even fazed by the fact that he clearly had no underwear on under those pants and his package was on full display. "What's in the bag?"

"Tacos," Jess said. "I picked up a few extra for you."

"I got something for you too," he said, falling back onto the couch. "Check the fridge."

Jess ambled off, but Sarah still couldn't move. Brian Hawkins was hot. Like, actually hot. As in, if they weren't mortal enemies and his sister wasn't her best friend, she would tackle him right then and there.

Fuck.

"Oh my god!" Jess exclaimed from the kitchen, shaking Sarah out of her stupor. "Is that iced coffee and... caramel syrup?"

Brian smiled, his eyes meeting Sarah's. "Wait for it..."

"Is that an espresso machine with a milk frother?"

"I brought you vanilla and toffee syrup too." His gaze intensified, lighting a fire in Sarah that she didn't like. "Happy belated birthday."

Something in her cracked at the words. The action was thoughtful. And though it wasn't just for her, it also was. He *had* been bringing her coffee all week because she asked—no demanded—that he do it. She pushed away the surge of emotions. They didn't have to be enemies, but they couldn't be whatever this was either.

She swallowed and softened her expression into as natural a smile as she could muster. "Thank you."

He nodded. "You only turn twenty-six once, and well, a proposal gone wrong shouldn't be your only present."

"Would you go to the fundraiser gala with me?" she blurted before she could stop herself.

His eyebrows rose exceedingly high on his forehead. "What? Did you just...?"

"I'll..." She paused, realizing it sounded like she'd asked him on a date. "I'll give you the bedroom for the weekend if you'll be my fake date."

He narrowed his eyes. "To make your ex jealous?"

She nodded.

"For the month."

No way. If she gave him a month, he'd never give the room back. And she could not stay in the living room, with no privacy, for a month. She just couldn't. Especially not when her period showed up. If there was ever a time she needed a bed and a place to hide away her bitchiness, it was then. But Brian was staring at her, straight-faced.

"A week," she countered.

He puckered his lips, considering. "Two weeks, and you'll let me use your car."

"You'll take good care of her."

"The best."

She stuck out her hand, already regretting this but knowing it was the only way. Brian *was* good-looking, and if they had any of the spark from the dressing room, Tyler would most certainly be jealous. Her eyes traveled down to his lips, and she quickly refocused on his eyes. "Fine, two weeks. And Betty gets a car wash."

Brian grinned and slipped his hand into hers. "Then it's a date."

Chapter 14

Brian

Brian untied his tie for the third time, his fingers rigid against the silk. He used to be good at this. Every game day for four years of high school, he had to wear a tie to school. His dad was out the door long before he left for school, and his mom, who knew exactly how to help him into all his football padding, couldn't tie a tie to save her life. So he'd learned—several knots in fact. But all that knowledge was failing him now.

Worry nagged at him. A fake date. With Sarah. Sarah, who starred in too many of his recent dreams. *What was I thinking?* After everything he'd gone through last year with his ex-girlfriend's fake marriage... but no, it wasn't the same thing. Sarah was single, and her ex was an asshole by all accounts.

He grimaced. He could imagine his ex's best friend saying the same thing about him. She probably had on that stupid podcast of hers. But he wasn't about to listen to the two-part special on the marriage pact to see how he fared in the retelling.

"Look at you, big brother." Jess whistled. "Fancy."

He glanced at himself in the mirror. The tux fit well for a last-minute rental. If only he could get this tie knotted properly. "Thanks, sis."

He fumbled with the tie again. Thank God Sarah had to be there early. He didn't think he could survive the whole preprom arrangement—corsage and all—his sister surely would have put them through.

"Let me do it." Jess stepped in front of him, her fingers tugging at the silk strands.

"Is this a good idea?"

She glanced up at him. "It was my idea so absolutely."

"It feels hypocritical."

"You're helping a friend out, nothing more."

He didn't correct her and say Sarah wasn't his friend. More and more, she was starting to feel like one. "Yeah, that's what Hannah's letter said."

"That fucking letter. She should've just let you think she'd left you for another guy for real without any further explanation. Because she did. And maybe you deserved it, but she didn't make anything better." She looked around the room—yes, the room he was finally back in, at least for the next two weeks. "I swear, Brian, if you still have that letter..."

He forced himself not to look at the dresser, where he'd stuffed the letter last night after removing it from its usual spot in his wallet. "It's long gone."

"It better be. And tonight is nothing like that. Sarah needs an escort for one night."

"I know."

Jess handed him a small box. "This is for her."

He opened it, finding a hair comb with jewels the same shade as Sarah's dress. "Where'd you get this?"

"It doesn't matter. Make sure you give it to her where Tyler can see."

"What if he just doesn't care?"

Sarah smirked. "He cares. Appearances are everything to him. Sarah embarrassed him by turning him down, and he's trying to push it back on her with his ridiculous model date, but when he sees you there with her—skimming her arm, putting this in her hair, dancing up close and personal—he's going to lose his mind."

"And want her back?" Heat—almost rage—roared through him, and he tamped it down as best he could, fixing his features back to normal.

"Maybe, but she's never going to take him back. She barely wanted him in the first place." She glared at him, pulling his tie too tight. "Not that you care."

He met her glare with one of his own but soon softened at the hint of a question in his sister's eyes. She still thought something had happened that first night, and it bothered her. He'd never thought he'd see the day when Sarah was right.

He shifted his gaze from his sister to his cuff links. "I care enough that I don't want her back together with a douchebag."

She shoved him toward the door. "All right, big brother. Have fun tonight but not *too much* fun."

He laughed, though her tone insinuated more than her words let on. "Seriously, Jess, it's not like that."

"That's what you said after playing seven minutes in heaven with Bella, and yet..."

He froze in the doorway, his fingers gripping the box she'd given him moments before. His sister hadn't mentioned Bella—his high school girlfriend and Jess's former friend—in years. Not since Jess had showed up at Binghamton his junior year and reminded him that he was under no circumstances allowed to date any of her friends.

"It's not the same thing," he said.

"Then I'd better find one of you on the air mattress in the morning."

THE ART MUSEUM AT NIGHT was spectacular. Manhattan had any number of museums, all beautiful in their own way. But this museum—lit up, with a crowd in fancy dress—was one of the most beautiful things he'd seen in Philadelphia. It made him want to see more—to stay long enough to know all the amazing things this city offered. Guests weren't entering at the famed Rocky Steps that led to the picturesque entrance—he could almost hear Sarah complaining about those stairs in heels—but the museum was still a sight.

He walked into the storied hall, taking in his surroundings. He fidgeted with his tux. Sarah hadn't told him how to find her once he'd gotten here, only handed him the ticket and told him no less than three times not to be there later than eight. It was 7:58, but he still felt late. It was clear from the thinning crowd inside that many people had already arrived. Finally, he reached the hostess, an older woman with a brilliant smile, who seemed to know every guest. Except, of course, him.

"Good evening," she said, taking his ticket. Her eyes narrowed at the number on the top of it, but her smile never faltered.

"Brian Hawkins. I'm Sarah Webb's..." He shifted in place, fumbling for the right word. "Date."

The woman's eyes widened, and a sly smile replaced her static greeter expression. "So you are, Brian Hawkins."

"Right." He swallowed. "Do you know where she is?"

"Last I saw, she was chatting with the event coordinator over by the platform." She waved to a woman closer to Sarah's age. "Can you take over, Leigh? I have to escort this fine young man to *our* table."

Leigh, who he'd heard Sarah mention more than once, ogled him, her eyes traveling from his head to his feet and back. Then she, too, smiled at him wickedly. "She did good."

"All right, Mr. Hawkins, this way," the first woman said.

"*Brian*'s fine."

She nodded. "I'm Maggie Clairmont, Sarah's boss and founder of Sophie's Wish Factory."

"It's nice to meet you. It's a great thing you're doing for these kids."

"We like to think so."

They walked past table after table until they were near the front. He spotted Sarah chatting with another tux-clad guy, and his heart stopped. They were standing close but not too close. His eyes skipped from the guy and his goo-goo eyes to Sarah. He froze in place. He'd seen the dress, but this was another level. Her hair was pulled back, but loose tendrils fell, framing her face. Though not as red as it had been, her hair glistened against her bare shoulder and the deep-red fabric. She glowed in the low lighting. He shifted, keeping his hands in his pockets. Feigning attraction wasn't going to be an issue. No, the opposite was going to be a huge problem. How was he going to keep his hands off her? Particularly when his job was to have his hands on her for all to see.

"Are you coming, Mr. Hawkins?" Maggie's eyes glinted in amusement at what he had to assume was an awestruck expression on his face.

"Yes, sorry." He closed the space between them and pulled his eyes from the gentle slope of Sarah's shoulder.

Sarah's eyes lit up as if maybe she was surprised that he'd shown up—or as if she was actually happy to see him.

"Bri," she said, taking one step then another.

Then her hands were around his neck, and she was squeezing him close, and he couldn't breathe from the heady scent of her perfume and her closeness and the silky softness of her skin under his hands. Blood shot down his body, and he took a steadying breath, which only made it worse as all his senses were overwhelmed by her.

"You look stunning," he said, stepping back but keeping a hand on her waist.

"Thank you." She straightened his tie and then cupped his face. "You look quite fetching yourself."

Her eyes never left his, but he saw the tiniest bit of mischief in them—her ex must have been nearby. He leaned into her so close her hair tickled his chin. He ran a hand up her arm and slipped a finger under the thin strap of her dress. She shuddered at the touch. *An act?*

"Where is he?" he whispered, his lips grazing her ear.

She laughed and pulled him in by the tie. Their lips were so close he felt every breath she took, tasted it. He'd never wanted to kiss someone so badly in his life. But then her eyes shifted from his for a millisecond, and the lust that had been there moments before faded into cunning and something darker.

"He's the douchebag in Armani at three o'clock."

He didn't want to look—didn't want to see the guy who only weeks before had Sarah's heart—but he couldn't help it. The ex had slicked-back hair, a fitted suit, and brogues that he could see from across the room. *What a dick.*

"I can't believe you dated that," he said, holding out his arm.

She hooked a hand around it. "We all make bad choices. Mine is Tyler. Yours is, like, the whole last decade of your life."

"Ouch."

She laughed. "Sorry, that was too much."

"Just a bit."

Sarah led them to their table, where her clutch already sat on a chair. His name in elegant script was on the place setting next to hers. And god, their names looked good next to each other.

"We have to mingle in a bit and dance," she said. "Get off your feet while you can."

He didn't have to be told twice. He took a sip of water and then turned to face her.

"So... I have something for you from Jess." He didn't look around to see if Tyler was looking, but he felt eyes on them. It would have to be enough.

"Oh? I love presents."

Brian laughed and pulled the box from his suit pocket. He handed it to her. "Yes, I know."

Her smile faltered, and she fingered the small box. Finally, with an audible breath, she opened it. "She didn't," she whispered so quietly he couldn't be sure of what she'd said.

He took in the flowered design and the red gems and how the comb sparkled in the lighting. It was a beautiful piece. Nothing like he'd seen in any of the stores Sarah dragged him to.

"What's wrong?" he asked, taking in her flushed cheeks and watery eyes.

"Nothing," she said. "It's perfect."

He picked the comb up and motioned to her hair. "May I?"

"It was my grandmother's," she said as he worked the comb through the knot of curls at the back of her head. "It lost a lot of the stones over the years and was pretty tarnished. My mom, she didn't know how to take care of things like this. I always said I was going to get it fixed, but it wasn't exactly in the budget."

His sister, always going above and beyond. Always knowing what everyone needed before they did. Like this night. And how much he needed one night of... if not normalcy then just not sitting on the couch being underemployed.

"It's beautiful," he said. She was beautiful. But he'd already said that. And saying it when no one was listening would give up the game. He stood and offered her his hand. "Dance or mingle?"

Chapter 15

Sarah

If Tyler didn't stop talking, Sarah was going to lose it. Ten minutes earlier, he'd wandered over to the group of donors she was chatting up. Brian had left her side for the first time all night to procure them drinks, and poof, her ex showed up. Monique was not on his arm—she was talking with another minor local celebrity across the hall. Tyler was droning on about some article he'd read in a recent medical journal. He had a captive audience in everyone but her. Everybody loved Dr. Ackerman, Philadelphia's finest pediatric surgeon. But she knew better. Tyler loved the sound of his own voice. He loved that these people pored over his every word. And he loved that Sarah had no choice but to nod and smile and be cordial. This crowd, at least, didn't know she and Tyler had ever been an item, but it would still look odd if she just disappeared.

She scanned the crowd for Brian but didn't see him, only the winding line for the bar. *Great.* Sarah wondered why exactly the bartenders were lacking and hoped that Brian would bring multiple drinks after waiting in that ridiculous queue.

Warm hands slid around her waist, followed by a lean body and the familiar scent of Light Blue, Brian's cologne of choice—a fact that she hadn't known until she threw herself into his arms earlier. Tyler stopped midsentence and glared at Brian. She couldn't see Brian's face, but his lips were so close to her that she felt him smile broadly and without shame.

"Sorry, folks, I just have to steal this beautiful lady for a dance," Brian said.

He led her away to a few chuckles and "young love" remarks from the older crowd. She didn't look back, and his eyes never left hers.

"Good move," she said, slipping her arms around his neck as they reached the dance floor. A few other couples were there, which was a nice change of pace from previous events. "But where are our drinks?"

"At the table. You looked like you were about to carve his tongue out with your bare hands."

"Close."

He pulled her to him and brought one of her hands down from his neck. His fingers traced a line down her forearm and over her wrist until their hands were clasped. His other hand went to her waist. Her senses were piqued, goose bumps sprouting on her arms as his warmth seeped into her. God, how she wanted him to move that hand farther down and ruck up her skirt and...

She was in so much trouble. Brian could not be doing this to her. And not on a fake date. But it didn't seem fake. There was none of his usual dickishness. He was pleasant and fun, and sure, there was banter, but it didn't have the same bite as before. He seemed happy, she realized. She hadn't seen him happy up close before. Not in all the years she'd known Jess.

"He looks like he wants to come over here and drag you away."

She blinked, almost forgetting who he was talking about and what they were doing here. Forgetting that they weren't in fact on a date. "Great."

"Want to give him a show?" His tone was playful, teasing even, and his eyes sparkled.

Her limbs went weak as his finger slowly trailed down her cheek and lifted her face to his. Before she could think to stop him or fall into him, he bent her into a dip. He followed her down and pressed his lips to her neck then pulled them both back up. His eyes blazed with what she swore was hunger.

But then he grinned, and that teasing was back. "You okay there?"

She shook her head. "Maybe we could get some air?"

SARAH SLIPPED OUT OF her heels and pulled a folded-up pair of ballet flats from her clutch. Maggie and Leigh would tease her endlessly if they saw her in these hideous things, but there was no way she was running up seventy-two steps in heels. Brian looked like he would already be at the top, jumping up and down like the millions of other tourists in this city. He bounced on his feet and loosened his tie. She waited an extra beat to see if he would start throwing fake punches, but no such luck.

"You ready?"

"Are you seriously excited for this?" she asked, handing Brian her shoes.

He nodded. "Running the Rocky Steps is, like, top of the bucket list."

"You realize you could've come here anytime, right? You lived ninety miles away for how many years?"

"And how many times have you been to New York City in the last three years?"

She shrugged. "A few, but going to the top of the Empire State Building isn't on my bucket list."

He paused, his eyes narrowed, as if he wanted to ask another question, but then he smiled. And it was breathtaking and contagious. She turned her attention to the steps. How many times had she and Jess done this over the years? Every time someone came to visit. It was literally the second request after cheesesteak.

"Winner buys dinner for the week," he said, leaning forward as if ready for a race.

She groaned. There was no way she was going to beat his long legs up these steps. "I hope you like Hot Pockets."

"Love them."

"Okay, on three."

Brian was fast, and he wasn't in a dress. But she really didn't want to live on Hot Pockets for the week. She sped up. Her feet felt every landing on those hard stone steps, but she didn't care. Free dinner for a week was at stake. And then she saw her opening—a misstep on his part. These steps weren't exactly normal. Sarah pushed ahead, sprinting toward the top. They were neck and neck at the last landing. Just a few more steps... but Brian pulled ahead and fell across the top step.

"Are you okay?" she screeched. That had to hurt. But he rolled over in that poor rented tux, his eyes brimming with tears, his body shaking in laughter.

His eyes met hers, and he grinned. "I prefer the ham and cheese and the pepperoni pizza Hot Pockets."

She rolled her eyes and sat down next to him. He shifted into a sitting position, resting his elbows on his knees, still shaking with laughter.

"You were supposed to let me win." She shoved him playfully.

His eyes shone, and that frenetic look from earlier was back. He leaned in close, his body taut, and pushed a piece of hair back from her cheek. She felt his breath on her skin and the warmth of his fingers against her arm. Her body urged her forward. *Yes*, it screamed. And *yes*, her mind screamed back. Because this was the most right she'd felt about something in years—righter than when she'd moved to Philadelphia to live with Jess or when she asked Tyler to dance that first night or when she left her small Midwestern town. Sarah pushed closer, and he did too.

His lips grazed hers. "Never," he whispered.

And then Brian kissed her.

Chapter 16
Brian

Brian's fingers tangled in Sarah's hair as their lips crashed together. Her hands wrapped around his neck, her breasts grazed his chest, and it took everything in him not to pull her onto his lap on this crowded set of stairs. She wasn't just kissing him back—she was breathing him in, urging him on with every flick of her tongue. This was like no kiss he'd ever had. He nipped at her lip, and a moan sounded from her that put him perfectly at attention. They couldn't do this here. They couldn't do this at all. Or could they? Sarah had most certainly kissed him back. She had welcomed him, parting her lips and letting him dance with her.

He pulled back, slowly opening his eyes to reality. He said her name in barely a whisper, but her eyes opened, and a blush brightened her cheeks—whether at their surroundings or their activities, he wasn't sure.

"You shouldn't have done that," she said. The words held no weight as she inclined her head into him.

He brought his hand back from her hair and cupped her cheek. "I had to."

She locked eyes with him, and a million questions passed between them, but she only asked, "Why?"

There were so many possible responses—"You're beautiful... I've wanted to since you fell into my lap... How could I not?"—but he didn't say any of them. They froze in his throat. If he said them, he couldn't go back. He wasn't ready to plunge into this dick first. Not when his living arrangements and her relationship with his sister and their own fledging friendship was at risk. He scanned the people around them—a combination of tourists and teenagers and gala guests—and his eyes landed on the one person he needed to be there in that moment.

"Douchebag at nine o'clock."

She didn't even look. Didn't even deign to pretend to believe him. "Take me home, Brian."

"What?" He couldn't breathe. Those words could mean anything.

She kissed him—hard and demanding and intentional, leaving no doubt. This wasn't a request. This was an invitation. An acceptance of the fate they had just tested. "Take me home."

IF ALL THE BLOOD IN his body hadn't already been rushing toward his dick, it most certainly was now. He stared at her for another heartbeat. Taking her home sounded like the best idea he'd had in his life, and Jess was at that bachelorette party. But if he did, what would happen next? And if he didn't, Sarah would never forgive the snub.

"Sarah?" a male voice said behind them—one he'd only heard for the first time less than an hour ago.

Brian stiffened, and across from him, Sarah did the same. He felt more than saw the snipped reply she was about to give her ex until they both glanced up at the couple standing before them, along with a stodgy-looking man.

"Sorry to interrupt," Tyler continued, not looking the least bit apologetic. "But this is Harold Rodgers, owner of Rodgers Talent Management, Monique's firm. He's hoping to set up some meetings and see how his firm can possibly work with Sophie's Wish Factory in the future. Maggie insisted we talk to you."

Sarah stood, a fake smile plastered on her face as if a potential donor hadn't caught her making out. Brian silently cursed whoever had decided that an outdoor bar was a good addition to the event as Sarah chatted up the man. Despite the model on Tyler's arm, his eyes swiveled between Sarah's breasts and ass.

Man, it would feel good to punch this asshole.

Brian watched as Tyler's model date sidled up next to the older man and Sarah. He kept a step behind and let Sarah do her job—the whole reason they were here in the first place.

"Good find," Tyler said, nodding approvingly at Sarah. "A little crazy but totally worth it in the bedroom."

Don't punch him. Do. Not. Punch. Him. "Yeah, I know, right? Picked her up a few weeks ago at some bar. She was on the prowl after some idiot who she clearly didn't love proposed to her. On her birthday no less. Woman was wound up tight like she hadn't had good sex in too long. Wildest night of my life, man."

He knew he was burying himself in a web of lies. But the look on Tyler's face made it worth it. Tyler was a dick. He deserved whatever pain losing Sarah had caused him because he obviously didn't deserve her. Not if he would call her crazy and discuss her sexual prowess with a stranger at a fundraising gala with his date less than ten feet away.

Tyler's hands clenched into fists at his sides, and Brian held in a laugh. Jess was one hundred percent right. Tyler absolutely cared and was infinitely pissed off that Sarah had a date. The act had worked.

Without another word to Tyler, Brian closed the distance between himself and the group. He stepped up next to Sarah, close enough that she would know he was there but far enough away that he didn't interrupt the conversation, which seemed to be going well.

"I can come to your office next week, and we can chat details," Sarah said, her smile burning at one hundred watts. She linked her arm with his without looking away from the task at hand, as if they'd been doing this forever and not for a few hours.

Harold nodded. "Lovely. Really. I want to hear all about the young talent."

Sarah nodded, her grip tightening on his arm in excitement. "Yes, of course, and I'll see if I can get some of Tessa's sketches."

"I'd love to meet her," Monique said. "Is that possible?"

"Yes, I can certainly arrange for that." Sarah paused. "She's in and out of the hospital throughout the week for dialysis, but I'm sure we could figure something out."

"I'm happy to come to the hospital if that's easiest," the model said as if it was nothing at all. Though Brian seriously doubted that.

Sarah's eyes lit up. "Let's talk next week."

They reentered the party, which had turned to the silent-auction part of the night. The lights were still dimmed but as not much, and couples no longer occupied the dance floor. Some stood by the auction items, but many sat chatting and picking at the assorted mini desserts that had appeared on each table. The donor gave Sarah a nod and a business card before melting into the party.

Tyler crashed their awkward gathering, picking Monique up and twirling her around. His eyes met Brian's in a challenge. "Sorry to break up the party, but I must steal this beautiful woman away." And then he kissed her, big and ugly and obvious.

Sarah rolled her eyes, turning her attention from the disgusting PDA. "I think you pissed him off."

Brian pulled her close, locking her in his embrace. "What now? Celebratory drinks? Do you still want to go home?" He hoped his voice sounded sturdier than he felt with that last question, but the blush on her cheeks proved that it didn't.

She stepped back from him, linking her hand with one of his, her expression thoughtful. Her eyes lingered on him, and he felt himself being undressed. "How about," she said, leading him toward the exit, "double or nothing."

Chapter 17

Sarah

"I can't believe you beat me again." Sarah gave him her best pout.

Brian laughed as they trudged up the stairs to the apartment, and she glowered at him. Feeding two people for two weeks on her budget was going to be nearly impossible, especially considering that Brian still ate like a teenage boy having a growth spurt. There had better be a sale on Hungry-Man meals or something.

He wrapped an arm around her waist as they reached the landing and pulled her into him. His breath stirred the hair at her ears. "You'd hate me more if I let you win."

She smirked and tugged him down by the tie. "True."

"I might be willing to let the double or nothing go for another week in the bedroom."

She glared at him. "Do not bargain with me, Brian Hawkins. You will eat every one-dollar frozen meal I buy you for the next two weeks, and you'll do it with a smile."

He laughed and tucked a piece of hair behind her ear. "Pinky promise, all smiles. Except if it's Salisbury steak. Then I'll throw up on you."

"Ew."

"My point exactly." His grin turned into something more serious. "Is there anything I can do to soften your loss?"

"Oh, I can think of a few things."

And oh, could she ever. Particularly with that tongue of his. If he could get her to the brink with a kiss, she could only imagine what he was able to do farther down. She kissed him, pushing up on her tiptoes and leaning into him until they were against the hallway wall. If she'd been worried that the earlier interruption and their second trip up the Rocky Steps had dampened Brian's want, she hadn't needed to. His hands skimmed the fabric covering her hips and waist and pushed it higher. She knew, by the growing need she felt from him, that if they hadn't been in this dingy hallway, the caress would be skin to skin and her dress would be on the floor.

"Should we...?" His eyes searched hers. There were so many questions and a desire so strong it bowled her over. No one had ever looked at her that way. His eyes told her the dirtiest thoughts he'd ever had—and that they were all about her.

"Yes," she said, "but first..." She freed her phone from her clutch and then pulled their faces back together. He smiled against her lips, and she swore she felt his eyes roll all the way to her toes. And it was so hot.

"More blackmail?" He fumbled in his pockets for the keys.

"No. Proof. If it's not on social media, did it even happen?"

"He saw it with his own eyes."

She added a few hashtags. "Don't worry. Look." Sarah held up the phone, and Brian squinted at it, his smirk growing wider.

"Best you ever had, huh?" He unlocked the door and pocketed his keys, his cheek dimpling.

Heat rushed through her, and she locked her gaze with his and licked her lips. "Dare to prove me right?"

A blaze rose behind Brian's eyes, and Sarah couldn't help the nervous giggle that escaped. Brian Hawkins was damn sexy. Desire practically radiated from his skin. He picked her up and buried his face in her neck. She wrapped her legs around him and brought his face back to her. They stumbled into the apartment. Every piece of her was a live wire sparking at each contact point. She had never wanted anything like she wanted to feel all of Brian on and in her, and god, she wanted him to possess her now. If she lived alone, the vestibule would be getting quite the show. But she didn't.

"Brian," she whispered against his lips. "The bedroom."

He pulled back, his nose crinkling. Not the mischievous expression she was expecting, but then she heard it—water running in the bathroom. *Fuck.*

"Jess is here." Brian's hand loosened on her waist, and soon, she was back on her feet.

This was a disaster. They looked like... well, two horndogs who'd been rolling around in the back of a car, which was exactly what they'd been doing.

"But she was supposed to be at that bachelorette party—they're staying at the Four Seasons. All night."

"Well..." Brian untied his tie and wrung it between his hands. "She's here, or we have a burglar that needed to pee."

Sarah held back the tirade of curse words she wanted to unleash and focused on the situation. Jess could not know what was happening. "How do I look?"

"Hot as fuck." Brian's husky tone warmed the ice-cold surprise that Jess being home had thrown on her senses.

"None of that. Your sister is here!"

"I really don't think she'll care that much."

"I'm telling you she will. And I'm not having secret sex with you across the hall. She's not stupid, and the walls are thin."

Brian rolled his eyes. "Jess and I wouldn't have survived high school or most of college without dealing with situations like this. Noise-canceling headphones. I'm sure she has them."

"I know she does, I gave them to her the Christmas after I met Tyler." Sarah didn't look to see if her words bothered him.

"Well, then, I don't see—"

The door to the bathroom screeched open as it often did. Jess stepped out. She wore joggers and a pink tank top. Her hair was thrown back in a messy bun. Mascara ran down her cheeks. Brian moved across the small space, his strides long and purposeful. In seconds, he was at his sister's side, a hand on her arm.

He leaned in, their foreheads practically touching. "Did something happen at the party?"

Jess shook her head and sniffled. "I never made it to the party."

Sarah saw Brian's shoulders visibly relax and felt her own do the same. She crossed the room and took up position next to him. He stepped back, meeting her eyes for only a second. So much passed in that moment. But she couldn't worry about Brian and what had almost happened—what she'd wanted to happen with every fiber of her being. If there was ever a sign that she should stay away from him, this was it. She focused on Jess. She hadn't seen her since that morning, but they'd texted all day. Nothing had come up. Nothing substantial, anyway.

"What happened?" She took Jess's hand as Brian backed away.

Cold seeped into the spot where he'd just been. Her arms, tingling with expectation moments earlier, were frosty. She kept her eyes trained on her best friend.

The moment the door to the guest bedroom closed, Jess fell into her arms, fresh tears wetting the bare skin at Sarah's shoulders. "I have so much to tell you."

JESS WAS DATING THE Herpes. Sarah didn't know how she'd missed the signs all these months. But it was so obvious now—the short-notice cancellations, the silence on her dating life, her "friend" who needed a ride to the airport more than once. She'd been dating him—Ryder—long distance for the last three months.

Three months. Sarah couldn't go three days without telling Jess about a guy. A rush of hurt and guilt flooded her veins. Her best friend hadn't trusted her with this news.

"Why didn't you tell me?" she said in a low voice, not sure she even wanted to know the answer.

Jess sniffled and repositioned on the pillow next to her. "After all the crap I said after our second date, he turned out to be so sweet, and he really cared. Like, he moved across the country and started a whole new life, and he still asked me about my day. He came back to tie up some loose ends, and..."

"So you like him."

She shook her head. "I love him."

A Jess Hawkins in love was a rare thing. A fragile thing. And Jess hadn't felt comfortable enough to tell her. Or Sarah hadn't been available enough. How much had she complained about Tyler in the last two months and Brian in the last two weeks? *Crap.*

"And the tears?" Sarah asked.

"We had a fight."

Sarah grasped Jess's hand. "Yes, I figured that part out."

"He didn't ask me to move to California." Her best friend had said it so plainly, as if it made perfect sense. Yet it couldn't be what it sounded like. In love or not, Jess couldn't be this upset because she *hadn't* been asked to uproot her whole life.

"What?"

Jess sighed and swiped at her eyes. "We were commiserating about how much we missed each other and how it sucked because I can't go out there for a few weeks and he's so tired of traveling back and forth. And I hinted that I could put out some feelers."

"In California?" The squeak in Sarah's voice was more than evident, but Jess didn't seem to notice.

Jess nodded. "And he didn't ask."

"You offered to move to *California*?"

Jess turned to Sarah and stared at her incredulously. "Yes, Sarah."

She tried to tamp down her panic. Her best friend could not move to California. "So, did you have a fight? Break up?"

"No."

"Then I don't understand."

"He was supposed to ask me, Sarah!" Jess pulled her hands from Sarah's and flung them in the air. "He was a Herpes for God's sake. He asked me to do long distance but not to close the distance. And I offered to do it after only three months, and he said nothing."

Sarah worried at the hem of her pajama shirt. "And so now you're the Herpes."

"Don't ever say that again." Jess laughed but soon smothered it with a groan. "How are we supposed to do this if we're three thousand miles apart?"

Sarah shrugged. "I guess you just do."

That had sounded better in her head, but Jess was nodding as if she'd said something profound. For a few seconds, Sarah considered that perhaps she had, but then Jess broke into a fresh batch of tears.

"I hate this."

"Come on." Sarah pulled her best friend to her feet and dragged her out into the living room. The space was mercifully empty. Some part of her had hoped that Brian would be sitting on the couch in only his suit pants and a bowtie like her own personal Magic Mike waiting for her. But no luck.

She pulled her phone out of her pocket and clicked on her music app.

"Nuh-uh." Jess shook her head. "No way."

Sarah clicked on the playlist she'd had since her last major breakup, the one that had sent her fleeing to Philadelphia in the first place. The first notes of Taylor Swift's "Shake It Off" rang through her phone's speakers. She blasted the volume before dropping the device onto the couch. Jess still stood across the room, shaking her head, but Sarah grabbed her by the hands and twirled her closer.

They danced and laughed and danced some more. They sang into their fists and tripped over pillows and clothing and fell into fits of giggles. The second song started, loud and full of foghorn before the familiar melody of one of Britney Spears's most popular songs from the aughts filled the small space.

"Be right back," Jess said as the door to the guest room opened.

Sarah hoped she wasn't going to try and recreate the chair dance from the music video for this song. They had downstairs neighbors after all, and Sarah was too tired after two trips up the Rocky Steps. She glanced over at Brian, who stood in the doorway with a sleepy but genuine smile on his face. Her eyes trailed down his cheekbones, stopping for too long on his lips before moving to the white ribbed tank top and leaving-nothing-to-the-imagination pajama pants.

"Were you sleeping?"

He shook his head and locked his gaze on her. "Waiting."

Something alive and raw and preternatural fluttered through her at that single word. It shot downward and almost bowled her over. Brian's usually light eyes were all darkness and desire. How she wanted to cross that room and jump into his arms. To feel the length of him against her. To push him back onto that bed and lock the door and forget all the reasons he was the worst idea she'd ever had—and to forget that her best friend had offered to move to California. She bit her bottom lip and watched him move from the doorway into the room.

Then Jess was beside her, handing over beers. "Hey, big brother."

"You okay?" His face softened into the expression reserved for little sisters and broken hearts.

Jess nodded as the song ended and another classic aughts pop anthem started. This wasn't technically a breakup situation, but the guy *was* gone. And Jess seemed happy enough. She jumped up on the balls of her feet, belting out the words. Without thinking about it, Sarah reached for Brian and pulled him into the shuffle.

"I'm not dancing to Kelly Clarkson," he said.

Sarah and Jess looked at each other, and then Jess stuck out her bottom lip. Brian rolled his eyes and threw his hands up in the air. A moment later, he caught the beat and was singing along, surprisingly on key, with the girl-power anthem of the last two decades.

Chapter 18

Brian

His head hurt. Brian squinted against the light and tried to roll over, but his arm hit something hard yet plush. He rolled the other way, but a body stopped him. A warm, soft, most definitely female body. *Holy shit.* Brian forced his eyes open and sucked in a breath at the chestnut hair next to him. They didn't. He would have remembered if they did, and anyway, they were in the living room. Still, her shoulder looked all too bare.

He ran a hand down his body. He wasn't naked. *Thank all the gods.* But he also wasn't dressed to be in bed with Sarah. Just the thought of her name sent blood rushing to his already erect cock. He resisted the urge to run his hand down her arm and pull her against him then nuzzle into her neck and wake her up with kisses and pleasure.

He sat up gingerly and immediately regretted it. A throbbing started behind his eyes, one he realized had been there the whole time. *Damn.* An arm hung off the couch, and he glanced up to see his sister sprawled out. *How much did we drink last night?*

"Hey, big brother," Jess said, her voice raspy and her eyes still half-lidded. "I think I'm still drunk."

He smiled at her, and the small movement made his head hurt even worse. "I *wish* I was still drunk."

She laughed and then stopped, a grimace twisting her face. She put a hand to her stomach. "Oh god. I think I might die."

"Let me get you some water." He said it before he'd really thought it through, but his sister's grateful expression made him get to his feet regardless. Brian untangled himself from the blanket and scooted to the edge of the air mattress. Sarah didn't even stir. He stared down at her incredulously. "Does she always sleep like this?"

"Yes, she does." Sarah's voice was scratchy and muffled by the pillow. Brian glanced over at his sister, who hid a giggle behind her hand. Sarah's eyes hadn't even opened, and she still hadn't moved.

"Need anything?" he asked just to see if she would sleep answer him again.

Her eyes cracked open, and she hit him with a glare so strong he had to keep from laughing. "Can you make pancakes?"

His stomach growled. "Chocolate chip or banana nut?"

Even with her eyes practically closed, he could see the eye roll Sarah gave him. "Is that a real question?"

Once in the kitchen, Brian crossed his fingers that there were even the ingredients to make pancakes. He knew his way around the kitchen well enough, but Jess didn't exactly keep a stocked pantry. Random condiments and snacks, yes. Food that added up to a meal, not quite. In fact, knowing Jess, she'd probably had a bowl of Raisin Bran the size of her head for dinner if she never made it to the party. He glanced at the sink, but she'd cleaned up the evidence of whatever she'd eaten.

He pulled open the cabinet closest to the oven. The few times Brian had seen his sister bake, he was pretty sure she pulled things from there. Which made sense—their mom had always kept the spices right next to the stove.

Yes. Hungry Jack pancake mix. Brian sent a silent prayer of thanks to whoever was listening and reached for a mixing bowl.

FIFTEEN MINUTES, A giant stack of pancakes, and a heaping plate of scrambled eggs later, Brian and Sarah sat in the dining room, still bleary-eyed but in better spirits. At least, he was in a better mood. Chocolate and coffee tended to have that effect. His sister had disappeared into her bedroom with more breakfast than one person should be able to eat and her cell phone pressed against her ear. She was talking in that low, indulgent tone some girls use during the makeup.

He turned his attention to the other woman in the room. The one who looked gorgeous even with bedhead and a mouth full of pancakes. The one whose bare shoulder sticking out of the thin cotton robe she'd slid into while he cooked was making him think too many dirty thoughts. He knew what that shoulder tasted like.

"What are you staring at?"

Brian blinked away the fantasy playing out in his mind. "Nothing. Looks like all will be well with Jess and her boyfriend."

"Ryder."

"What?"

"That's his name—Ryder." Sarah pushed a piece of pancake through a puddle of syrup. "Do you think she'd really move to California?"

Brian had only gotten half the story between their dance party and viewing of a god-awful *Dirty Dancing* prequel, and California hadn't been part of it. But that made sense. Jess and Ryder couldn't live at opposite ends of the country forever.

"Why not if she loves him?" Brian asked.

"How about because she has a life here?"

He shrugged. "I had a life in New York."

"It's not the same. Your life blew up—hers is thriving."

"Is it?"

"And," she continued, speaking over him as if he hadn't asked the question. "You are just itching to get back to your life in New York, so don't act like it's so easy."

He was ready to get back to his real life—to subway rides and too-long hours and overpriced beers with friends and coworkers. Staying in Philadelphia had never been an actual option. All the jobs he'd applied for recently had been in the New York area. But he also had to admit that *some* things about his current stopgap appealed to him.

He reached across the table and let his fingertips just meet hers. "I don't know. Philadelphia is kind of growing on me."

She shook her head, but her hand stayed where it was. "Listen, last night..."

He inched his fingers between hers so slowly that it was almost erotic. This was the best bad idea he'd ever had. And maybe after the past year, he needed a good bad idea. "Could be continued?"

"No, it can't." Sarah pulled her hand into her lap. "Last night was just the wine and tricking Tyler and all the endorphins from running up those stairs. It wasn't real."

Wow. There were plenty of things she could have said that Brian would have accepted—including that in the light of day, she thought it had been a mistake—but their activities not being real wasn't one of them.

"It seemed pretty real when you had your tongue down my throat."

Her eyes shifted away from him. "I'm sorry if it seemed like more than what it was."

"And if we *hadn't* been interrupted last night...?"

"But we were." Sarah stood and brought her plate over to the sink, never once looking back at him.

Brian wanted to stop her from walking away—to pull her to him and make her remember exactly how real last night had been. But something about her tone kept him in his seat. He was ignoring the fact that Sarah was giving him an out. He didn't want it. He was so tired of telling half-truths and skirting the issues. He didn't even know what this issue was. It couldn't all be about his sister's disapproval because Jess was a marshmallow, when it came down to it, and Sarah was one of the biggest parts of the fluffy and gooey middle. The stern look she would give the two of them would be worth figuring out whatever the hell was going on between him and Sarah, even if it ended up being nothing.

"That's a crap answer," he said to her retreating form.

She stopped on the cusp of leaving the room, her back still to him. "Well, it's the only one you're going to get."

Chapter 19

Sarah

Sarah lifted her head at the sound of gentle knocking. She'd asked Leigh to wake her up after twenty minutes, but a glance at the wall clock told her an hour had passed. And it wasn't Leigh standing at the door but Maggie. Her boss's face was twisted in concern. Rightfully so—Sarah wasn't one to literally sleep on the job. And she was in Maggie's office since her boss was supposed to be out at a prospective donor luncheon all afternoon. Sarah wondered if Leigh had intentionally let her oversleep, but it didn't seem like her.

"Everything okay?" Maggie asked.

Sarah sat up and ran a hand through her hair. "Yeah, sorry. I've been banished to the air mattress at the apartment and haven't been sleeping well."

It was a half-truth. She was sleeping on an air mattress, but that had nothing to do with her exhaustion. That inflatable bed was more comfortable than the bargain mattress in the bedroom. No, it was Brian who was keeping her awake. Or rather his absence. Since she'd rejected him three days earlier, he hadn't spoken to her. If he was home, he was in the bedroom. There were no more surprise dinners or banter or even dirty looks. There was just nothing. She knew she could fix it with a few words, but she wouldn't. Brian wasn't staying. And Jess was most likely leaving. Panic swelled in her again, and she swallowed it down, dry and harsh.

"Do I want to know why you are sleeping on an air mattress in your own apartment?"

Sarah laughed. It sounded brittle even to her own ears. "Lost a bet."

It wasn't exactly the truth, but she couldn't say she'd given her room away in exchange for a date to the gala.

"To whom?"

"Brian." The name flew out of her mouth before she could stop it.

To her coworkers, Brian was still the hot guy who had dazzled donors at the gala and brought Tyler to heel. It wasn't any more complicated than that, which was how she'd intended for it to stay before she blurted out his name, but the gleam in her boss's eye said there was no backtracking.

"Ah, I didn't realize you two were roommates."

"For the time being, but Jess only has the one extra room."

"Which you lost in a bet to your *date*." Her emphasis on "date" implied all sorts of things, including one glaring question of why someone who seemed so enamored with her would let her sleep on the air mattress.

Sarah shrugged. "The bed's too small to share."

"A bed is never too small to share with a man who looks like that and who looked at you like that man looked at you. There wasn't another woman in the entire ballroom."

"Brian," Sarah cleared her throat, "is Jess's older brother."

Maggie gave a nod of understanding, her eyes widening. Over the years, she'd seen enough of the dynamic duo, as she called Sarah and Jess, to understand the subtext with nearly no context. "I see."

"Yup." Sarah stood and walked toward the door. "Anyway, sorry I fell asleep in here. It won't happen again."

Maggie put a hand on her shoulder to stop her. "I have a spare room if you need a place to stay for a few days."

Brian had the bed for approximately ten more days, but even a few nights out of his circle of silence could be refreshing, especially considering that Jess's boyfriend had flown in that day for a long weekend as if their fight hadn't even happened. Jess and Ryder had made up swiftly and thoroughly, and he was coming to town for five days to meet the Hawkinses. Sarah was, of course, counted as one of the Hawkinses, but for the first time ever, the idea of spending a whole weekend with her second family felt suffocating.

"Are you sure?" Sarah asked. "Because that would be amazing."

"Consider the room yours."

"I'll only need it until..." She tried to remember when Jess's parents were descending on Philadelphia. "Saturday? I can be out first thing Sunday morning."

"Sounds great. I'll pick up some groceries and teach you how to cook so you can stop living off takeout and Ramen."

"I *can* cook. I choose not to." And it was the truth. She'd been cooking for herself long before she should have been allowed to use the stove, but that was privileged information.

Her boss gave her an incredulous look. "What exactly can you cook?"

Sarah met her gaze defiantly. "What do you want to eat?"

"WHAT DO YOU MEAN YOU'RE not going to be here this week?"

Sarah didn't look up at her best friend's surprised and somewhat hurt tone. One look at Jess's pout would have her unpacking her duffel bag. "It's just a little crowded in here. Don't you want some alone time with Ryder?"

"Brian will still be across the hall."

"Yes, and according to him, that situation is one you two are well accustomed to."

"So are we."

Sarah stopped stuffing underwear into the already full bag and looked at her friend. "I just need a little space."

"From...?"

"All of this." Sarah waved a hand to indicate the apartment and to try to move the conversation away from the fact that she simply didn't want to be around the guy who was taking her best friend away from her and the other guy who was bound to leave before they ever really had a chance to see what could be between them.

"Did something happen with Brian?"

"No."

"Because you two have been..." Jess's nose scrunched in that way it did when she was unsure how exactly to define something. "Weird."

Sarah barely refrained from throwing her hands up in the air. "Weird how? It's not like we're friends."

"Aren't you?"

"I really can't do this now."

"Did you sleep with him?" Jess's tone was more curious than angry, and her expression was placid if not a little wary. That normally would have been a positive thing, but the sense of inevitability on her best friend's face hit like a gut punch.

"When exactly would I have slept with him? At *the gala*, where I was working, or at *home*, where you were *crying* about how you didn't get asked to move across the country?"

Jess flinched, and a part of Sarah felt good that her words had landed as intended. The rest of her wanted to take them back and run into her friend's arms. She wanted to bury her face in Jess's shoulder, as she had so many times before, and let the lavender scent that always came with Jess comfort her. She wanted to tell her everything—from the kiss on the stairs to the making out in the Uber to the seconds-away-from-naked show that Jess had interrupted.

But she said none of that. Instead, she zipped up her bag and shouldered it. "I'll see you on Sunday. Give your parents my best."

Chapter 20

Brian

After only an hour, Brian could see why Sarah had deemed Ryder a Herpes. Brian truly hated that phrase, but it was inescapable. All that time with Hannah had hammered it into his vernacular, and now Sarah and Jess used it regularly. The two of them literally played Herpes or Not for every TV show and movie they watched. Tom from *500 Days of Summer*— totally a Herpes. Javier from *Dirty Dancing: Havana Nights*—not. Dawson Leery? Herpes. Pacey Witter? Not so much.

How was this his life? Again.

Although Ryder wasn't really a Herpes. He was more like a cinnamon roll—another phrase he'd added to his vernacular since arriving in Philadelphia.

"So, Brian," Ryder said, pulling him away from thoughts of all the other ridiculous habits he'd picked up in only a few weeks with Jess and Sarah. "How are you liking Philadelphia? Jess said you're in the market for a new job. Any bites?"

Brian had to keep himself from laughing. Bites? He'd barely even found a suitable position to apply to within a hundred-mile radius of Manhattan. He was going to have to widen the perimeter of his search area or seriously consider taking the job Corey kept offering. Working at an architectural firm wouldn't be the worst thing in the world. Despite its small-town home base, Scott and Johnson Home Design was a well-known name in certain parts. And they were looking to upgrade their systems, which meant Brian would be building something from the ground up. By all accounts, the job would be a great résumé builder. But Fairford was a hundred miles and another life from Manhattan. He had barely survived the summer there. How would he survive a year or more?

"Philly's nice," he said finally. "I haven't gotten to see much of it yet, but the company's good." He smiled at his sister. "Nothing on the job front at the moment. I might have to look beyond opportunities that are New York adjacent."

"Ain't that the truth." Ryder nodded enthusiastically. "That's how I ended up in San Diego. Don't get me wrong—I love it there. But if I'd had my way, I'd still be here with my family and friends and Jess."

Gooey inside and out. *The perfect dessert*, as he was sure Sarah and Jess would say.

"So, California was luck of the draw?" Brian asked, honestly interested. He didn't want to go back home, but he also couldn't imagine moving thousands of miles away from everyone he knew. Which was why he was hesitant to change his search radius. But if Jess was going to move...

"Not exactly." Ryder shifted in his seat. "I had connections through some fraternity brothers that got me out of the slush pile and in front of the right people. But yeah, I had the choice of moving to San Diego or Phoenix or Seattle. California just seemed the best fit. I had a few brothers out there. No one I knew directly, but we've connected now, and they've become great friends."

"That's how Sarah ended up an honorary Hawkins," Brian's dad said with the contented smile he got whenever anyone talked about the bonds of brotherhood—or sisterhood in Jess's case—that Greek organizations wrought.

Brian shifted uncomfortably at his father's mention of Sarah. She'd been a no-go topic for much of the night after Jess simply shrugged and said Sarah had other plans. The haughty flip of her hair gave away the fact that all was not right, but even Ryder, the newest to Jess's ways, knew better than to push it further.

"He knows that, Dad." Jess rolled her eyes.

"Right, yes. Jess has told me all about Sarah and all of you. How's the car rebuild going by the way?" Ryder asked.

Oh, this guy was good. And his sister was eating it up—her eyes were saucers of love. His mother looked like she was already planning the wedding and imagining summering in California with her grand-kids. And his dad could talk about that car for hours. It was practi-cally a third child—the rebuild had certainly taken long enough for the car to be an ornery teenager.

As his dad started in on the latest update on the car—the same one he'd been working on before Brian left for Philly—Brian tuned out. The car was yet another thing he and his father had never con-nected on. They had a fine relationship, but they had never meshed in the ways some of his friends had bonded with their parents. Or even the way Jess and their father seemed to connect. She'd sit for hours while he tinkered with the car, and she'd joined a Greek orga-nization when Brian hadn't. She'd left home but always loved com-ing back—she had been on the planning committee for her graduat-ing class's five-year reunion and would help plan their ten-year one in a few years. Brian had thrown away the invitation to his. But Brian had always wanted out, and Jess had literally been the homecoming queen.

His phone buzzed in his pocket, not for the first time, and he took his dad's distraction as a chance to finally check it. A desperate part of him wanted all the texts to be from Sarah. There was no way she didn't want to know what was happening here after her weird ex-it. But it wasn't Sarah's usual trail of stacked missives—seriously, the woman couldn't put more than four words in one text bubble. In-stead, the message was from Tasha.

They worked together most days and had quickly become friend-ly. Not hang-out friendly, but texts from her weren't strictly out of the realm of normalcy. Their conversations mainly consisted of memes and GIFs. It was fun in a way things hadn't been in so long.

How's dinner with your sister's beau? she asked.

She would use that word.

Boring AF. He's got Dad talking about his decades-long car rebuild.

Kiss ass, she said.

Yup.

Tell them there's a coffee-related emergency at the store and come hang. We're having a Kart party.

For real?

Fuck yeah. If you can get here in twenty, I can slot you in next round.

Send me your address, he wrote.

Bring your shit for tomorrow if you want. Couch is free.

If it wasn't Tasha, he'd have a total gamer boner. As it stood, it *was* Tasha, and she was most definitely not inviting him over for tawdry reasons. If anything, she was giving him an out from having to sleep with soundproof headphones. Sarah had had one thing right when she'd made her escape.

He glanced at Tasha's address. He'd known she lived near the store, but he hadn't realized she lived *that* close. He would be able to practically fall out of bed and be at work in the morning.

"Sorry, everyone," he said, cutting off whatever asinine question Ryder was about to ask his father, "but there's an issue at the store, and they need me to come in."

"Isn't there already a shift on duty?" Jess asked, her eyes boring into him with a sisterly rage that said she knew what he was doing and would make him pay for it later.

"Well, that's the issue." He stood and pocketed his phone. "The shift has to leave, and he needs someone to cover." Brian leaned down and gave his mother a kiss. "I'll see you tomorrow."

Jess quirked an eyebrow. "You won't be back tonight?"

"Just gonna crash at a friend's. Not worth it to come back here just to have to go back there for opening." It was stretching the truth, but no one was going to check whether he was at the store before sunrise or after—though he could tell his sister was already considering it.

"Will you get enough sleep?" His mother's eyes were so full of a maternal concern that it almost made him feel bad.

"Yes, Mom. I'll be fine." He gave his sister a half hug and nods of recognition to his father and Ryder. "Nice to meet you, man."

With his sister's eyes burning a hole into his back, Brian practically ran to his bedroom. He packed a bag, barely even noticing what clothes he was stuffing in it, only concerned about getting out of the apartment before someone drew him back in. When he turned to head to the bathroom for his toiletries, he found Jess standing in the doorway, her arms crossed.

"Yes?"

"Will you be back at any point during their visit?"

He nodded. "I'll be back tomorrow night if you want. Or I can stay with a friend."

"Tasha."

"Fine, Tasha. Or I'm sure Mom and Dad will get me a room at their hotel if you want some privacy."

"You're not going because you hate him?" She'd stepped into the room and dropped her voice so as not to be heard at the table.

"He's nice. I can totally see why you love him and why he's worth the long distance."

"But...?"

He smirked. They knew each other too well. "But I can't listen to Dad talk about that rebuild for another second. And if I have to talk about my job prospects, you know it'll turn into a campaign to get me to return to Fairford."

She considered this for a minute and then dropped her arms to her sides. "Fine. Go do whatever. But there'd better be *several* free lattes in my future."

He kissed her on the cheek. "Anything for you, sis."

BRIAN JAMMED HIS FINGERS into the controller as he maneuvered Toad around the course. He'd wondered on his way over if he'd be stuck trying to manhandle a Switch controller and was pleasantly surprised to find that the tournament was on an old-school Wii. The controller felt familiar in his hand, and the game soothed his angst as it always did. He'd dominated since he stepped in and was currently facing off with the hostess. For a second, he considered driving himself into a banana, but Tasha would know better, and there would be hell to pay for the rest of time.

"I got you now, Supe," she said, her fingers moving as fast as his on the buttons.

Brian laughed. There wasn't a chance she would beat him now. "In your dreams."

"Why does she call you Supe, man?" the guy next to him, Ethan, asked. His eyes went wide at his own joke. "I guess you have a Clark Kent vibe, but where are your glasses?"

Brian rolled his eyes. He felt Tasha laugh beside him and prayed that she wouldn't tell the Tinder story. He liked these people. He didn't need them knowing his sister occasionally perused his Tinder app.

"I'm the shift Supe-ervisor." Toad slid across the finish line seconds before Yoshi. Brian grinned. "And I'm Supe-er good at my job."

Tasha groaned. "Yeah, that's totally it. I couldn't remember his name, so I just called him Supe."

"And it stuck."

She placed fifty dollars—many of them singles—in his open palm. "That's, like, all my tips for the week, jerkoff."

"You invited me."

"Never happening again," she said.

"Oh no, he's totally coming back. I have to redeem myself, and he kicked your ass." Ethan stood. Tasha shot him the finger, and he gave her a shit-eating grin. "Brian, it's been a pleasure—see you next week for *Halo*."

He nodded. Ethan lived two doors over from Tasha, and apparently, he had some guys over regularly for Tuesday night *Halo*. Brian was more a *Call of Duty* guy, but he wouldn't turn down the offer. Friends outside his sister and his nemesis would be nice, and if he was really going to start applying to jobs outside his comfort zone, maybe he'd even find a roommate out of it.

Once Ethan left, the exit train started. One by one, people left, and then all at once, the apartment cleared out. He felt equally exhilarated and exhausted. It was after midnight, and while that wasn't late, he had work in seven hours, and he was back to sleeping on a couch. At least it was a comfortable couch.

He dropped six beer bottles in the recycling bin. "This was fun, Tee. Thanks for inviting me."

She nudged him with her hip as she was wont to do. "You're welcome. That couch pulls out, by the way."

"I think I love you."

"Of course you do. I'm fabulous."

He laughed. "Now you sound like Sarah."

She glanced at her watch. "Three hours."

"What?"

"You lasted three hours without mentioning her."

"I don't—"

"You do. Now, I have to open while you get to sleep for another hour, so blankets are in the hall closet, and God help you if you snore."

Chapter 21

Sarah

Sarah plopped down into the most comfortable armchair ever. She sat cross-legged, a bowl of fresh fruit in her lap and a cup of coffee on the table next to her. This was the life. Maggie's house was gorgeous. It was somehow petite but big, empty but cozy. The colonial-style home had three bedrooms upstairs, a dining room, a living room, and an eat-in kitchen down below, plus a small den that Maggie had set up as an office. But the selling point was the sunroom she'd added to the back and the expansive lawn. The property was surrounded by trees—she couldn't even see the closest neighbor. Sarah hated to admit it, but suburban living had its benefits—like watching the extremely hot guy who was currently mowing the lawn. He was too far away for her to make out much, but his rippling and sweaty abdomen said enough.

She turned her attention away from the heavenly sight out the windows and back to her conversation with her mother. They weren't the weekly-call type of mother-daughter duo—not like the Hawkins clan. Jess had talked with her mom on the phone every week for as long as she'd been in Philly, and even Brian had called his parents in the few weeks he'd been in town. Sarah and her mom could go weeks, sometimes months, without meaningful communication, and then her mother would pop up with a stream of consciousness update that made Sarah's phone explode for hours.

This was one of those mornings. Sarah had barely typed the words *Tyler and I broke up* before her mother was overlapping her frowning emojis with updates on her own love life. Which was never good. Her mom had awful taste in men. There'd been the baseball player who couldn't even make a farm team, the hillbilly, the married doctor, and so many other bad choices that Sarah often wondered how she and her mom hadn't lost their house in a scam involving a mysterious prince halfway across the world or, even worse, in a pyramid scheme. But they hadn't. And Jeanine always bounced back, eager as ever.

How'd you meet? Sarah typed.

She'd only half read the series of texts that had come through from her mother. They'd mentioned a name and how good-looking he was and that he was the *real deal* and *not like my other boyfriends*, but there weren't any actual details.

At Tommy's.

Tommy's was the local bar and grill her mom still frequented—even after a disastrous fling with the bartender—but Sarah was hoping the answer would be at the county fair or at church. As if Jeanine would be in church when it wasn't Christmas or Easter.

Stop making that face, Sarah Marie Webb.

I'm not making a face.

You most certainly are. You may live 1,000 miles away, but I still know these things.

Sarah sent her an eye-roll emoji while she fought the smile she could feel tugging at her lips. Her mother was a character—an annoying one who disapproved of every choice Sarah made that wasn't moving back home and getting married, but she loved her all the same.

What's he— Sarah dropped the phone as a shadow fell over her. A sweaty, sexy shadow. The panic that had caused her heart rate to spike receded as she took in the familiar face of Maggie's nephew.

"Jace?" she asked.

"Sorry, I didn't mean to startle you." He wiped his forehead with the gray shirt he had crumpled up in his hand.

"I just... I didn't realize that was *you* outside."

He smiled. "Yeah. Aunt Mags asked me to do some work around the house this weekend. Though she didn't mention that you'd be here." He pulled the sweat-stained shirt over his head, mushing his dirty-blond locks. "I would've kept my clothes on."

"Don't feel obliged to do so on my account."

He narrowed his eyes, and his expression fell, the corners of his mouth tugging down. "Don't you have a boyfriend?"

Crap. "I actually do not."

"But there's a guy."

It wasn't a question. Jace had been at the gala and was talking with her minutes before Brian arrived and practically undressed her with his eyes in front of the entire party. And if her boss's less-than-subtle hints were to be believed, Jace had been watching because he was interested—and had been for a while. Sarah had ignored all the hints and that picture-perfect face because dating her boss's beloved nephew was an awful idea. She wasn't looking to become a wife in the foreseeable future, and she liked her job. But in hindsight, it seemed a much better option than falling for—*not* that she was falling for—her best friend's brother.

"He was just a date for the gala." The half-truth was the easiest angle. It wasn't a lie, but it didn't give away the game. "Definitely not a reason that you need to stay clothed in front of me."

"Let's agree to disagree." Jace pulled a bottle of water out of his back pocket and took a swig. "Why *are* you here, anyway?"

Of course that would be his next question. Somehow all possible answers seemed awful. Even the truth would lead to the question of why she didn't have other friends she could crash with.

"My roommate's boyfriend is in town, and your aunt offered the guest room for a few days."

"Good old Aunt Mags." He shook his head. "Always taking in you wayward souls."

She rolled her eyes. "I'm hardly wayward."

"Guess it depends which synonym you use."

"And which one do you use?"

"Hmm... seven letters, starts with an *N* and ends with a *Y*, and there's *U* in the middle."

A smile worked its way free despite the wholly nerdy joke. Jace was a well-read high school English teacher, so the wordplay could be expected, but she thought he'd be better at it. "Naughty?" She arched an eyebrow. "Untrue, and poor execution. If my mother wasn't obsessed with crossword puzzles, I would never have figured that out."

"Well, it's hard to come up with a good wordplay when someone is ogling me."

"I was not ogling you."

He stretched up and grasped the top of the doorjamb. She tried not to look, but even with his shirt on, his taut abdomen was visible. And then his shirt rose the slightest bit. The hint of defined hips peeked out from under the hem, still gleaming with sweat. She glanced lower, where his joggers sat low on those delicious hips. Her imagination ran wild as she noted that there was no sign of boxers or boxer briefs or any type of underwear that she certainly would have seen by that point. Her gaze dipped even lower before a laugh snapped her attention back to his face. His brown eyes—so light they were almost golden—danced with amusement. She shifted her attention but landed on his mouth, where the tip of his tongue just met what she imagined were soft and well-trained lips. His left ear would have to do, then.

Jace settled his arms across his chest and stared at her with a satisfied grin that only highlighted the subtle stubble on his jawline. "Ogling."

Sarah flushed. There was no denying it. "Whatever." She turned away, fishing around the chair for her phone, which only made him laugh harder.

"Good morning, you two."

Maggie stood in the doorway in workout clothes, a yoga mat slung over her shoulder. Her hair was in a messy ponytail, and her tank top read "Any yoga I do is hot yoga." Her pants were bright pink. She'd seen Maggie dressed up and dressed down and everything in between, but this was something else. Sarah had never been invited to her boss's inner sanctum or seen the truly unfiltered version of her. But here it was.

"Hey, Aunt Mags." Jace pulled his aunt into a hug. "Nice to see you this morning. How was Sven?"

"As flexible as ever." She winked.

Jace laughed at his aunt's completely inappropriate joke, and they both broke into ridiculous smiles. Aunt Mags was clearly the definition of the cool aunt.

"I'm glad you're both here, because I need you."

"Both of us?" Sarah asked, eyeing the sweaty man to her left.

It was the weekend and her last day of distance from Brian. The next morning, she'd be in the apartment again—back to pretending she didn't care that she'd hurt Brian and talking her best friend through the ups and downs of a relationship that would tear her and Jess apart. And back to the air mattress. All she wanted to do was sit in this sunroom and read about her mom's latest conquest and roll her eyes and forget her own life. And maybe spy on Jace as he did his "work around the house."

"Yes, sorry to take your Saturday, but Leigh has the flu." Maggie shrugged. "She said she texted you first but..."

Sarah pulled out her phone to argue that Leigh most certainly hadn't texted her first, but hidden among the missed texts from her mother sat an unread message from her coworker sent about thirty minutes ago. There was even a screen shot of a doctor's note from that morning.

Great. She put on her biggest, realest fake smile. "Here it is. I've been chatting with my mom. I must have missed it."

"It's not a big deal, but I'll need you to go to the game today in her place. You too."

"Why do you need me?" Jace asked, arms crossed.

Maggie's face went from determined to exasperated in an instant, an expression Sarah hadn't seen her boss make before but knew well from being around Jess and Brian. Only a family member could make someone that annoyed with one question.

"Because we need someone there who knows something about baseball. That is Leigh's area of expertise, certainly not mine, and Sarah doesn't even know what *walk off* means."

The look Jace gave her made Sarah think that perhaps she should know that simple phrase from the classic American pastime.

"Football is more my thing," Sarah said.

"*You* like football?" Jace asked.

"No. But we were each assigned a sport we had to be well versed in. Leigh is baseball. I'm football."

"And I'm basketball." Maggie waved away whatever question Jace had been about to ask. "Kayla was hockey before she quit."

Jace's expression hardened for only a moment, and Sarah looked between the two of them as they had a silent standoff. Kayla had left shortly into Sarah's tenure, but apparently, there was a bigger story than her taking her skills to a larger charity. Jace looked away first with a nod, and Maggie turned back to Sarah with a tight smile.

"Anyway, the game starts at one, and clients are arriving by noon. So chop-chop."

Before Sarah could protest, Maggie was out of the room. The sound of her footsteps on the stairs and the slam of her bedroom door made it clear there was no room for negotiation. Yet Sarah would need to go home to change and get a few things. Which meant she really needed to have left already. And she hated driving

Betty in the city on the weekend. And parking was going to be a bitch. And then she would need to take the train to Citizens Bank Park. It would literally be a miracle if she was at the stadium and in the suite before any donors. Which Leigh had known when she texted thirty minutes ago. And Maggie had known before she even walked in the door.

"Why do you look like you're about to throw up?" Jace asked.

She glared at Jace, who would probably be able to shower and throw on clean clothes in ten minutes and no one would know the difference. Men had it so easy. "Just trying to figure out how I'm going to get home, get dressed, and get to the stadium before noon."

"It's a baseball game. You don't need to look like a prom queen."

"Well, I can't go in yoga pants and a camisole either." Suddenly aware of what she was wearing in his presence, she pulled her cardigan tighter around her shoulders.

"No, but you can go in jeans, and I'm sure I have an old Phillies shirt that would fit you well enough. We can buy you a hat... no, a visor at the stadium."

She eyed him. He was tall and built, but with her curvy frame and boob size, a shirt of his might just fit her. It might also hug in all the inappropriate places.

"My place is technically on the way, so we could just stop in and change before heading over to the stadium," he continued.

"All right," she said, standing up and trying not to look directly at this sexy and kind man. "Let me get ready."

Her phone pinged as she walked up the stairs. She glanced down at two notifications. The first was from her mom: *So, who's the guy on your Instagram?*

The second was from Maggie: *Fair warning, Tyler will be there.*

Chapter 22

Sarah

"Here, try this." Jace adjusted the Velcro strap on the visor in his hand and then pulled it over her head. He grinned at her as she lifted the rim back above her eyebrows.

"What do you think?" she asked.

He curved the rim—which she assumed meant it was a keeper because if not, the salesperson was going to be pissed. "It's cute. Better than the pink hat."

"I could've told you that two pink hats ago." She adjusted the official Phillies red visor, pulled her ponytail over the back, and tightened the strap.

He frowned at the row of ladies' hats next to the visors. "I really wanted it to work on you."

She laughed and adjusted the royal blue Phillies shirt he'd given her to wear. Despite being unisex, it fit snugly in all the wrong places for a work event. "Are you getting anything?"

"Nah." He pulled a well-worn cap out of his back pocket. The rim was faded and the *P* frayed. Jace slipped it on. "They almost never lose when I wear it to a game. And it's more than proven itself as an effective rally cap."

Sarah's eyes widened. She had no idea what he was talking about, but clearly, it was some weird sports belief. "I didn't peg you for the superstitious type."

"Rally caps are the real deal."

"Are you wearing socks you haven't washed since their winning streak started too?"

Jace winced. He handed the cashier exact change, and they headed toward the box they'd rented for the event. "My socks are clean, but I always wear my Grumpy Cat boxers when Nola pitches. They're *usually* clean."

"Wow, this is a whole new side of you."

He side-eyed her. "Not really."

Sarah walked past him into the suite, where fortunately no one was waiting, and the food was already set up. A blush crept up her cheeks. She and Jace had been working at events together for nearly three years, and while she thought of him as Maggie's affable nephew who was good with donors, he was right—she didn't know him at all. Sure, they chatted at events and spent some time together during setups or cleanups because Jace was the kind of guy who was the first one there and the last one to leave even though he was unpaid. But no, she wouldn't have seen this side of him. In fact, she'd purposely stayed away from thinking about that because it was clear how easy it would be to fall for that smile, and she couldn't risk her job for a set of abs. Tyler had been risk enough.

Fortunately, her phone buzzed before she had to respond. Her heart—that traitorous organ—jumped at the photo of Brian that appeared on the screen. He was holding a paper-towel roll up to his lips and singing along to "Single Ladies." She didn't remember changing his photo to that, especially not after blowing him off the morning after. But apparently, she had. At least the photo cut out all the fun bits—aside from those damn dimples.

"Hey," she said.

"Hey, sorry, I just saw your text. What's up?" He sounded distracted. But he'd called. She wasn't sure she would have responded if the situation were reversed.

"How fast can you get to Citizens Bank Park?" There was a protracted silence on his end of the line, and she wondered if Brian even knew the name of the stadium where the Phillies played.

She was about to clarify when he spoke. "Considering I have about two hours left on my shift? Probably about two hours and however long the subway ride is to the stadium... you *can* take the subway there, right?"

Crap. "Yes."

"Why are you at the Phillies game?"

Well, that answered that question. "I have to fill in for Leigh at this fundraiser." Sarah glanced at Jace, who was watching her intently, and then took a step away from him. "Tyler will be here."

She thought she heard Brian laugh, but it was hard to tell over the blood rushing through her ears. He was going to say no. He had every reason—every right—to say no.

"So, you disappear all week after basically blowing me off after the gala, and now you want me to come be your fake boyfriend at a Phillies game?"

"Basically."

This time, she did hear him laugh, and it was cynical and not at all positive. "You realize I'm a Mets fan."

That statement meant nothing to her, but she could infer enough. She couldn't even remember who the Phillies were playing that day, but the odds that it was the Mets had to be slim. Sarah glanced at the scoreboard and saw those four dreaded letters. *Crap.*

She took another step away from Jace and lowered her voice. "I'll give you the bedroom for another two weeks. And full Betty privileges."

"Do I get any *other* benefits?"

"Brian..."

He snorted, and she could feel his eye roll through the phone. "I'm not wearing Phillies apparel."

Sarah's hand unclenched from around the phone. He could come in his Starbucks apron, reeking of espresso, for all she cared. "Thank you."

"What else are fake boyfriends for?"

SARAH TAPPED HER FOOT and glanced from the group in front of her to the door to the suite and back again. She honestly had no idea what anyone was saying or why they weren't watching the game. As far as she could tell, with her limited knowledge of the sport, it was an exciting game. A legendary rivalry. And these men were standing around eating sliders and talking to her.

She picked at her pretzel, glad that Leigh had ordered stadium food instead of fancy catering. Sometimes a person just needed a hot pretzel and syrupy fountain soda. She turned back to the man directly in front of her and smiled. He was a frequent donor who made a point to learn about the kids in the program and not just drop money. And he didn't do it for show or due to proximity, like certain people. Said *certain person* had been waylaid by Maggie and was now standing just behind the last row of seats with Jace, watching the game. Monique was not on his arm, but Sarah would be forced to deal with the both of them in another week or two once they nailed down the details for Monique's visit to the children's floor. At least the woman seemed genuinely interested in meeting Tessa—she'd personally followed up about the visit before Sarah had even had a chance to call her manager. It had been a quick text explaining that she got the number from Tyler. Of course, it was more than fine for her ex to give her personal number to celebrities. Maybe he could do Chris Evans next.

As if sensing her eyes on him, Tyler turned and started toward her. Jace followed with an apologetic look on his face. Sarah hadn't told him the Tyler story, but he'd been at the gala, and Tyler had made a point of asking after Brian when he first arrived at the game. When Sarah held up the photo of Brian cheekily grinning behind the espresso bar, Tyler's eyes quirked in interest, and she'd realized her mistake. Brian was hot, but going from a doctor to a barista wouldn't be a step up to Tyler. Things like love and ambition and orgasms didn't matter to Tyler. Not that Brian himself had ever given her an orgasm, but the dream version of him certainly had.

"Ah," Tyler said, his eyes skipping past Sarah and landing somewhere directly behind her. "Here's your barista."

"He's…" She trailed off because honestly, she didn't know what Brian's actual job title was or what it entailed besides staring at a jumble code she would never understand.

"Hey, babe." Brian's lips were soft against her cheek, and his hand was warm as it slid into hers. He still smelled faintly of coffee, the scent now welcome and familiar and completely Brian.

Her whole body curved into him of its own volition. And it all felt so perfectly natural—which was what worried her. "You made it!"

"I told you I would. Just had a little holdup at the will-call window."

"Why? I gave them your name."

He smirked, making her heart thud against her rib cage. "Guy didn't like my shirt."

Brian was in a button-down that Sarah had never seen before. Under it, he wore a royal blue shirt, and she could just make out the ridges of letters.

Jace whistled. "Brave man."

She stared at the shirt a second longer. Mets. He'd worn Mets apparel. Of course he had.

Brian grinned and stuck out his hand. "Brian Hawkins, Sarah's boyfriend and Mets fan."

She started at the word. He'd said it on the phone, but she'd assumed he was being glib. But here he was, announcing himself as her boyfriend only one week after the gala, and she couldn't refute him.

"Jace Clairmont, Maggie's nephew and Phillies diehard." His eyes slid to Sarah's with a hint of accusation.

She looked away. There was no explanation she could give with Tyler standing there, and what would she even say? Was she supposed to apologize for checking out his six-pack? As if he hadn't checked out her rack when she came out of his bathroom in his T-shirt.

Jace cleared his throat. "I see my aunt is waving me down, so I guess that's my cue."

Brian turned to Tyler with a perfunctory nod. "Nice to see you again, man."

Tyler quirked an eyebrow. "Hawkins, huh? So, Sarah's boyfriend and Jess's brother, if I'm not mistaken?"

Sarah barely held in the squeak that rose in her throat. Once she'd made their relationship social-media official, it was an easy jump from Brian to Jess. That kind of information didn't stay quiet.

"Guilty as charged, I'm afraid," Brian said.

"I thought you hated Jess's brother."

"I... I never said I *hated* him. More like mutual respectable dislike."

"And now he's your boyfriend." Tyler's tone was dry and disbelieving.

"You know what they say." Brian laughed. "You can't hate someone you don't already love. And that whole sharing-a-bed thing... mutual respectable dislike throws off a lot of pheromones."

"You live together?"

"My sister, love her to death, overbooked her guest room. And Sarah, here, is just so stubborn. She wouldn't give up the bed or let me sleep on the couch. Well..." He laughed, and Sarah braced herself for whatever was about to come out of his mouth. "At least not after she saw me in a towel."

So many lies. How was she ever going to keep this straight? And she'd have to because Tyler was certainly going to try to pick it apart.

"That's an awfully cute story," Tyler said, his voice dripping with sarcasm.

"Hopefully, we'll have to edit it for the kids one day."

Sarah nearly choked on her soda. "I'm just... I think I'm going to go watch the game." She tugged on Brian's arm. "Coming, *honey*?"

She practically dragged him to the seated section before pulling him down into one of the chairs. He immediately put his arm around her shoulder. The urge to shove him off shot through her, and irritation flooded her veins.

"What is wrong with you?" she asked.

"Whatever do you mean, dearest?"

Sarah glanced over her shoulder, but Tyler had merged into a conversation with several other donors. *Thank God.* "You can cut the act. No one is watching."

He didn't move his arm. "I highly doubt that."

"Don't you think that was a little over-the-top?"

Brian shrugged. "We're supposed to make your ex jealous. Well, he's sufficiently jealous."

"You think?"

"You turned down his marriage proposal what—less than a month ago? And now you have a *boyfriend* who you trot out to events and who worships the ground you walk on and apparently lives with you and is your best friend's brother." Brian leaned in close, his lips brushing her ear. A shiver worked its way through her. "I'd be jealous."

Sarah turned to look at him, and their lips were so close she could smell the minty scent coming off his breath. With the smallest of movements, she would be lost. Whatever irritation had flared up was long gone. His touch didn't chafe but burned. Goose bumps sprouted on her arms, and a spark of something she wouldn't name settled low in her belly as he ran a finger down her cheek to her neck and settled at the collar of her shirt. She braced herself for his lips against hers—yearned for it, ready for the explosion of desire she knew would follow. But his lips met her cheek, and then he sat back, keeping his arm securely around her shoulders.

"I have to get back to it in a few," she said breathily.

"I know. Let's just watch the bottom of the inning. Then I'm yours to parade around." He pulled his arm from the back of her chair and buttoned another button on his shirt. "No one will even know I'm an enemy spy."

She laughed despite all the feelings stirring inside her. Why did he do this to her? "Thank you for coming."

"Free food and free baseball—I'd have to be a fool to turn that down."

"Right."

"Honestly, it's really fun to mess with your ex."

"Uh-huh."

"And, well, I kinda missed you this week, Chestnut."

The nickname was so unexpected that she snorted. "Well, I'll be home tomorrow."

"Promise?"

That was an unexpected response. "Yes, I'll be home in the morning. I told Jess I'd go with her and Ryder on the mural walking tour. You're coming, too, right?"

He nodded. "Yeah. I'm having breakfast with my parents, and then I'll meet you guys at the first stop."

"Good. I was kind of dreading spending the day with just the two of them on their last day together."

His eyebrows arched in curiosity. "Even though you are now being forced to spend the day with me?"

"Even though," she said and meant it.

"Gotta love those mutual-respectable-dislike pheromones."

She giggled. "They're undeniable."

Chapter 23

Brian

Philly was growing on him. It wasn't New York, but it had a vibe all its own. He could see himself here—for a while at least. If he got a good job, a nice place, and a bike, he could be happy. New York City had never been sustainable. Every day was an adventure and a milestone. Rents were sky-high, competition was fierce, and there was never a dull moment. It was exhilarating but exhausting. Philly had that, but it was different in a way he couldn't quite define. Philly suited him. Partially employed, squatting at his sister's, and in a tangled mess with someone he shouldn't be, Brian was happier than he'd been in a long time, if he was being honest. Happier than he'd been in his last relationship.

He stood shoulder to shoulder with Sarah in front of a mural that took up the entire side of a building in Old City. It was exquisite and awe-inspiring. In jeans and a sorority hoodie, she was beautiful. In that moment, there was no place else he'd rather be.

"How do you even create something like this?" she asked.

"Piece by piece." He watched her take in the mural, her eyes moving across the expanse of the wall before sliding over to Ryder and Jess, who were standing a few feet away, looking at the map. "I know you want to hate him, but he's a good guy."

Sarah crossed her arms and shifted her gaze back to the mural. "What did you mean when you said she wasn't thriving here?"

With everything that had happened, Brian had nearly forgotten that part of their conversation that dreadful morning after. Sarah had said Jess's life in Philadelphia was thriving. And he'd questioned whether that was true.

"How long did you live with Tyler? A couple of months? She never even tried to rent out that room or downsize. I'm not sure she even thought about doing it. I had barely finished explaining why I needed a place to stay before she was saying yes and asking when I could be in town. I mean, she says she did it to stop me from whining, but she wanted me there." He stepped closer to Sarah. Her scent hit him like a sledgehammer, but he didn't move. "And then you showed up, and I don't know about you, but if I had yet another long-term house guest taking up my living room for an undefined period of time, I'd be less than happy, but for the most part, she was thrilled."

"She was lonely." Sarah's words were barely a whisper, and when he looked over at her, her eyes were watering.

"Most people aren't offering to uproot their whole life after a few months if they're happy."

Sarah sniffled. "Why didn't I see it?"

"She didn't want you to see it." Brian wrapped his hand around hers. "But I've had a lot of practice studying my sister. She forgets to put on an act for me because she doesn't think I notice."

"But you do."

"I do."

She squeezed his hand. "What do you observe about me?"

"You let Jess think she's the one taking care of you, but really, you're holding her together." He waited to see if she'd refute him, but she just turned to him with glassy, sad eyes. "You can have the bed back."

"What?" Her voice was scratchy with emotion.

"It's your room. She was always saving it for you."

Sarah's arms were around him before he'd even finished the sentence. He held her lightly, his hands skimming down her back. She rested her head over his heart, and it felt right in a way nothing had in his whole life. She fit. Sarah Webb, the bane of his existence for the last eight years, fit perfectly.

Chapter 24

Brian

Brian knocked on the open door to Sarah's room, which was back to polka dots and pastels and so much pink. It was fun seeing her personality bleed out into every part of her bedroom. She stood out against the brightness of the room in black leggings and a Wish Factory zip-up hoodie. On her feet were those fuzzy socks he'd gotten her.

He knocked a second time. "Hey, Chestnut."

Sarah pulled an earbud out and lowered the screen on her laptop. "What's up?"

"You busy?"

"Just checking through everything for the Eagles game tomorrow." She stuck her bottom lip out in a pout. "You're sure you can't come?"

He nodded. "I'm closing tomorrow so Tasha can go to her brother's engagement party."

Her pout deepened into a full-on frown. "That's too bad. Didn't you used to be a football star or something?"

"I was *on* the football team, but baseball was more my specialty." He felt her eyes graze over his body and resisted the urge to cross his arms.

He was fully clothed this evening, even wearing his favorite hoodie, which was old and frayed and emblazoned with his college logo. It was quickly becoming that part of the year when the mornings were chilly and by afternoon you were stripping off layers, which meant, like his and Jess's parents', the apartment thermostat was still set to frigid.

Sarah's eyes returned to his. "Yeah, I can see that. Did you need something?"

"Do you think I could keep some of my stuff in here?"

He wasn't entirely sure she'd agree, but he *had* given her the bedroom, so it seemed like a fair trade. He honestly didn't have that much stuff. Most of his life had stayed at his parents' house. But he was getting awfully tired of living out of a laundry basket.

"Oh, sure. Why don't you take the top drawer or two? And just shove my stuff to one side in the closet."

"Thank you. Seriously."

She shrugged and shut her laptop. "You gave me the bedroom, and I think Jess is going to let me pay rent soon."

"Yeah, she finally stopped giving back half the Venmo payments I send her." He pulled open the top drawer. "What should I do with these?" He held up a pair of lacy red underwear.

She turned, already halfway inside the closet, moving things around. "Just move everything down. The bottom drawer is just books. You can move those... I don't know, here?" She pointed to a shelf near the bottom of her closet. "Is this enough space?"

He tried to focus on her question and not the fact that she'd given him permission to touch her underwear. He wondered if that was a good thing or a bad thing. "Yes, more than enough. Thank you."

"When you're done, did you want to watch a movie or something?" Her voice hitched at the end, and he thought—though he couldn't tell in the dim lighting and all the pink in the room—he saw a blush rise on her cheeks. "Jess and I were thinking of having a *High School Musical* marathon."

Okay, that had to have been a flush because she'd said the last part quickly as if she should have led with it. Despite the movie choice, he wished he could stay. Now that they weren't enemies or potential lovers, they were kind of friends. And Sarah was fun. She always made him laugh, she actually listened, and her taste in movies wasn't too bad when his sister wasn't around. But their schedules had been off lately. He was gone before she was awake, and then there were his new friendships with Tasha and Ethan, and the days were moving quickly. If he wasn't working or with his friends, he was job hunting. He'd put in a few applications but had gotten no offers yet.

He focused back on her, realizing she was waiting for an answer. "Well, that does sound fun, but I'm having dinner with the guys, and then we're going to Terror Behind the Walls."

She shook her head. "Such a tourist."

That was true, but he *was* technically a tourist in this city, and who didn't like to be terrified in a haunted penitentiary? "You could come?"

"To guys' night?"

Right. Why did he feel like he'd just asked her to prom? He rolled his shoulder. "To the thing at Eastern State. Tasha's coming."

"Oh. I'm pretty sure you need tickets in advance. It's super popular, and I think I'd rather stay in with the Wildcats."

"I'm going to pretend I don't know what that means." He grinned, and she smiled back with another shake of her head as if he amused her to no end. Maybe he did. He scratched the back of his head, the hair there in need of a trim. "We could have breakfast tomorrow. I'll make pancakes."

She frowned. "Jess and I are going to yoga later in the morning."

Damn. "All right. Well, maybe next weekend."

"I'll pencil you in." Sarah crawled back into her bed and pulled her laptop onto her lap. "I have to finish this, but feel free to organize around me."

Before he could respond, she was already back in the zone. He watched her for a few seconds, allowing himself to appreciate the moment. Maybe what had happened at and after the gala was a good thing. Maybe it needed to happen. Because this version of him and Sarah was much better than any that had come before. And maybe that was enough. His stomach roiled in protest, but he ignored it. Sarah was here, and she was happy—that was what mattered. After one last look, he headed out to the living room to grab his things.

Chapter 25

Sarah

Sarah had been walking the halls of Cedar Crest Hospital for three years. When she'd first started dating Tyler, there'd been whispers and stares, but it was nothing like today. Conversations stopped and heads turned as she led Monique Miller through the hospital. Tyler was noticeably absent—conveniently called in to a case at the exact time his "girlfriend" was meant to arrive—but that didn't stop the talk. Cedar Crest might as well have been a small-town high school the way the gossip mill churned.

But she refused to let the talk bother her. Today was a good day. Maggie had told her that her numbers were looking good after the event at the Eagles game, and Jess had let Sarah cut her first rent check. If she was paying rent, she was an official tenant. Everyone agreed. And maybe that meant her best friend wasn't going to move across the country. Or maybe it meant Jess needed to save money to be able to afford to move. But either way, Sarah was officially Jess Hawkins's roommate again. Life was good. For once, everything was coming up Sarah.

Even the fact that Monique had shown up with her own camera-man didn't bother Sarah. Nor had she cared when she explained to the photographer that he needed parental permission before snapping any photos of Tessa and was met with a grouchy "Yeah, I know, kid." She hadn't minded when he kept asking Sarah to step out of his frame so he could get a shot of Monique with a nurse or a doctor or just standing in a hospital hallway, looking elegant in a tan trench coat and strappy heels that accentuated her long, lean legs. Sarah could take the stairs for the rest of her life and never have calves like that.

"How many Wish Factory kids are in the hospital now?" Monique asked as they passed room after room of the children's wing.

"A few. Wish Factory doesn't require them to be critically ill, so a lot of our kids are home but missing out on something."

"Like...?"

Sarah thought through recent Wish Factory kids. "Well, we had a kid last month, Teddy, who broke his arm. He's thirteen and was supposed to be the starting quarterback for his junior high team. We arranged for him to go to an Eagles game and meet some of the players. They all signed a jersey for him. It was a great day."

"He must have been ecstatic." Monique's smile was genuine, as was her interest. From the moment she stepped through the doors, she had seemed engaged and open, friendly even.

Sarah knew that it wasn't the model's fault that Tyler was being an ass, but her being awesome was not helping Sarah dislike her. And she so wanted to dislike this beautiful woman if only because it would make it easier to stomach Tyler's public rebound.

"Ty was there, right? I think he showed me a picture the other night when he was telling me about the organization."

Ty? Sarah's untouchable good mood had just been touched. She had never called Tyler "Ty." Ever. No one called him that—no one but Monique Miller apparently. *Just how friendly are they?*

Monique glanced at her when the silence between them extended into uncomfortable territory. "Everything okay?"

"Yes, sorry." Sarah paused, looking back at the cameraman, uncertain if she should really say what she was about to say. "It's just... this is kinda weird, right?"

"It wasn't until you said that."

"Oh, right." Sarah tried to laugh, but it came out strangled. "It's just, I'm his ex-girlfriend, you're his new girlfriend…"

Monique's eyes narrowed, but then her expression smoothed out. "It doesn't have to be weird. This is about Tessa, not us."

"Right."

"And we're grown women. Does it really matter who we're sleeping with? From what I hear, you didn't want Ty anyway, so it shouldn't matter. And if your actions at the gala are any indication, you didn't waste any time jumping into someone else's bed or flaunting that fact."

Ouch. There were two sides to every story, and Sarah hadn't stopped to think about Tyler's or the fact that she might have hurt him by saying no. He'd been so harsh afterward that it had colored everything.

Sarah pointed to a room down the hall, where Tessa was set up for her dialysis. Her little brother and stepfather sat outside, passing a Nintendo Switch back and forth. Her mother, Sarah knew, would be sitting next to the bed reading whatever Tessa was meant to read for school so that she could supplement the hybrid schedule her illness demanded.

She turned to the cameraman. "You'll need to put that away for now." Once it was tucked back in his bag, she turned back to the model who had just royally put Sarah in her place. "If you'll follow me."

Sarah knocked on the door, inching it open so that Monique was out of view. The father-and-son duo barely glanced up. Tessa's face lit up as Sarah entered the room. Sarah's eyes surveyed the small space and fell on Tessa's mom sitting with Tyler.

Is Tessa his case? Tessa had been waiting for a kidney for a short while and would continue waiting until she came up on the transplant list. For a once super-active sixteen-year-old, she was doing so with impeccable patience. But Mrs. Carlton didn't look excited or nervous, and Tyler, though in doctor mode, was relaxed. He even gave Sarah a cordial smile and nod. Perhaps he just wanted to be here for the moment. Maybe bringing Monique to the gala had been enough payback for him. She could only hope.

"Hey, Tessa," Sarah said, plastering a smile on her face. "There's someone here who would like to meet you."

Tessa stared at her in confusion until the door opened and the six-foot-tall model of perfection sauntered in. Tears burst from Tessa's eyes as Monique walked over and sat down on the edge of the bed. A camera flashed behind Sarah, and she turned to see Mr. Carlton signing a photo release against the wall.

"Oh my god." Tessa's voice was squeaky with excitement. There was a celebrity sitting on the edge of her bed, but Tessa only had eyes for Sarah. "How did... I mean, how is this happening right now?"

Sarah grinned. "Surprise."

"Ms. Miller, I am, like, your biggest fan."

"Monique, please."

"Monique?" Tessa squeaked.

Sarah moved to the side of the room, letting Monique and Tessa have their moment. She leaned against the wall, and her eyes clouded over. The pay might suck, and the work might be hard, but this was why she did it. She hadn't known what she was getting into when she'd joined Sophie's Wish Factory. But she was good with people and had been one of those student employees who called alumni for donations in college, so it had seemed a good fit. Sarah had never counted on the beauty it would bring to her soul or how connected she would feel to the kids. So many of them were in and out of the program before she had a chance to really know them. A few were terminal, though Maggie usually worked directly with those children and their parents. But Tessa was different. She'd been on their radar as a Wish Factory kid for a few months. She'd gotten to do some group events, but her specific wish had been to sit in the front row at a fashion show or go to a photo shoot. They'd been working on it.

A small part of Sarah wanted to yell at Tyler for never mentioning he had this connection to pull. He'd known Monique for a while, if their familiarity was any indication. Sarah couldn't imagine world-class pediatric surgeon Tyler Ackerman letting anyone new to his life call him Ty. But then, Sarah probably wouldn't have called in a favor from an old sex buddy, either, especially not when the favor was on behalf of a new significant other.

Tyler stood and walked over to the bed. He hooked an arm around Monique's waist and gave a goofy grin to Tessa.

"Doc Ack, you sat there this whole time and didn't say anything?" Tessa asked.

"I didn't want to ruin Sarah's surprise." Her name from his lips sounded so natural, but the way he curved into Monique said everything that wasn't said.

Tessa's eyes went wide and slid to Sarah for a second before going back to the happy couple. "Well, I'm definitely surprised."

"I do have one more surprise." Monique stepped out of Tyler's embrace and started on the buttons of her jacket.

Sarah hadn't thought anything of the jacket, but now that she was taking it off, she realized it was peculiar that a fashionista had been so plainly dressed. The jacket slipped from her shoulders, and a gasp escaped Tessa that had everyone in the room on their feet.

"My dress!"

"Surprise!" Monique's tone was giddy. "Sarah sent over some designs you did, and I just loved this one, so I had it made. I hope you don't mind."

"Mind? Mind? No, I don't mind!"

Mrs. Carlton, who had moved to the bedside at Tessa's gasp, pushed Tessa's hair back from her forehead. "Breathe, honey."

"I have to go to an event this weekend," Monique said. "Do you mind if I wear it?"

Tessa shook her head, and even from across the room, Sarah could see her hands shaking. "You want to wear my design?"

"I do. Johnny loved it too. He's getting a suit made like the one in your sketch. The side design that matches the dress—it's a daring move."

"Johnny... Midolo?"

Sarah knew that was some actor, though she couldn't exactly place him besides knowing that he had dark hair and blue eyes for days. And it was interesting that Monique was mentioning another guy after Tyler had been cozied up to her minutes before.

"Yeah, he's my date for the premiere." She didn't look back at Tyler, but he was certainly watching her, and he seemed none too happy.

"I thought..." Tessa looked around the room before coming back to Monique.

Sarah could see the triangle turning into a square in her head. If only she knew about Brian. A love pentagon was exactly up Tessa's alley. She'd be talking Sarah's ears off for days.

"You're really going to wear my design to a movie premiere?"

Monique pulled out a sheet of paper that Sarah recognized as one of Tessa's designs. This one was a jumpsuit that hugged in all the right places. "We thought perhaps *you* could wear this one."

"What?"

That came from every single person in the room other than Monique and her cameraman. No one had cleared this with Sarah, but that wasn't technically required. Celebrities added surprises in all the time—just not usually ones this big.

"If it's okay with your parents and your doctor." She looked pointedly at Tyler. "I'd love for you to be my guest."

"With you and Johnny Midolo," Tessa said.

"Yes."

"Mom?"

Tessa's mom turned to the only one who could really give an answer. "Dr. Ackerman?"

"I don't see why not," Tyler said, mussing Tessa's hair. "If she can go to school for a few hours, she can certainly walk the red carpet and watch a movie."

"That's settled, then." Monique handed Mrs. Carlton a card. "My manager will be calling you to arrange everything. Tessa, I'll see you on Friday."

"Let me walk you out," Tyler said, placing a hand on the small of her back.

"That'd be great. I wanted to chat with you about something anyway." The look Monique shot Tyler made Sarah certain it wasn't going to be a fun conversation. The possibility that Monique hadn't known Sarah was Tyler's ex-girlfriend sat heavy on her shoulders.

Clearly, she'd known some of the facts, but maybe Tyler had left out the part where he used Monique to make his ex look bad at a charity event. *Or could it have been the "new girlfriend" comment and Tyler's touchy-feely bit back in the room? Did Tyler lie about how he's connected to Monique?* The questions spiraled through her mind, and the part of her that read the monthly edition of *Talented* really hated that she would probably never know the answers.

Sarah followed them into the hallway, closing the door to the room behind her. Tessa's little brother still sat there playing what looked like *Animal Crossing*. Tyler and Monique looked to already be having the necessary conversation, and neither one looked too happy.

"Monique." Sarah waited until the woman turned to her. "Thank you so much. That was wholly unexpected, and I can't begin to say how grateful we all are."

"Of course. It's nothing really. Don will email you all the photos from today and the premiere. Do you need anything else from me?"

Sarah pulled a folder and a pen out of her tote bag. "We have these certificates that we hang in the office. Could you sign this?"

Monique's smile grew as she looked at the certificate. "Can I have a copy? Not many people are *that* excited to meet me. I'd love to have the commemoration."

"I'm sure that's not true." Sarah took back the signed certificate and tucked it away. "But absolutely, I can work one up and get it sent over to you later this week."

"Thank you, Sarah." Monique took her hand. "This has been an illuminating experience, and if there's anything else I can do, you know how to reach me."

"WHY DO YOU SOUND OUT of breath?" Sarah sat down at one of the tables in the hospital cafeteria and tucked her phone between her ear and her shoulder. "Lugging around bags of espresso beans?"

Brian laughed. "No, I'm walking home."

She glanced at her watch—it was only two thirty in the afternoon. "Already?"

"That's how it works when you open with the sun."

"Well, isn't that nice."

He grunted. "You get up at four thirty in the morning and tell me how nice it is."

"No, thank you."

"That's what I thought. So, what's up?"

"Oh..." She fiddled with the Jell-O sundae she'd just purchased—a hospital staple she never passed up.

She'd planned to call Jess, but her bestie hadn't been in the best of moods lately. Whether that was related to work, life, or Ryder, Sarah didn't know, because Jess had clammed up again. She hid out in her room after dinner while Sarah and Brian cleaned up and watched TV. Last night, Brian had slept at Tasha's since he was opening in the morning, and while Jess spent the night next to Sarah on the couch, she hadn't said much, even when Sarah pried. So when Brian had texted her some silly meme, she'd dialed him instead of Jess.

"I'm just taking a moment before I have to drive back to the city and thought I'd say hi," she said.

"Hi."

"Do you want to grab dinner tonight?"

"I can't. It's *Halo* night with the guys."

Right. Because now he has friends. A part of her hated it. She finally wanted him around—even if only as a friend—and he'd gone and gotten himself a life. The rest of her was torn between excitement that perhaps the distance would help dissipate whatever the hell was happening between them and hope that if he started to build a life here, Brian might just stay. If nothing else, Sarah could admit that she didn't want him to leave Philadelphia.

"Can you do tomorrow night?" he asked.

She could, but her stomach was already doing flips of regret at her impetuous call. An invitation to "grab dinner" didn't scream date, but she'd also never asked him to eat food out of the house with her before. And he'd followed up with an alternate option, which meant he was invested in going.

"I have Zumba on Wednesday nights."

"Since when?"

"Since always." Not that she had been to class lately. Even before the Tyler debacle, her attendance had been haphazard, but her class pass never expired.

"You know just wearing the yoga pants doesn't constitute a workout, right?"

"Don't be a jerk. It's been a busy few weeks with moving and turning down a proposal and my needy fake boyfriend."

"You wound me, Chestnut."

That nickname. By his tone, she could already tell it was going to be a thing. "Stop it with that!"

He laughed. "I'm down for Zumba."

"Seriously?"

"What? I like to shake my butt as much as the next guy."

"I don't think I've ever seen a guy in this class."

"That won't bother me." He paused, and she could hear him move the phone around and then the clinking of his keys. He must have gotten home. "Unless you don't want me to come..."

Could I make this conversation any more awkward? All she'd wanted was someone to talk to while she ate this Jell-O cup, and instead, she was making platonic dates with a guy who had shown up in her dream last night in only a towel. And she knew exactly what that looked like because even if she hadn't *liked* Brian that first night, her libido had ingrained every inch of that torso in her memory for all time. And how those hips had rocked against her... *Stop.*

"No, no, it's a date."

"Is it, now?" he asked.

Sarah stared at her Jell-O cup and clamped her mouth shut. Her mind raced with equal parts panic and inevitability. *Yes* had been her first thought. And that couldn't happen. She could not go on a real date with Brian ever.

"Teasing," he said over the sound of a door slamming. "Anyway, I need to wash the gleam of espresso off my skin. I'll see you tomorrow night?"

Now she had *that* visual in her mind. She crossed her legs. She really needed to get a grip. "Yeah, see you tomorrow night."

Which, she realized a moment too late, meant he wasn't coming home tonight. Again.

Chapter 26

Brian

"I can't believe you agreed to go to a dance class." Ethan picked up three empty beer bottles and the bowl that had once been full of Fritos. Most of the guys had left, minus Sam, who was still glued to a joystick and had put on headphones the minute Ethan and Brian started talking. "The sex better be phenomenal."

Brian threw a Funyun at Ethan. "It's not like that. We're *friends.*"

"Right, *friends* like me and the girl in 5A."

"No, not like that."

"Dude, you are so whipped," Ethan called out as Brian headed for the kitchen.

And maybe he was. But he'd take the heckling. It meant he had a friend to heckle him—not that Tasha didn't have that covered most days.

He picked up the rest of the garbage from the living room and walked it into the kitchen. He scanned the apartment. Much like Tasha's, it was on the smaller side—though anything was bigger than the studio he'd rented in Astoria, which had practically been a closet. But Ethan's apartment, while mainly the same style as Tasha's, didn't have comfy, well-loved pullout couches and dining room table scratches dating back to childhood. It barely had the clutter of life. This space was well furnished and sleek. There was a bowl for the keys, a mat for his shoes, and a hook for his coat. Everything else—before a troupe of men had invaded the living room—was orderly and clutter free. At least everything Brian could see.

A yearning gnawed at his chest. Closet or not, his apartment had started to feel like a home, and he'd loved having it to himself. He could see himself living here when he got back on his feet. If Tasha and Ethan could afford it, with their varied types of employment—Ethan was a financial advisor—then certainly, eventually, Brian could too. He could get a bike so he didn't have to pay for public transportation all the time. He could almost picture it.

"What's this place run you?" Brian asked.

Ethan kicked the garbage can toward him and raised an eyebrow. "About eighteen hundred." Brian's studio had been more than that. "Why? You looking to relocate?"

"From my little sister's living room floor? Hell yes."

"As if you aren't crawling into Zumba chick's bed every night."

Brian shook his head. "We're just friends."

"I saw that photo of you two up against the wall." Ethan side-eyed him. "Wish I had *friends* like that."

"What about the girl in 5A?"

"If she posted pictures of me like that on social media, she wouldn't be the girl in 5A. She'd be the girl in my bed."

Brian rolled his eyes. He'd told Ethan about the fake dating as there wasn't really any harm in it and he didn't need his new friends thinking he was a douchebag after one of Tasha's friends had given him her number. His social media was so damning with how much fake stuff Sarah had posted as well as real stuff from the last few weeks of just cohabitating.

"You know we were acting."

"So you say." Ethan stuck a cup in the dishwasher. "How's the job hunt going?"

"All right, I guess? I have an interview on Halloween with a SaaS company in Princeton."

"Oh yeah, my brother works for one of those out in St. Louis. They do HR systems or job application systems? I don't know. They have offices all over, though. I'll get the name if you want to check them out."

"That would be great. There haven't been too many bites here, and forget about New York."

"Yeah, man, I get it. Are you picky about what you do?"

Brian shrugged. "I'd love to be, but right now, it's just about getting a salary and some health insurance and an apartment."

"Have you looked at Myer? If they have anything that suits your skill set, I'm happy to put my name behind you—not that it has much weight, but it might get you a foot in the door."

Myer was a financial firm. But corporate America survived because of its IT and systems teams. It might be soul sucking, but it could work. "That would be awesome. Thank you."

"I'm being completely selfish here. I don't want you to leave my city. You're the only one who can best Tasha at any game."

"Well, I appreciate it all the same," Brian said with a laugh. Myer wasn't ideal, but it wasn't in Fairford, and it wouldn't make him smell like coffee constantly or require him to wake up at four thirty in the morning. "I'd take anything at this point."

"Get me your résumé, then."

BRIAN PUSHED OPEN THE door to the apartment as quietly as he could, which in his sister's older building wasn't quiet at all. It was late, and he at least wanted to try to be considerate since Jess and Sarah weren't expecting him home.

"Hey," he said, spying Sarah sitting cross-legged on the couch, Chuck curled up in her lap.

"I thought you weren't coming back tonight."

He shrugged. "I needed my laptop for something."

"Watch porn?"

"No." He sat down next to her, pulling Chuck into his arms. The cat purred like the happiest creature alive. "I missed you, too, buddy."

"Do you two need a minute alone?"

He ignored her and glanced at the television. "Is that Britney Spears?"

Sarah crossed her arms and let out a harumph. "We can turn it off if you need to go to sleep."

"It's okay. I'm working the midmorning shift." He picked up the DVD case from where it was wedged between the couch cushions and grinned—so Sarah's taste in movies *was* as awful as his sister's when no one was around. "I can't believe you're watching this. How old is this movie?"

"I'll turn it off."

He picked up the remote and moved it out of her reach. "I want to see how they're going to win the money to fix the car and finish their road trip to California."

"Give me the remote."

He laughed and pushed it farther away. "No, no... I love me some rock and roll."

She flushed. "I hate you."

"You love me, Chestnut."

She rolled her eyes, but no denial came from her lips. "Why do *you* know the plot of *Crossroads*?"

"I have a sister?"

"Somehow, I don't think it's that." She leaned her head on his shoulder. "Jess is coming down with something. Could you bring home some tea tomorrow? We only have black tea, and we need—"

"Magic tea. I know." His childhood had been full of the calming mint, green tea, and chamomile concoction. In all this time, he hadn't found a better home remedy.

"Are you feeling okay? I have some echinacea." He shifted to look at Sarah, and Chuck jumped out of his lap and curled into a fluff ball next to him.

She smiled. "You would."

"Guy without health insurance here."

"Oh." She gave him a commiserating look. "I'm feeling fine. She probably got it from Ryder and all his airport germs. But she had a fever, which is unusual for her."

Brian wouldn't have known that about his sister. He got a fever at the slightest sign of a sniffle, so he would assume his sister would be the same. But Sarah knew these things. Sarah had been with Jess all these years. And while he'd always thought of her as the wild child to Jess's calm grown-up, he was starting to think it was Sarah who took care of Jess rather than vice versa. Maybe the caregiving dynamic was mutual in a way that Brian would never fully understand. It wouldn't be the first time he was clueless about women's friendships—he certainly hadn't understood the fierce bond his ex had with her best friend.

He stroked Chuck's back. He'd have to make sure to wash his hands before bed, or he'd wake up with puffy, itchy eyes, but he couldn't help it. Chuck demanded to be petted. Most nights, Chuck slept on the couch above Brian's head, pawing him in the early hours of the morning for breakfast. And damned if he didn't kind of love it.

"Does she need anything else?" he asked.

"No," Sarah said with a yawn. "Magic tea, Nyquil, and rest usually does the trick."

"Thanks for taking care of my sister."

"We take care of each other."

He hooked an arm around her shoulder that she didn't shrug off. If anything, she burrowed deeper. His heart fluttered then calmed. The résumé could wait until the morning. "Thank you nonetheless."

Chapter 27

Sarah

The gym was starting to fill up. And the more it filled, the more she fidgeted—with her water bottle, the *Bitching about Boyfriends* tote she'd forgotten to swap out, the hem of her "I don't sweat, I sparkle" tank, her hair. Every woman who walked into the room scanned the small space, spotted her, gave an enthusiastic wave, and then turned, wide-eyed, to the tall mesh-shorts-wearing man next to her. Brian was all man tonight. He'd asked to come early so he could use the rest of the gym, and his expression had been filled with so much excitement at the mention of a rowing machine that she couldn't say no. So now he was a glistening behemoth throwing off sweaty pheromones. *Kill me now.*

"Why are you so fidgety?" he asked, wiping his face with a hand towel. "We're not expecting Tyler, are we?"

"At Zumba?" She laughed despite the nerves building up in her. "That would never happen. Plus, I told you, we don't usually have guys in class."

He glanced around, turning back to her with a smirk. "I do seem to be quite the commodity."

She rummaged through her tote again without answering, and her hand stumbled upon the plastic bag she'd shoved in there and totally forgotten about in the few hours since she'd picked up his gift. She thrust the bag at him. "I got you something."

His smile alone was worth the price tag. She watched him as he pulled out the heather-gray tank top, his eyes landing on the words printed on the front: Torn between wanting a snack and looking like one.

"Wow, Chestnut." A small smile played on his lips, and she could swear his cheeks were a bit redder than before. "Tell me how you really feel."

"It's a thing." She pointed at her tank, which she realized a moment too late gave him permission to stare at her boobs. "Regulars wear funny shirts."

Brian, to his credit, barely looked at her shirt before turning his attention to the numerous graphic tees reflected in the mirror. He nodded in understanding before reaching for the hem of his shirt.

"What are you doing?" she hissed as his torso—shiny and taut and far too tantalizing—appeared in front of her. As if it wasn't something she saw at home nearly every day, her body jerked to life, heat blossoming in her lower abdomen. She cursed him and his stupid workout body.

"See something you like?" he asked, the tank top bundled in his hands.

"No." Sarah motioned toward his body. "Put that away."

He obliged, though the slim fit of the tank did little to change the view. It showcased his pecs, the nice shape of his biceps, and the complete lack of sag in his triceps. She felt more than saw all the eyes currently on them and tried to rearrange her face into something more neutral.

"Sarah! Hello!" Layla said, and Sarah turned away from Brian. She'd been taking class with Layla pretty much since she arrived in Philadelphia, even moving gyms one time to keep going to class. The instructor pulled her into a hug. "I'm so glad to see you back! We missed you the last few months."

Months. Had it really been months? She tried to remember if she'd been to Zumba since moving in with Tyler, but the classes blended together—those months were a blur of late nights, canceled plans, and Tyler. There'd been less of everything over the summer, but she thought that was to be expected with a new apartment and a live-in boyfriend with an erratic schedule. Even her time with Jess had been more limited. Sarah's weird schedule had seemed normal until Layla's statement.

"Life got a little hectic."

Layla nodded. "As it does. Welcome back. And welcome…"

"Oh…" Sarah stepped closer to Brian. "This is Brian. He's my…" No one present needed to think Brian was her boyfriend—Tyler didn't use this gym, didn't know these people—yet it felt weird *not* saying it. Between maintaining the relationship on social media and using the word at work, it had become almost natural.

"Her roommate," Brian said as Sarah's silence stretched. He tucked her into his side, his arm coming around her and his hand settling on her waist. "We're still figuring out the rest."

Layla laughed. "Well, welcome, roommate Brian. Have you attended a Zumba class before?"

"No, but I've taken dance lessons before, so I think I'll be okay."

"Perfect. We're mirror image, and you can follow me for queues and counts." Her eyes turned toward his shirt, and she leaned in close. "I don't think you need to worry about either of those things."

With a wink, she moved back toward the front of the room, stopping a few times to chat with other students. Brian didn't let Sarah go. She glanced up and found him watching her, a confused expression on his face.

Before she could question it, he smiled and pulled his phone out of his pocket. "Selfie?"

"You're supposed to take the selfie after your workout."

"Come on." He held the phone up. "This one is for me. My first Zumba class ever. We can take a sweaty one later if you want and put some inappropriate caption on Instagram about how we got that way and how you are hungry for a snack or something."

She leaned into him. "You know just how to sweet-talk me, Brian Hawkins."

He laughed, shaking his head, and then snapped a few photos. "Any other requests?"

Before she could answer, the music blared through the speakers almost loud enough to shake the mirrors. Layla's voice followed, calling a start to the class. Sarah tugged Brian onto the floor a few rows back from the front as the instructor worked to lower the volume.

"You ready?" Sarah asked over the music.

Brian grinned. "You sure you don't want to stand behind me? The view would be better."

She followed the steps she used to know before her skipped week had turned into months, glad that she wasn't tripping over her own feet—yet. She turned to her well-coordinated partner. "I knew I should've gotten the shirt that had a stubby-armed T. rex."

"Your mistake." Brian shimmied along with the rest of the class and then easily transitioned into a salsa step with the correct foot.

Meanwhile, Sarah was already half a step off the beat. *Lucky coordinated bastard.*

"YOU GET YOUR TIPS?"

Brian held up a bank envelope along with a plastic cup with two straws sticking out of it. "And this fabulous concoction."

Sarah eyed the venti Frappuccino that didn't look like anything on the menu. "That kind of defeats the purpose of the workout, doesn't it?"

He shrugged. "The shirt speaks the truth."

She took a sip of the drink. A mix of flavors hit her tongue—the sweetness of caramel, hazelnut, coffee, and chocolate followed by a lingering saltiness. "What is this?"

"A frozen salted caramel hazelnut hot chocolate."

"This should not be legal."

"Secret menu, baby." He took a sip. "Well, my secret menu at least. It's kind of a barista rite of passage."

"So, I guess that means we're not picking up Mexican?"

"We are totally getting Mexican."

"How... *men*."

"What? We promised my sister El Vez. She gave us money. If we don't come back with it... well, you know what she's like when she doesn't get her guac."

"That poor server at Chipotle."

"Right?" Brian said.

"Well, let's go, then. She's probably already hangry." She grabbed for the drink again. "Gimme that."

"Kind of defeats the point of the workout, no?"

"You did not."

He laughed, bent over, the cup held out to her. "I couldn't resist. I'm sorry. Your face."

"We are not friends anymore. That dresser drawer I so graciously offered you is no longer yours. And this"—she hugged the drink to her chest— "is now mine."

Brian wrapped an arm around her and pulled her into him as they walked through the crowded streets. Center City this time of night was madness, and commuters eyed them with distaste as they fouled up pedestrian traffic. Part of her didn't care because she felt warm and cozy next to Brian, and his charm was magnetic. But she forced herself to step away from him.

"What can I do to earn your forgiveness, Chestnut?" He stuck his lip out in a pout.

She scrunched her nose up as if she was thinking. "Free lattes for a week."

"I already give you free lattes."

She held up a hand. "Delivered to my office as your breaks allow."

"Done."

"Really?"

He shrugged. "Nothing I haven't done before. And lately, I spend my break sitting in the back of the store, trolling Indeed for jobs."

"Then consider yourself forgiven." Sarah stopped in front of a rack of bouquets outside a local food mart. She bypassed the roses, her eyes going to the fall bunch. She fingered mums, lingering a moment, enjoying their beauty.

She looped her arm back through Brian's and started forward, but he pulled her back and asked, "Do you—"

"Want another sip of this drink? Why yes, I do, thank you." She took a long sip, the cold reaching her toes. She handed it back to him. "Too cold."

He laughed. "Wimp."

A few blocks later, they reached the restaurant, and for a few minutes the only conversation between them was about the menu. They ordered too much food and more chips, salsa, and guac than was humanly possible to consume. And still, she knew there'd be nothing left in the morning. They sat outside the restaurant, waiting for their order in companionable silence. The night was cool, and she tugged her sweatshirt tighter around her.

Brian zipped up his hoodie. He leaned back on the bench, crossing his legs at the ankle. She ignored the expanse of legs and the way his shorts rode up too high. At least her eyes averted themselves, but her mind was imagining straddling those legs right there in public.

"What are you doing for Halloween?" he asked, turning toward her.

"In the afternoon, I always visit Cedar Crest and give out presents."

"Presents?"

"Well, not all the kids can eat candy. We give some candy and some small gifts. As part of their intake, we ask about their interests so we know what they like, and then there's a small fund to pick up stuff for them for Halloween, Christmas, and birthdays, depending how long they are in the program."

"That's really sweet. Want some company?" he asked.

"You don't have to—"

"I want to. Halloween season is the only time I get to break out my costumes from Comic Con."

Halloween season. She couldn't argue with that designation. "Then yes, I'd love company."

"Any plans after?"

Sarah shook her head. "Since Jess will be at Ryder's sister's wedding, I'll probably put together a witch costume and hand out candy. If we sit on the stoop, we'll get a lot of kids."

"Then we shall sit on the stoop, but the following Saturday night, you're coming to a party with me."

"Oh, am I?"

"Yes. My sister will be catching the bouquet. Don't laugh—you know it's gonna happen. And I know you don't have plans."

"It's still two weeks away. I could make plans."

"Come on. I need a partner for my Han costume," he said.

"So, I'm to be your Princess Leia?"

"Yes?"

"Sounds fun. I am dying to meet these friends of yours."

He laughed. "Not as much as they are dying to meet you."

The pager from the restaurant buzzed on the bench between them before she could even formulate a response. She wondered what exactly he'd told his friends.

Brian stood and held out his hand. "Is my sister already in a Nyquil coma, or is she sitting at the table, staring at the door, fork at the ready?"

Sarah glanced at her phone and then back at him. "Both."

Chapter 28

Brian

Brian stopped outside the doors to the hospital. When he'd offered to go, he'd meant it. What Sarah and everyone at Sophie's Wish Factory did was an amazing kindness, but he hadn't thought about seeing the sick kids and what that might mean until the night before, when Sarah started telling him a bit about them. His memories of hospital visits were limited—a broken arm, stitches from that time he slid into second wrong—and nothing like what these kids were experiencing.

His phone buzzed in his pocket. It was probably Sarah asking where he was despite the fact that he was still ten minutes early. But no, it was a Fairford number on his screen.

"Hello?" he said even though he knew who it was from the business card he'd stuffed in his sock drawer.

"Hey, it's Corey."

"Hey, man. What's up?" He palmed his face. *Man* was not the way you addressed the person offering you a job. Even if it was a job you didn't want.

"I just saw your sister, and she mentioned you were still on the job hunt."

Brian hadn't thought that Jess and Ryder would stop in Fairford. It was decidedly out of the way, but then, Ryder seemed the kind of guy who would insist they stop and see her parents if they were even remotely in the vicinity. And his sister was the meddling type, particularly if she wanted her living room couch back. "I am."

"Well, listen. I know you're not keen on Fairford and coming home and all that, but maybe we could figure something out. I mean, there's no reason you technically *have* to be up here to be our senior systems engineer, is there? We have a shared workspace in downtown Manhattan—I mean, it's really just one office with two desks, but I'm sure we could make it work if you're interested. Now that Andi is moving up here, I won't be in the city quite so often, so you'd have the space to yourself."

Senior systems engineer. Mic drop. He would not be a senior anything anywhere else. "No, I suppose not."

"Listen, I'm going to be in the city next week, getting the rest of Andi's things packed and such. We should meet up."

"That sounds like a great idea. I'll text you on Monday to set something up."

They hung up after a few more pleasantries. Brian texted his sister an angry series of emojis that went unanswered before he reached the fourth-floor wing, where Sarah was waiting for him. She wore a witch costume that she must have pulled together from clothing she owned—black tights with the outlines of three witches on them, a pleated black-and-purple skirt, and a tank top with a black vest over it. A glittery witch's hat adorned her head.

"I thought you were dressing up," she said by way of greeting.

Brian dropped his briefcase onto a chair in the waiting area and shrugged off his jacket. He unbuttoned his cuffs and rolled his sleeves up to his elbows. Next, he pulled a black-rimmed pair of glasses out of his suitcase and slipped them on. "Oh ye of little faith."

He loosened his tie and unbuttoned his collar. Sarah stared at him wide-eyed, with what looked like intrigue and heat and amusement competing for attention in her expression. Another button came loose and another.

"I had a job interview this morning, but..." He pulled open his shirt, exposing the costume underneath, a large *S* emblazoned across its chest. "Superman does not disappoint."

She laughed, a warm and real smile brightening her features. "Did you wear that to your interview?"

"Maybe."

Her smile grew somehow bigger, and God, she was beautiful. She tugged him forward. "Okay, Clark, let's go. The kids are waiting."

That smile didn't last long. He saw it start to fade as they approached the nurses' station and then completely disappear when the woman sitting behind the counter—Susan, according to her name tag—handed Sarah a note. Rage replaced all other emotions on her face as she read it.

"You can't be serious." This was directed at the nurse, who blinked up at them innocently. "I know you read this, so stop acting like you don't know what it says."

"What's going on?" Brian asked, though most of it was obvious enough. Tyler had struck again. *Bastard.*

"My jackass ex left a note requesting that I have someone else handle today's festivities."

If Brian saw Tyler today, the shit was going to hit the fan. *The man had better hide all day in his office or in a freaking OR.* "A little late for that request, no?"

Sarah glared at him, the nurse, the note, and the wall and then stomped a foot. "I'm going in there. This may be his department, but those are my kids."

Susan shrugged. "I'm not going to stop you. But if he sees you, it would be great if you could say you slipped past while I was in the restroom. I really can't deal with his attitude today."

"Oh, he'll see me."

Brian barely had a chance to utter a thank-you to the nurse before Sarah had him halfway down the hallway. The words she mumbled were not complimentary or appropriate for a children's hospital. He reminded himself to never, ever piss her off. If her angry words were even partially true, Tyler was in for a world of hurt. Not that Brian understood what Tyler and Sarah were doing. Brian's ex had dumped him and married another guy in less than a week, and still, Brian had kept Hannah's secret about her marriage pact. He hadn't even thought of telling anyone about it. And his and Sarah's situations were similar—they'd both been in relationships that clung to hope, that weren't working, and that never would have moved into something more. Nothing about Tyler and Sarah seemed a fit. Yet they'd lived together, and the man had thought enough of their relationship that he'd proposed. Still, it all seemed too much. Instead of letting them both keep their dignity when their paths were forced to cross, they'd strewn their laundry all over the hospital and the gala and everything.

"Sarah," he said. She didn't stop. "Would you just stop for a minute?"

"What?" Her face was a tornado of emotions, anger being the most prominent, but he saw fear in the set of her jaw.

The hallway they were in was oddly deserted, and he hoped that meant most people were in whatever room they were supposed to be going into for the event. He stepped closer to her and put a hand on her shoulder.

"Call a truce."

"Are you serious? He just tried to keep me from my kids."

"Exactly. This is no longer you two showing each other up at a gala with competing hot dates. Apologize and call a truce."

"Apologize!" she said.

Brian took a breath and hoped he didn't get smacked for what he was about to say. "He proposed to you, Sarah. Do you know how much courage it takes a man to propose? He has to think pretty solidly that the person is going to say yes. Engagement rings aren't exactly refundable, and proposals aren't planned in a vacuum. You broke his heart and gut punched his pride. And he handled it awfully. I'm not saying he didn't." He leaned in closer to her, dropping his voice to just above a whisper. "But how were you two so far apart that he didn't know you wouldn't say yes?"

Sarah's jaw snapped shut. Her eyes went wide, and color sprouted on her cheeks. Then she shoved the bag of supplies at him and pointed to a room with an open door to the right. She stuffed a piece of paper into his breast pocket. "Start face painting." She wheeled on her heels and strode back down the hall.

Brian watched her until she turned a corner and was out of sight. Then he pulled the crumpled piece of paper from his pocket. *Schedule* was written in Sarah's curly handwriting at the top. After face painting, there was pumpkin decorating and a costume contest and music, all ending with a viewing of the Halloween classic, *Hocus Pocus*. Even Brian could get behind that.

He walked the short distance to the room. Voices filled the hall, young and high, girls and boys, a few deeper and older—teenagers most likely. Wilderness Weekend, of all bands, filtered out of the room. Sarah had spent a long time the night before talking about *her kids*. Chris G. was the Wilderness fan, and his wish was to meet Leonard, which was nearly impossible now that he was retired. Johnny K. loved Superman. Dylan N. was a gamer. And Tessa C.—well, Sarah had spent a lot of time talking about Tessa. Brian raked a hand through his hair, adjusted his glasses, and made sure the Superman symbol was visible.

"If it isn't Clark Kent."

Brian looked up to find a young woman, probably fifteen or sixteen, standing in the doorway. He recognized her from the photos Sarah had shown him, though she looked quite different in leggings and a tank top, with kitten ears adorning her head.

"Tessa, right?"

"Sarah's boy toy, right?" she said, and Brian flushed. "I follow her on Insta—not that she knows that."

Great.

"Doc Ack is not going to be happy to see you."

Brian shrugged. "He's going to be even less happy to see Sarah."

Tessa laughed, and it was a wonderful, musical sound. She was so vibrant, yet he knew that she was here more than anywhere else in her life and would be for much longer. His insides twisted.

She motioned toward the paper he still held. "What's the plan, Superman?"

He smiled. It was obvious why Sarah liked Tessa. Brian liked her already. "How are you at face painting?"

Chapter 29

Sarah

The door to Tyler's office was closed, but she didn't knock. She plowed in, her death glare on full power, harsh words at the ready. But Tyler wasn't waiting for her at his desk as she'd thought he would be. He wasn't in an important meeting or on the phone. No, Tyler was passed out on the couch in his office, in a sleep mask he'd gotten as a white elephant gift at last year's holiday party, which read, "If you can read this, go away." His chest rose and fell in slow, even breaths. She almost didn't want to bother him. Almost. Instead, she slammed the door shut.

He bolted upright, as if he'd been shot, and ripped the sleep mask off his face. His expression neutralized at the sight of her, as if Sarah standing in his office was the best possible outcome. And maybe for a pediatric surgeon, a pissed-off ex-girlfriend was high on the list of people to wake up to.

But then his lips flattened into a line, and his eyes narrowed. "What the hell?"

She leaned back against the door with her arms crossed. Brian's advice played through her mind, but she ignored it. Faces like Tyler's didn't get truces. "Morning, sunshine."

"Get out."

"I would, but someone asked me to abandon the Wish Factory kids. Maggie is going to be pissed if I have to tell her that we didn't have our Halloween party because you were acting like a jackass."

"I agree. She's going to be royally pissed at *you*."

"This isn't a joke, Tyler. You don't speak for the hospital. And you certainly don't speak for Sophie's Wish Factory. And why would you do something that was going to hurt the kids?"

"Getting Leigh instead of you wouldn't hurt the kids."

"Leigh hardly knows them, and you made sure I got the note on arrival, which means I would've had to postpone or cancel if I even considered honoring your asinine request."

"Did you ever think that maybe I need a break from you?" His voice broke on the last half of the sentence, and it almost softened her. But it wasn't *enough*. He could have just stayed in his office like he was doing anyway. He didn't have to get Wish Factory involved.

"After you summoned me here forty hours after our breakup to tell me about your sex buddy? No, the thought hadn't really crossed my mind."

"Yeah, well, your little truth bomb blew up my relationship with Monique."

She rolled her eyes. "How was I to know you lied to her about our history?"

"Fine. Whatever." He waved toward the door. "Go see the kids. I need to get some sleep anyway. I had a twelve-hour surgery last night."

She refrained from asking for more details. She loved to hear about his surgeries—each story was like *Grey's Anatomy* in real life—but it wasn't her place anymore. "This can't happen again, Tyler. This is my *job*. You can't screw with my life."

"Why not? You screwed with mine."

Brian's words—"how were you two so far apart that he thought you'd say yes?"— came back to her.

"I never meant to," she said.

"That doesn't really help."

"Can we...?" Sarah swallowed back the revulsion at what she was about to ask. Brian had been right.

This had gone too far. And for what? They both knew they were better off apart. She'd known it the moment he kicked her out of his apartment, and if Tyler hadn't known it then, he certainly knew it now.

"Can we call a truce?" she asked.

"A truce?"

"Yeah. I will stop being a bitch to you, and you'll stop being an asshole, and we'll just coexist."

Tyler stepped toward her. "As if it never happened."

"No. As if it happened, and we moved on graciously like the mature adults that we are."

"You're wearing *Hocus Pocus* tights."

"Your point?" she said, hands on hips.

He smiled, and it might have been the first real smile she'd seen on him in too long—longer than the weeks they'd been apart. Her heart did a little flip, and an ache settled in her chest. She didn't want to be with Tyler, but she didn't want to regret him either.

He took her hand in his. "Nothing. Truce called."

"Thank you."

BRIAN WAS FULL-ON SUPERMAN when Sarah finally arrived in the common room. He'd discarded the rest of his clothing, and the full suit was visible, which meant he had worn a spandex body suit—albeit a hidden one—to a job interview. For her. Someone, probably Tessa, had sprayed his hair with one of those cheap temporary hair colors, and his usually brown locks were jet-black. He stood in the back of the room, taking photos with the kids. Johnny K. hung off Brian's flexed arm. There was a box under Johnny's feet, but no one would see that if they took the photo right. And of course, Tessa would take the photo right even with that beat-up old Polaroid.

Sarah sighed. She would miss Tessa after the girl got her kidney. Maybe they could sign her on as an intern.

"Behold, it's my lady love," Brian said, giving Superman a weirdly Shakespearean accent.

"Sarah!" A horde of kids gathered in front of her. Sammie hugged her legs, and Ruth burrowed into her rib cage. Tessa snapped another photo.

"It's Lois Lane today." She held up her notepad and tapped the pen against her lips. She batted her eye lashes and, escaping the clutches of the kids, mock ran across the room and into Brian's arms. "What would I do without you, Superman?"

Brian laughed in a fake, haughty way, his voice deep and his tone over-the-top. "You would actually stick to the schedule."

Sarah took the crumpled paper he offered her and rolled her eyes. From the looks of the room, the kids had dived into everything. Half-painted pumpkins littered the table, the face-paint set was still out, and cornhole bags were everywhere. And she'd barely been gone for twenty minutes.

"All right! It's time for the parade!" she called.

Kids scrambled to get their costumes arranged and made a makeshift line by the door.

"Doc Ack!" Sammie yelled as he knocked into Tyler's legs with a thud.

Sarah glanced behind her to find Tyler standing in the doorway in a black robe with a yellow-and-maroon scarf. His normally well-coifed hair was messy, and a rounded pair of glasses sat on his nose.

"Can someone tell me the way to Platform Nine and Three Quarters?"

Wow, his British accent is bad.

Tessa leaned in close to her. "Do you think they're going to battle for your hand?"

"It's not like that." Sarah looked back at Brian, who seemed more than content helping Tyler corral the kids into a line.

"It's most certainly like that. That man is smitten."

Sarah really didn't need to keep up the fake-dating ruse anymore. It didn't matter what Tyler knew. He'd seen enough. And too much of it had been real enough.

Yet she still had to force the next words from her mouth. "He's not."

"He is. And you're smitten with him."

"We've barely interacted with each other. You're projecting."

"No, I have eyes and ears and *social media*."

"Tessa," Sarah groaned.

"Hey." Brian came up to them, and the grin on Tessa's face grew so wide her jaw had to hurt. He held out his hand to Sarah. His eyes, thank God, were only on her. "You ready?"

Sarah did not want to take his hand. Not with Tessa standing there as if her one true pairing had just declared their love for each other for the first time. But she couldn't *not* take his hand either. She slipped her hand into his, and her whole body felt the touch of skin to skin as his fingers slid between hers. Her eyes went to his eyes and then to his lips. The memory of his mouth on hers sparked something in her. Something she was losing the battle against. Something she no longer wanted to fight.

Pushing on her tiptoes, she pressed her lips against his cheek. "I like the hair."

He smiled. "Knew you would."

Chapter 30

Sarah

"This *will* wash out, right?" Brian sat down on the stoop next to her, dropping another bag of candy into the bowl on her lap. "I have job interviews next week."

Sarah took in his half-brown, half-black mess of hair. "Take a few extra showers, but I think you'll be fine. Tessa used some really cheap stuff."

"I'm going to have to deep clean the shower after this."

"Oh yeah. I should've warned you. Also, don't wear any shirts you're particularly attached to."

"I learned that the hard way."

She frowned. "Sorry. Where are your interviews?"

"I have a virtual one with this SaaS company in St. Louis."

"Saz?" She hoped her voice sounded steady as panic chilled her to the core. Brian couldn't move to St. Louis.

"Sorry, software as a service. The other one's in New York on Wednesday."

The third Elsa they'd seen in the last half hour approached. This one was maybe four. Her pink pumpkin overflowed with candy. "Trick or treat."

"Happy Halloween!" Brian dropped two Hershey's kisses into her bucket.

The mother, who stood a few feet back, mouthed a thank-you and held out her hand for the little girl. Sarah watched them go, her thoughts on the awful possibility that Brian wouldn't find a job in Philadelphia—if he even wanted to stay in this city. Jess was leaving soon. It was obvious to everyone, though none of them would say it. The band was breaking up before it had even really started.

She cleared her throat and wrapped her arms around her legs. "First time back?"

He nodded. "I don't miss it as much as I thought I would. It always felt like this rite of passage—this privilege—to work and live in New York City. And now that I've been away from it for a few months, it's just another overpriced city with a lot of tourists."

"Says the New Yorker."

"Fine. It's the best city in the world. But that doesn't mean I need to live there again."

Sarah's phone pinged, and she picked it up, her eyes skimming over the email she'd been waiting for all day. "Dammit."

"What?" Brian leaned over, and she let him read the email on her screen.

"I've been trying to get a visit with Wilderness Weekend set up for Chris, but Leonard's agent just wrote back that he's not accepting appearance requests for the foreseeable future."

Which made sense, considering the man had just retired from the public eye, but that didn't make it any easier to take. Chris had entered the program the day after the final Wilderness Weekend show. He was one of the sick ones, in and out of the hospital with cancer treatments. Sarah wasn't a Wilderness aficionado, but she knew enough to know that if she could just get five minutes with Leonard Nulty, he'd be at the hospital in the few hours it took to drive from Boston to Philly. But she couldn't get around his damn agent.

"Sorry, Chestnut. That really sucks."

She could tell Brian meant it, too, because these were no longer just names on a paper to him—they were kids, real and fragile and important. She thought about the way Brian had sat with Dylan and talked video games after the parade. Everyone else had been watching Max, Dani, and Binx duke it out with the Sanderson sisters, and Brian and Dylan had been huddled in the back, talking *Kingdom Hearts*, which she only knew about because it had Disney characters in it.

A fairy and a Harry Potter approached, bags open, smiles plastered on. "Trick or treat!"

Sarah dropped a few pieces into each of their bags. "Happy Halloween!"

She watched the two walk back to their dad. Memories of those earliest Halloweens before her dad fled and her mom stopped making her costumes blossomed, unwanted, as the fairy wrapped her arms around her dad's legs. Sarah had loved those costumes, as cheesy as they were, and there'd been something special about that night with her dad.

"I was, like, a Crayola crayon at that age. I wish I could've had a cool character costume," she said as the family crossed the street.

Brian leaned back, bracing himself with his hands. "I was a pirate or a ninja for most of my childhood."

"Nice."

"Speaking of costumes…" He turned to her, his gaze discerning. "Things seemed better with Tyler."

"That was an awful transition."

"Come on. What happened?"

She shrugged. "I called a truce."

His eyebrows practically hit his hairline. "You listened to me?"

"Don't sound so surprised. It was good advice."

"Well, I'm glad." He handed a few candy bars to the tween ninja standing in front of them. "This turned out to be an amazing Halloween."

Sarah dropped a candy into another bucket, waving at the ballerina who had stayed back with her parents. "I'm sure you've had better. What did you do last year?"

"Nothing. Everything with my ex had just happened. I stayed in and watched horror movies all night. Didn't see a single person or eat a single piece of candy."

"What happened there?"

"You know. You've heard the podcast."

"That's her side of the story—and honestly, you're barely in it. What's your side?"

He pulled out his wallet and took out a folded sheet of paper. It was creased and worn. He handed it to her. "I've been walking around with this letter for a year."

She unfolded it carefully, her eyes raking over the girly scribble.

Dear Brian, I know what you must be thinking. I'd be thinking it too. You may never believe me, but I swear that I wasn't cheating on you. Whatever you hear in the next days and weeks and months, it's a lie. Will and I had a marriage pact.

"She told you about the pact?"

Brian nodded. "She did, and I kept her—their—secret until she blasted it all over the internet."

"I wouldn't say all over the internet. *Bitching about Boyfriends* doesn't have that big of a following."

"Not the point."

"Right. Sorry." Sarah quickly read through the rest as Brian handed candy to yet another Elsa. "She asked you to marry her first?"

"Hannah and I... we never fit. We started out as a fun fling, and it became more."

"Sounds familiar."

"We would take breaks, but we always came back to each other. But she never let me in. I was never her priority. Between her and Kate and all their traditions and her job and her cat hating me... she never made room for me. Then about six months before it all went to hell, she mentioned something about engagement. I mean, we were so far from that. We didn't live together and hadn't even talked about

it. I took some time to consider if I could be with someone like that long-term. If I could find a way to fit into her crowded life. I decided it was worth it. So I made time for her. I respected her time with her best friend, and I worked around her job. I started staying at her place even though her cat made me sneeze and bit my toes in my sleep. But nothing changed. I still always felt like I was intruding. Then she asked me to marry her. At first, I thought maybe this was her making the effort. But then she added, 'I know we're not ready to be married.'"

"She did not," Sarah said.

"It was the truth. We both knew it. We'd known it for a long while at that point."

"So why keep the letter?"

"Read the last line."

"I was never going to be that person for you, and you couldn't be that person for me," Sarah read.

Brian grimaced. "You and Tyler were too far apart and wanted different things. Hannah and I knew exactly where we stood but couldn't come together to make it work. It was really painful to know she got married literally days after we broke up, even if it was just for convenience. And then when it came out that her marriage had turned into true love, it was like I was back to the last time I saw her standing in my doorway in a white dress, wearing someone else's engagement ring. I keep the letter because sometimes I really need the reminder that Hannah and I were never going to be anything more than we were, and we both knew it."

"I can't believe you kept her secret."

"How many people have you told that Tyler proposed and you said no?" Brian asked.

"That's different."

"Not really if you think about it."

"You're always the villain in someone else's story." She kneaded the paper, seeing the words again. Brian had been Hannah's villain, or at least one of them, but Hannah had also been his. Sarah folded the letter back up. She held it out to him, her eyes still on her lap. "I guess you'll be wanting this back?"

Brian took it and then cupped her face with his free hand until she looked at him. Without a word, he crumpled the paper into a ball and dropped it into the garbage bag at their feet.

Chapter 31

Brian

Brian's watch ticked another minute past nine. They were going to be so late—if you could technically be late to a Halloween party. Maybe it wouldn't be too bad. If Ethan's place was already crowded, then him arriving with Sarah on his arm might not be the declaration he was worried it would be. They hadn't kissed in weeks, not since the night of the gala, yet something had most certainly changed for them in the last few days. He felt it, and he could tell she did too. Her eyes softened whenever she looked at him, and he noticed the indulgent way she said his name and the way she curved into him when they sat on the couch and watched television until all hours of the morning now that Jess was out of town. She'd fallen asleep with her head on his lap during *Scream*, and it had physically hurt him to wake her. He was falling for her hard and completely.

His phone buzzed. Brian pulled it out of his pocket, his heart thrumming at the appearance of the text he'd been expecting since the day before. *Does 2 pm work? At Blue Bottle on 53rd?* He sent back a confirmation before pocketing his phone.

Another minute passed, and still, Sarah did not come out of the bathroom. *How long does it take to throw on a white Leia dress?* "Just come out already!"

There was a shuffle behind the bathroom door. "I'm having trouble with my... buns."

He rolled his eyes. "I've been to enough Comic Cons to know how to do Leia buns. Just come out and let me help you."

He swore he heard a giggle through the door. But then it opened. Brian's hands stilled on the button of his jacket. He blinked a few times, but no, this was real. His eyes trailed a course down Sarah's body, from the golden straps of her bikini top to the oh-so-bare skin of her torso and farther down to the golden shorts and sheer cover-up. She was Princess Leia all right. Princess Leia from *Return of the Jedi*. Blood rushed down his body, and there was no stopping his erection. He swallowed and leaned against the back of the couch, hoping his hands covered the obvious bulge.

"Hey, scoundrel."

Holy. Shit. His cock was going to fall off.

Sarah's gaze went from him to her costume, and she looked up at him with feigned innocence. "Did I do it wrong?"

"I think I love you."

She grinned. "I know."

He stared as her eyes told him a truth that he really should have already figured out. No one was that bad at identifying celebrities. "I thought you said you didn't like *Star Wars*."

Her grin widened. "I said no such thing."

He swallowed. A million fantasies he'd had about that very outfit—one as recent as last night and featuring Sarah—filtered through his mind like a damn flip book. "Did you need help with your buns?"

"Not *those* buns. But I got it. Just needed a little tape."

"Tape."

"Yes, tape." She walked toward him, and he tried to look anywhere but at the abundance of skin on display. "What's going on with your hair? It's not Han."

"I think I know what Han hair looks like. I've only been cosplaying him for a decade."

She stepped between his legs, as close to him as she'd ever been. She must have felt him against her, but if she did, she didn't let on. He wrapped his arms around her and clasped them behind her back, locking in the closeness. Her fingers ran through his hair, moving it, parting it, and it felt like heaven.

"Is that stubble I see on your face?"

With him sitting down, they were finally eye level with each other, and he saw the mischief in her expression. He freed one of his hands and rubbed his jawline. "No-Shave November. Ethan and I have a bet on who will cave first."

"I like it." Sarah brought the hand that had been playing with his hair to his cheek.

His eyes dropped to the blush across her cheeks. She licked her lips, and he became impossibly harder. He rested his hands on the bare skin of her waist and pulled her closer. "Sarah."

Her name on his lips was an oath, a prayer, a request. And he knew between one moment and the next that he was going to kiss her—that until they saw where this madness went, they couldn't go back. He couldn't go back. He tilted her chin so she had to look at him.

Her eyes were dark with hunger and wide with trepidation. Her lips parted, and his name fell on a whisper as she brought her lips to his.

Chapter 32

Sarah

The way he'd said her name—the unfiltered reverence in his voice and the want in his eyes—had undone her. She'd known for days, but her name from his mouth... weeks' worth of emotion had been put into that word. And the rest was pouring into her as his tongue danced with hers. The simple act of kissing bringing her to the brink like no kiss ever had before. Her whole body was at attention. She pushed up against his hardness, feeling the length of him against her. He groaned against her mouth, and then he stood, pulling her into him and changing the angle. His mouth slanted over hers, deepening the kiss. Warmth shot through her as his hands skimmed the sides of her body, from the curve of her shoulder and lower across the crest of her breast until they splayed across the expanse of her back.

Goose bumps sprouted wherever his fingers went, a spark following their motion down her side. He shouldn't have been able to do this to her with a simple touch. She pushed the vest off his shoulders and raked her nails down his plain white T-shirt until she grasped the hem. He pulled back and met her gaze, and his eyes, clouded with lust, gave her permission. Sarah pulled the shirt over his head and let it drop to the floor. She sucked in a breath. Brian Hawkins was gorgeous. She'd known that. She'd seen him in his underwear for weeks now. But this was different. She touched his chest, softly, slowly crossing the ridge of his pecs and down his firm abdomen and then back up.

He pulled her back to him, his hands on her ass as he lifted her up and into him. She wrapped her legs around him, and the thin fabric of her shorts did nothing to dull the sensation of his hands on her. She nuzzled into him, kissing the tender spot below his ear.

He jerked to attention as her tongue hit the right spot, and she pulled back with a grin. "Are we going somewhere, or were you just leveling the playing field?"

He laughed, and it was pure and happy and sexy as hell. He took a step away from the couch. "This seems like a bedroom conversation."

She nodded. "An all-night conversation."

He crossed the short distance to her bedroom—their bedroom—and backed her against the door, placing her on her feet. Brian worked his way down her neck and over her collarbone with his lips, eliciting noises from her that encouraged him further. His fingers crept under the soft fabric of her golden bikini top and teased at the soft, sensitive skin as he shucked it off. His hands cupped her breasts, and his lips followed, his tongue flicking over her nipple.

"Brian," she rasped as his tongue traced a line across her chest and he took her in his mouth. Her legs shook as desire rocketed down her body. She reached for the doorknob and pushed the door open before tugging him into the room by his belt buckle.

This was moving fast, but that was exactly how she wanted it. Slow could come later. Right now, she wanted to learn exactly what she'd been missing since the gala. And then she wanted to know it again, to memorize it and perfect it. She wanted to make him gasp and moan and call out her name.

Sitting down on the edge of the bed, she undid his belt buckle. She grasped him, running her hand down his length. And *holy shit*, he was well-endowed.

Brian stilled her hand after a few moments, his eyes glassy but focused. "You first." He leaned over her, pushing her back onto the bed.

He moved down her body, lavishing attention on each part until his lips rested above her lower abdomen. He snuck a finger and then two under the thin gold fabric of her costume. "May I?"

She nodded. He pulled them off, careful—even in the moment—of the tape she'd mentioned earlier. He tossed them to the floor and then kept his gaze locked on hers as he fitted himself between her thighs. Nothing had ever felt so right in her life. His breath against her inner thigh nearly broke her, each inch closer bringing new waves of pleasure and surprise. By the time his tongue touched her soft center, she was throbbing. She arched into him, her fingers tangling in his hair. It had been too long since she'd had sex this good—she might never have had sex this good—and he wasn't even inside her yet. She felt herself cresting, losing all sense of time or place or self until he made her scream his name.

Pulling him back up, she wasted no time freeing him from his pants. He sprang to attention. This was going to be fun. A smile formed on her lips at his rumpled appearance and the triumphant look on his face. But now it was her turn. She rolled on top of him, stroking him as she kissed down his body.

"Sarah," he moaned as she sped up her touch. She kissed lower, but he put a hand on her shoulder and urged her back up to him. "I need to be inside you."

He grabbed his pants from the floor and pulled out his wallet. Sarah's eyes widened at the golden-foil wrapper—the one no other man she'd been with had ever had the need for. Well-endowed indeed.

Sarah positioned herself over him, and they moved together gently until he was deep within her. He kissed her then, soft and sweet and agonizingly slow. He reached up and tugged at the hair ties keeping her buns up until her hair hung free, cascading down her shoulders.

"That's better." Brian ran a finger through her hair and then down across her chest. He caressed her breast. She urged him still deeper, and he obliged, moving faster and teasing her with his tongue, each kiss more urgent than the next. Sarah breathed him in and opened herself to him. The warmth of his hands, gentle yet rough against her skin as he brought her still closer to the edge, spoke of the weeks between this kiss and their last. The look in his eyes radiated a heat that said he'd do this forever if she let him. And she wanted to let him. Brian fit in so many ways. He took her banter, accepted her shit, and gave it all back to her. He stayed when she pushed him away.

She changed the angle, and her desire peaked as he moved with her, his lips never leaving hers except to say her name again and again. Pleasure washed over her, and she braced herself against the bed, Brian's hand keeping her steady until he followed her into oblivion.

They lay next to each other, their intense breathing the only sound in the room until he sat up. She watched his back as he cleaned up, and then he returned to her and tugged her into his arms. He kissed her forehead with his eyes closed, and a smile played at the edge of his lips. "I guess we're not making it to the party."

She laughed and nuzzled into his neck. "I mean, we could. If you prefer."

Brian tightened his grip on her and then kissed her lightly and lazily as if they had been kissing for their entire lives. "I believe we agreed to an all-night conversation."

Her body came back to life, and she coiled a leg around his. "That we did."

"Then I guess that means we're sharing the bed." His hand strolled up her side, his fingers tracing circles on her skin.

"How about..." She rolled on top of him and pinned his arms to the bed. "Double or nothing?"

Chapter 33

Sarah

Sarah had never lived alone. Honestly, the idea had only appealed to her in that terrifying time back in her childhood bedroom between college graduation and hightailing it to Philadelphia to move in with Jess. But sitting here half-clothed and lazy on a Sunday evening, with dinner still strewn across the table, football playing in the background, and Brian's hands on her, she could get used to not having a roommate. At least one who required clothing and a little bit of discretion. Because after this morning, Sarah was never going to be able to look at the kitchen counter the same way again. Or the couch. Or her bed for that matter. She thought of Brian's strong arms bracing her against the back of this couch... the length of his body against her back.

"Mmm..." she said as Brian ran a hand up her leg, stopping at the edge of her shorts. She sank down into his touch as his fingers kneaded her hamstring into relaxation. "How'd you learn how to do that?"

He looked up at her, his face scratchy with a few days' worth of stubble. The slow ache of desire started as she remembered it scratching against her thighs. He gave her a half smile. "Dated a massage therapist for a while."

"Really?"

Brian laughed and tugged her up onto his lap. His lips found the spot on her neck that always set her squirming. "Jealous?"

"If it'll make you keep doing that, then absolutely." She felt him laugh against her before kissing his way down her shoulder and arm, finally bringing the palm of her hand to his mouth. "I'm seething."

He slanted his lips over hers, teasing her with his tongue. She gave in, losing herself in him. He slipped her bra straps off her shoulders. Her whole body shuddered at his touch. It had never been like this before. Even she and Tyler, who had started out hot and heavy, hadn't been like this. This was all-consuming and right and oh so wrong. Jess was going to kill her when she found out. And she was bound to find out if Sarah went into heat from merely looking at Brian's new beard.

Jess. Sarah broke their kiss, but Brian's hand didn't stop moving. Instead, he skimmed his fingers down her stomach and under her shorts. Her body urged her to arch into him, to give him access, but she stilled his hand. "We can't."

"Oh, but we can." He grinned. "I picked up more condoms when I went to get the cheesesteaks."

Of course he had. "Jess will be home soon. We can't be midsex on the couch."

"So let's go to the bedroom."

"I can't be having sex with you when your sister walks through the door, bedroom or not."

His hands dropped to his sides, and he grimaced. "Fine. But in the future, please refrain from talking about my sister when I have my hands in your pants."

"I'm sorry. Won't happen again."

"But we *are* going to have sex again?"

"So much sex." She kissed him. Too quickly, it started to deepen into something urgent, and God, she wanted to do something about the bulge under his sweats. This time, he pulled back and slipped her bra into place. It was a concession, and she loved that she didn't have to ask it of him.

She slid off him and back onto the couch. "We'll just have to be sneaky about it with Jess here."

As if they'd conjured Jess by uttering her name, the key sounded in the door. Brian, still in only sweats, jumped off the couch. Sarah pulled the first shirt she found over her head, cursing because it was Brian's. The bathroom door slammed shut a moment before the front door swung open. Sarah plastered on a smile and scanned the living room. Fortunately, they hadn't gotten dressed that morning, so most of the evidence remained in her room. *Fuck.* A condom wrapper sat in plain view on the coffee table. She grabbed her now-ice-cold coffee from the table and swigged it then shoved the wrapper between the couch cushions. Hopefully, Jess wasn't in a cleaning mood.

"Hey, roomie." She put the mug back down and crossed her legs. Jess hardly glanced up. "Hey."

"How was the wedding?"

"It was nice." Jess plopped down next to Sarah.

It took all the power she had to not move away. She had to smell like Brian—she was wearing his shirt, for fuck's sake. But if her best friend noticed anything was amiss, she didn't react. Hell, she had still barely looked up from her phone.

"Ryder's family is intense."

"Huh. I wouldn't have guessed that."

"I know, right?" Jess dropped her phone onto the table. "Are you watching football?"

"Your brother. But he paid for dinner, so I couldn't protest." Sarah hoped she sounded nonchalant—Brian buying her dinner wasn't anything new, nor was Sarah eating it with him. But the air in the room felt supercharged.

"Okay, but why are you wearing his shirt?"

Holy crap. Sarah glanced at the writing on the shirt, which she hadn't bothered to read all day: "The cake is a lie." There was no denying that it was his. This shirt was one of his favorites.

She scrambled for a reason that would make sense. "Oh. I won it off him in a bet."

"Another one?"

"Yup. He didn't think I could properly finish quotes from the original *Star Wars* trilogy. And of course, I can. So I won the shirt off his back, and I've been flaunting my winnings all day." Yes, that sounded like something she'd do.

She tried not to stare and gauge Jess's reaction. Nothing gave away a lie like checking to see if it stood up. Instead, she flipped through Netflix on her phone and cast *The Greatest Showman*. Her bestie would be distracted in approximately thirty seconds.

"I guess it's good that you guys are getting along now." Jess's tone was wry, definitely not playful or teasing. Sarah glanced at her friend sideways. Jess picked at food on the coffee table. "Is there any other food in the house?"

The bathroom door opened, and Brian stepped into the room, still in his sweats and, she knew, sans boxers. The V of his hips taunted her with his obvious lack of underwear and the prize that waited underneath. He was also still shirtless. They were so screwed.

"Why are you walking around like an ad for Old Spice?" Jess asked, turning to face her brother.

Brian's gaze shifted from his sister to Sarah, and that quick look told her he'd been listening to their earlier conversation. "Well, after Sarah *stole* my favorite shirt—it's not winning if you cheat—I felt it was only appropriate to go shirtless for the rest of the day. And I have leftover Chinese food and pizza in the fridge if you're desperate."

"Hmm... you don't pay rent, so technically, that's my food."

Sarah glanced at Jess again. She often ribbed her brother, and he gave it back, but this was different and a bit below the belt. It wasn't like Brian didn't contribute. Sarah had seen him slip all his tips for the week into Jess's purse more than once.

"My mistake." He held up his hands in supplication, his smile faltering. "Please eat the leftovers of the food I bought with my hard-earned money from my part-time hourly position."

"Thank you." Jess stood. "I think I will."

As soon as Jess was gone, Brian took her place. "Here's what I'm thinking," he whispered, his lips too close to hers. "I'll tell her I'm sleeping at Tasha's tonight and then after she goes into her room, I'll pretend to leave and sneak into your bed. I'll be up and out before she wakes up for work."

Sarah shook her head. "Not tonight."

"Why not?"

The fridge door slammed. "Because we need more than thirty seconds to develop a plan."

"It's a fine plan." He tugged at her hair. "You know you want to."

The microwave door clicked shut. "It's a recipe for getting caught."

"We could just tell her."

"Brian."

"Okay, how about I sneak in your room, have my way with you, and then return to the air mattress."

"How about we talk more about this over lunch when you bring me my latte." The microwave beeped.

"Fine. But I'll miss you." He kissed her so quickly that his lips barely touched hers, yet her whole body felt like it was on fire.

She swatted at him. "Stop that. And go get dressed. I can't have you looking like sex on a stick with your sister here."

He stood with a shit-eating grin and then winked at her, and *holy hell*, her ovaries exploded. A wink and a dimple—it was more than any woman could handle. She was in so much trouble.

Chapter 34

Brian

"He lives!"

Brian rolled his eyes at Ethan's over-the-top impression and motioned for him to continue. "Come on. Get it all out."

"Whatever do you mean?"

"Look, I'm sorry I missed the party." Brian shrugged. "Something came up."

"Oh, I sure hope it did."

Brian narrowed his eyes. No one knew what had happened between him and Sarah, and not showing up to the party because he was getting laid was a big jump in logic.

Tasha walked into the room and handed him a beer. "I totally told him."

Brian shot her a look. "Told him what?"

"That you came to work Monday and Tuesday looking like a rumpled sex puppy."

Freakin' Tasha. He might have been in a good mood on Monday, and maybe on Tuesday there was a little pep in his step since Sarah had agreed to an early-morning rendezvous in the shower, but he'd been mum on the topic. He hadn't even mentioned Sarah or Jess to Tasha.

"And it wasn't a far leap to figure out that you finally navigated Sarah's asteroid belt."

"I don't know." Tasha nudged him. "I was surprised. The odds really weren't in your favor."

Brian shook his head at the bad transition in pop-culture references. "Now, that's just bad form."

Tasha laughed. "That's what she said."

He'd walked into that. "Are we done now?"

"Oh, I could go all night." Ethan snickered.

And Brian officially hated his friends.

"Stop. Please." Brian took a swig of his beer and almost choked. He'd been expecting their usual cheap IPA, but this was hoppy, with hints of citrus and floral. He looked down at the bottle—Dogfish Head 120 Minute. Hard to find and expensive. Brian sat down between them on the couch. "What are we celebrating?"

"You finally getting laid." Ethan clinked his bottle against Brian's.

"Hardy-har-har."

"Oh right, you *missed the party* and, hence, my news. I put in an offer on that townhouse in Fishtown, and it's been accepted."

He bumped fists with Ethan. "Nice. Congratulations, man."

"I'll be looking for someone to take over my lease once I know when I'm closing and such."

An apartment in falling distance of his job would be nice, except that he couldn't afford it on his part-time salary. He wasn't even sure he could afford it on the full-time salary—Tasha was an assistant store manager, not an hourly shift supervisor. But it would be nice to be out of his sister's place. Grown siblings were not meant to cohabitate in small spaces, particularly when one was sleeping with the other's best friend.

"As if," Brian said.

"As if what? You have a job interview tomorrow."

"In New York."

"Fair. But I have it on good authority that you can expect a phone call this week from my brother's boss."

"That's fantastic. Thank you for setting that up, man." Brian took a drink. "But neither of those options lets me keep an apartment in Philadelphia."

"So you're *not* interested?"

After this weekend, there was only one answer he could stomach, even though he wasn't naïve enough to think that meant he could turn down a job for love. Hell, if push came to shove, he couldn't even turn down a job to stay out of his hometown. He'd set his deadline, and it was quickly approaching. He didn't want to leave Philadelphia, but that didn't mean he'd be able to stay.

"I didn't say that," Brian said. "Let me know when you need to know about the place."

Tasha flopped back on the couch dramatically. "I guess I should be ready to hire your replacement?"

"I didn't say that either." Brian picked up the controller. "Are we playing or what?"

"I thought he'd be in a better mood, you know, now that he got some," Ethan said, leaning across him to talk directly to Tasha.

She nodded. "Seriously, right?"

Brian shoved the controller into Tasha's hand and took another swig of his beer. It was going to be a long night.

BRIAN STOOD IN FRONT of the door to Sarah's bedroom. Never had a door looked so formidable and so dangerous. He scratched at his new and itchy facial hair. *To knock or not to knock?*

"What are you doing?"

He flinched at the sound of his sister's voice too close behind him. "I thought I told you not to do that anymore."

Jess laughed. "And I believe you signed a document that said it was my right as little sister if you snooped in my room." She motioned toward him. "You skulking in your underwear outside my best friend's bedroom qualifies."

Crap. Crap. Crap.

"Twelve-year-old you was the worst."

She crossed her arms and hit him with a glare so intense that it almost made him take a step back from her. "Don't skirt the point."

There had to be several logical reasons he could be standing there, hand poised to knock. But his mind was blank except for the obvious and the truth. "I just—"

"Are you sleeping with Sarah?"

Holy fuck. Sarah would never forgive him if he told Jess. And what would he even tell her? They'd barely had time to figure it out themselves in the three days since it started. And looking at his sister—eyes blazing, cheeks flushed, and foot tapping impatiently—Jess might never forgive either of them. When he'd told Sarah his sister wouldn't care, he'd mostly believed it, but then, before the gala, Jess had mentioned his high school ex—Jess's former friend, Bella. The implication had been clear: Brian had to keep the promise he'd made to Jess and not date her friends. But the situation with Sarah was different, and he hadn't made any decision about her lightly. His sister's expression, though, left no room for gray areas.

"No." The lie felt heavy on his tongue. "How could you think that?"

"I don't know," she said, her voice rising slightly. "Maybe because since the gala, you two have been acting weird. You couldn't even be in the apartment together, and now you're always hanging out, and you visit her at work, and you gave her back the bedroom."

"So? We became friends. That should be a welcome change of pace. What did you think was going to happen when I agreed to be her fake boyfriend?"

Jess grimaced. "I walked in on her wearing your shirt while you strutted around half-naked, and the apartment smelled like... I don't even know what. And now you're outside her bedroom door in the middle of the night, half-naked again!"

Brian shifted his gaze to his bare feet and legs, and his brain finally started working again. *Thank God.* "I just need my pajamas, Jess." He tugged at the hem of her cardigan. "It's too cold to sleep in my underwear."

"Likely excuse."

"Jess, chill—"

"She's probably up watching Netflix." His sister's fingers angrily swiped across her screen. "If she doesn't answer in less than a minute, just go in and get them." Jess's phone pinged. "I'm trusting you, Brian." She turned and headed to the bathroom without another word.

Her words echoed through him, and he stepped toward the bathroom. Maybe it was better to tell her now. Maybe he should crawl under the comforters and forget he was ever going to knock. But then the door opened, and Sarah stood there in pink satin shorts and a matching cami with lace trim. She was hot. So hot. He pulled up stats from the last football game, anything to take his mind off what his dick was doing.

"Did you knock?" she asked, glancing around, but Jess was still in the bathroom. "I was watching *Outlander*. Sorry if I didn't hear."

He shook his head and motioned toward the bathroom so Sarah would know where his sister was. "No, Jess came out before I could."

Her eyes narrowed, and she glanced at the bathroom door. "Did she suspect anything?"

He nodded, not wanting to lie to Sarah. "But I think she believed me about needing my pajamas."

He watched her consider her options, her teeth sinking into her bottom lip. And then she entered his personal space, running her hands down his chest before grasping him through his boxers. Oh god, he was in so much trouble. He leaned into her, her scent overwhelming him, which only made him harder.

"Make a fake person out of pillows and get in my bedroom." She grinned. "Here's your pajamas," she said, pitching her voice loud enough that it was clear she wanted Jess to hear. "Do you need anything else? Because I'm going to bed now."

Brian shook his head, and when she gave him an annoyed look, he added, "No, thank you. Good night."

The toilet flushed, and she released him then backed away. "Good night."

She didn't close the door all the way, though in the dim lighting, his sister wouldn't be able to tell. He pulled the shirt she'd handed him over his head just as Jess exited the bathroom. She gave him a stern look before heading back into her bedroom. He was in trouble. He could see all the ways this might end in disaster, but right then, he chose not to care. Because all Brian knew was that he was going to take those itty-bitty pink shorts off with his teeth.

He shoved some pillows under his comforter, turned off the light, opened and closed the bathroom door, and as quietly as he could, shut the bedroom door. "See? My plan was a good one."

He sat down next to her and pulled her in for a kiss. He'd missed her. The whole night since the moment Ethan started teasing him, he'd ached for her. It had only been two days, yet he'd come home for the explicit purpose of knocking on her door.

"We'll have to be quiet," she whispered.

"I can be quiet," he said, brushing his lips against the soft skin of her neck. Sarah giggled. "What? I *can* be quiet. This weekend I just *chose* not to be."

She kissed him, pulling him down on top of her. "And afterward, you go back in the living room."

"I believe we had a double-or-nothing bet, and I more than doubled your pleasure."

She rolled her eyes. "You have to be back in that living room before the sun comes up, or Jess will see your pillow man."

"Is four thirty early enough?" Brian picked her phone up off the bedside table and pulled up her alarm app.

"Make it earlier. Just in case."

He scrolled to four o'clock with a sigh. That was going to hurt, considering how late it already was, but Sarah was right. They couldn't take any chances after his encounter with Jess. He could sleep on the train to New York tomorrow.

"Now..." He crawled back over her, leaning into her on the bed and kissing down her body until his teeth landed on the band of her shorts. "Let's see how quiet *you* can be."

Chapter 35

Brian

"Look, I'm not going to beat around the bush." Corey sat back in his chair, and Brian braced for the "but" that had been hanging over their whole conversation. He wouldn't call it an interview—Corey had known long before today what he was going to do. It was up to Brian to accept or not. "You know my story. My mentor gave me and a lot of others in Fairford a chance when no one else would. I try to live up to that legacy every day—that's why we're here. But I'm looking for a career person. We're a family company, and while I'm not asking you for a decade, I would need to know that you were in for the somewhat long-term."

That kind of commitment was the one thing he couldn't promise, and Corey knew it. Brian closed the folder of Scott and Johnson Home Design materials that had been waiting for him and met his friend's imploring gaze. "I *am* interested, especially if you were serious about me being able to do it in the city. But we spent all of high school talking about getting out. And I did, and I never looked back. I've never even wanted to. You turned what could've been a dire situation into a thriving company and a partnership. But for me, being back home this summer was awful. It felt like failure."

"I know—I get it. I've been there. But you wouldn't be unemployed and living in your parents' spare room this time. You would have a leadership position at a reputable company. You would be well compensated."

Brian scratched at his scruffy face. He'd promised himself last night that he would openly consider this offer. But then he'd woken up before the sun with Sarah wrapped around him. And if Corey was really looking to bring his IT and systems needs in-house, a person working a hundred miles away was not going to solve that problem no matter what Corey said, and forget about living two states away.

"I just don't know if that's a promise I can make."

Corey nodded and stood up. "That's fair, but I can't wait forever. I need to open the position up if you aren't interested."

"I understand." Brian followed Corey out into the hall and to the elevator banks. As the elevator dinged their arrival at the first floor, he stopped himself from saying anything because if he did, he might take this position and break a promise and jeopardize a life-long friendship.

When the doors opened, a woman Brian would recognize any-where stood with a young girl clutching an oversized, and surely overpriced, dinosaur plush—Andi Scott with Corey's daughter, Emily.

"Daddy!" The girl ran into Corey's arms.

"Hey, sweetie. How was the museum?"

Brian tuned them out as Andi approached. He grinned at his once friend. "Are you interviewing with Corey too?"

She laughed and flashed her left hand, where a crown of dia-monds adorned her ring finger. "I got the job last night."

This did not surprise him. The entire Fairford gossip chain had been waiting for it to happen for the last six months. "Wow. Con-gratulations!"

Corey wrapped an arm around her waist. And just like that, the CEO he'd interviewed with was gone, replaced by a smitten man ex-uberant about his engagement. "Thanks, man. We're excited."

Brian grinned. "So, when you said you were 'getting the rest of Andi's things packed and such,' that was code for proposing?"

"Well, she was in the room when I called you." Corey glanced at his watch. "Anyway, we have to get to the matinee of *Frozen*."

"That sounds fun."

"We'll see you at the reunion?" Andi asked with a smirk that said she knew exactly how he felt about said reunion, and she felt it, too, but *Fairford*.

Their ten-year high school reunion was Thanksgiving weekend, which meant practically the entire class would be in town. He might have thrown out the invitation, but it was always the same weekend. And he would be in town, so there was no way he *couldn't* go.

"And miss Dustin reenacting his amazing homecoming winning throw, marking the first time we beat Liberty in forever? Never."

"I happen to like that reenactment," Corey said with a grin.

"You would." For a moment, Brian could see how it would all work out, how his life would be reshaped and formed by taking this job. He could resist, but eventually, he'd be pulled into their orbit. And he might even forget why he'd resisted in the first place.

Corey's daughter rolled her eyes at the adults and stomped off down the street. "We're going to be late!"

"Guess that's our cue." Andi gave Brian a quick hug and then started after Emily.

Corey shook Brian's hand. "Think about my offer and let me know by the reunion."

STEPPING ABOVEGROUND in Midtown felt like coming home. It also smelled like pee and street meat and all the things he'd once loved about this city. How easy it would be to fall back into it if he got the right job and found a good place. His friends would welcome him back, and life would go on as it had—as he'd wanted it to until a few weeks ago. Now he wanted to get back on the train. He wanted to have guys' night with Ethan and be mocked by Tasha. He wanted to spend his nights with Sarah and be tortured by his sister before she inevitably followed her heart across the country. No one who knew them would have pegged the Hawkins siblings as hopeless romantics. Yet there they were, with Jess looking to uproot her whole life and Brian ready to dig in, all because the right person had looked their way. Maybe that was all it took. It had certainly worked out for his ex. Though convincing *his* right person that it was time to go public was going to take some finessing and maybe even some scheming. He could worry about that tomorrow.

He stopped in front of Blue Bottle Coffee. It was teeming with people, as most places were at all times of the day. At least it wasn't Starbucks, though there would have been something fitting about that. He took a deep breath to steady his nerves. He'd felt confident when he'd requested this meeting the morning after Halloween, but now nervousness flared in his chest. He scanned the tables near the window and spotted his intended companion, Hannah, inside with her headphones in, staring intently at her laptop. She sat crosslegged, and the tips of her Chucks were visible on her chair. Same Hannah, still completely oblivious to his presence.

He dug into his pocket for his phone. An all-caps emoji-filled text from Sarah greeted him, but he didn't reply as his attention turned to the next notification—an email from MyHR. Right on time, just as Ethan had said. He scanned it and sent back a quick thank-you and a confirmation on the time of a video conference call on Friday afternoon. That was one benefit to working an opening shift—he was free most afternoons. The clock on his phone rolled to two. Brian loosened his tie and shrugged out of his jacket. Part of him wanted Hannah to see him all dressed up and professional, but mostly, he just wanted her to see him. He unbuttoned his cuffs and rolled his sleeves to his elbow.

Enough stalling. He pulled open the door and, skirting a few exiting patrons, headed for her table. Brian slid into the seat across from her.

Hannah glanced up at him over the top of her laptop, bringing her headphones down around her neck. Their eyes met, and her expression softened. "Nice beard."

It hardly constituted a beard yet, but he wasn't going to argue with her before he asked a favor. "Thanks. It's growing on me."

"Literally."

He laughed. So much had changed in their lives, but it was nice to see that their banter hadn't disappeared. "It's good to see you, Hannah."

"You too. You seem different somehow."

He shrugged. "A few months back in your childhood bedroom will do that."

She shook her head. "I don't think that's it."

"Congratulations by the way," he said, deflecting. "I hear you and Will got married—again—last month."

Her face scrunched in a way that used to turn him on to no end. "You heard how...?"

"We still have some mutual friends online, and Sarah listens to Kate's podcast..." He hedged for just a moment, and her expression changed from intrigued to exasperated in an instant.

"You saw it on *Page Six*, didn't you?" She palmed her face. "Dammit."

"For what it's worth, the socialite life seems to suit you," he said, not confirming or denying that he had indeed read the gossip website.

"More like society rebel." Hannah laughed. "Who knew that the storyteller would one day become the story."

He refrained from giving the retort that waited on his tongue. "It looked like a beautiful wedding."

"Thank you. Now..." She smiled a mischievous and damning grin. "Who is Sarah?"

He'd walked straight into that. He'd gotten so used to being able to just talk about Sarah with Ethan and Tasha—two people so disconnected from the rest of his life that it didn't matter—that it hadn't even occurred to him to call her *my sister's best friend*.

"Sarah is actually the reason why I'm here."

Hannah's eyebrows rose in interest, and she sat back in her chair. "Do tell."

Chapter 36
Sarah

Sarah read through the article she'd crafted about Tessa's big night for the third time. It was no use—her brain was in New York City. It was sitting in a job interview, alternately wishing all good things for her lover and praying he completely flubbed the interview. Not that he could mess up an interview with an old friend who just happened to run his own company and who wanted to hire Brian specifically for a brand-new position he was making for him.

She'd texted him right before the scheduled interview time with good-luck wishes and emojis, but he hadn't responded. And it had been more than two hours. Brian couldn't possibly still be in the interview. Did his friend convince him so hard he left for his hometown straight away? No, he was probably just reuniting with his friends and remembering how much he loved *his* city. *Dammit.*

"Sarah." Maggie's voice pulled her out of her spiral. "Come here when you have a second."

That did not sound like a good-news beckon. *Double dammit.* This day needed to end. She pocketed her phone and started toward her boss's office. Leigh gave her a commiserating smile from behind the stack of papers she'd walked out of Maggie's office with an hour earlier. Direct mailing was still a thing at Sophie's Wish Factory. Their digital newsletter was strong, but they invariably got extra donations from people on the mailing list as the holidays neared. Sarah was just glad she wasn't stuffing the envelopes this year. Her fingers had been bandaged for a week after last year's campaign.

"Sit down, please."

Sarah's heart practically skipped out of her chest. "Is everything okay?"

Maggie's expression gave nothing away. Not a hint of what the hell was going on. She pulled a sheet of paper out of the printer on her desk and handed it over. "This came in today."

Sarah didn't want to touch it. It couldn't be good. Maybe Tyler's behavior at Halloween had just been a temporary thing. Was he pulling his donation—or worse, had he done something to get Cedar Crest to void their partnership? No. He wouldn't do that.

Maggie waved it in front of her, and reluctantly, Sarah took it, her hands shaking. She scanned the paper and then started back at the top. Rodgers Talent Management—Monique Miller's agency—had signed on as a Gold Partner. Gold partnerships came with a hefty donation and a guarantee to participate in the program. That meant they would have access to any client on the RTM roster, and the buy-in donation meant more than she could even imagine. She'd never brought in a Gold Partner on her own before.

When she looked up, Maggie was grinning at her, teeth and all. "Congratulations."

Sarah exhaled loudly. Satisfaction bloomed in her chest where panic had just been—her first Gold Partner and in an autumn that had been such a mess. "That was so mean."

Her boss's smile turned devious. "I know." Maggie handed her a second sheet of paper. "This also came through today."

It was a basic donor form—the same one she'd delivered to the hospital all those weeks ago. From the signature line, Tyler's messy scrawl greeted her. He was making an extra one-time donation, and the staff of record was her this time. A three-thousand-dollar donation. It wasn't what she would have gotten had he not taken her recurring fee from her, but she would more than accept the gesture.

Her eyes misted over, and she brought her hand to her heart, which had finally stopped pounding and was fluttering like a giant pair of butterfly wings. She felt numb and tingly all at once from the shock of all this good news. "Wow."

"I think you deserve the rest of the afternoon off with all this good news. Go celebrate with that boy of yours."

Maggie's words hit hard. *That boy of yours.* And now he really was hers—she couldn't even try to deny it—and she had no idea what to do about it. "He's in New York today actually." She shrugged, but she knew the nonchalance didn't reach her expression. "Job interview."

"I see. Well, the afternoon is still yours." Maggie slid a credit card across the desk. "Go get your nails done or something relaxing. You've earned it." She tapped the papers in front of her against her desk as if they weren't already in a neat stack. "I have to be honest—I didn't think you were going to be able to recover from Tyler, and I worried what that meant for you and for Wish Factory, but you really turned it around."

"Thank you."

Maggie thrust the card into Sarah's hands. "Now, shoo. I don't want to see you until tomorrow morning."

Sarah stood and slipped the credit card into her pocket. "Thank you, Maggie."

Her boss waved her away. "That card better be back on my desk first thing in the morning."

PINK REALLY WAS HER color. Nails, hair, pajamas, it didn't matter—the color called to her. She fanned her nails out in front of her, taking in the clean, soft look of her manicure. It had been ages since any of her budget had gone toward nail care. Highlights were an expensive fashion choice after all. But man, she could get used to this.

Sarah sidestepped to get out of the way of one of the women from her Zumba class. There were a few minutes before the session started, and while she would probably be relegated to the back, she wanted to try Brian one more time. His silence had extended through the afternoon and into the evening. From what she could tell when she swung by the apartment to change, he hadn't yet returned. She wasn't worried per se—just mildly concerned. It wasn't like him to disappear, but it was like him to want to give her news in person. Which meant he'd taken the job. She dug in her gym bag for her phone to no avail. *Shit.* This was fine. She must have left it at home. Maybe in the bathroom when she'd changed... or on the kitchen counter.

She pulled the bag around until she could see into it. *How much crap do I have in here?* Her fingers closed around the smooth surface of her phone, tucked into a secret pocket on the side of the bag. *Thank God.*

The music picked up from inside the studio, the opening notes reaching her each time the door swung open. Class would start in another minute or so. She scanned her notifications for any sign of Brian, but there was only a text from Jess, reiterating that her mother was more than happy to host Sarah for Thanksgiving even though Jess wouldn't be there. Because that wouldn't be awkward on so many levels. First, she'd never been to a Hawkins holiday without Jess. Second, it would be like inviting herself to her fuck buddy's family event. For the first time in a long time, she wished she could go home, but plane tickets this close to the holiday were out of the question, and the sheer amount of time it would take for her to go by car, train, or bus just didn't make sense.

Sarah navigated back to her text chain with Brian. *Where is he?* A warm hand clamped down on her arm, and she jumped, ready to use all the knowledge her semester of self-defense classes had taught her. "Don't even think about it, ass—"

"Hi, Chestnut."

Brian. Her heart slowed down but only slightly. Adrenaline coursed through her for a different reason now. He was here. In the flesh. In mesh shorts and a Giants hoodie. Sarah jumped into his arms, not caring who saw or that she had no chill. She'd missed him. Since the moment her boss had handed her those papers, she'd wanted nothing more than to drag him to her favorite restaurant, which she could rarely afford, and tell him all about it.

She pulled back but kept her arms wrapped around him. "What are you doing here?"

"It's Wednesday. On Wednesdays, we Zumba."

She giggled. "We do."

He unwrapped her hands from his waist and tugged off his sweatshirt. Underneath, he wore a tank top with a flexing Gaston holding up a bench with three beautiful women and the words "No one lifts like Gaston."

"Oh my god. Where did you get that?"

"Hot Topic," he said with a completely straight face. That made perfect sense. He did seem like the Hot Topic type. "Should we go in?"

"Actually..." She glanced at the door and then back at him and then back at the door. "What do you say to a dinner instead?"

His face softened into the most beautiful smile she'd ever seen, and he pulled her back into his arms. "I say, how do you feel about Talula's?"

THE WAITER REFILLED her wineglass and seamlessly slid the remnants of their desserts away. The crème brûlée was the sole reason Talula's Garden was her favorite restaurant. The entire meal, she'd been trying to figure out how Brian had known. Talula's wasn't exactly budget friendly, and Sarah certainly hadn't eaten there since he'd been in town. They'd walked past it on their mural tour with Ryder, but she didn't remember mentioning it. And she wouldn't have named it as a takeout option, considering Brian was working part-time and she budgeted for Hot Pockets. Maybe she'd made a joke about it when he'd watched the end of *High School Musical* with her after Terror Behind the Walls. There were plenty of crème brûlée jokes in there. She didn't know how he knew, but he knew. Why else would he have suggested a restaurant so clearly out of their way and asked her what was good there? He'd even ordered wine after she told him what happened at work.

"So..." She sipped her wine, hoping to further steel herself for the answer to the question she was about to ask. "Are you going to take the job with your friend?"

He'd done a terrific job of describing everything about the position and the interview while still telling her nothing at all—like, whether he was about to move hundreds of miles away from her. She supposed it was better than a thousand.

"I don't know." He put his wineglass down and locked eyes with her. His expression was open, his features relaxed. "It's not like any other job that I can just quit if I change my mind or find something better. But it's an amazing opportunity to craft something from the ground up, and as hard as I try not to see any benefits to a job in my hometown, where all these people from my high school work, I can see the allure of being part of something special like that."

"But I thought you said you had the option to work remotely."

He nodded. "I do, but that seems pretty lonely. My whole company would be in one office, and I'd be in Manhattan, sitting in a single-man station all day by myself."

"Which puts you back to your hometown."

"Even if I live in a neighboring town, there's no city close by—a few college towns, sure, but I'm not quite ready to give up on city living just yet."

"There is a certain allure to living in the epicenter of something." She laughed. "I'm particularly fond of the less-than-livable salaries."

"And spending more than half your income on an apartment the size of a master bath."

"And the tourists."

"The fucking tourists."

"Why do we live here again?" she asked.

"There is a certain allure to living in the epicenter of something." Brian smirked, and that dimple teased her with its perfection.

She gripped her wineglass so that she didn't reach across the table and pull his lips to hers. This had been the best date she'd ever had. And it *was* a date. That had been clear from her invitation to his choice of restaurant and the way he had just casually handed the waiter his credit card, even though this would take a chunk out of his income. She knew from the way his knee kept bumping into hers and his eyes kept falling to her lips.

She put her wine down and reached for his hand across the table. Their fingers intertwined, and her whole body went up in flames. The hair on her arm literally stood up from the tension. She crossed her legs as his thumb ran a circle across her palm. "Thank you for dinner."

"It was my pleasure." He kissed her hand, his eyes staying on hers. That look promised too many things—sexual things and emotional things and words she knew all too well but that neither of them could say out loud. Not tonight. Not with his decision looming over their heads and his sister waiting for them at home.

Chapter 37
Sarah

Brian's hands skimmed down her body, slick with soap, as shower water beat down around them. His fingers passed over the supple mountains of her breasts and lower through the soft terrain of her stomach until he reached her valley. She braced herself against the hard tile as he parted—

"Sarah!"

She jumped to attention, the memory of exactly what Brian had done to her in the shower that morning vanishing. His scratchy face and piercing green eyes transformed into a clean-shaven soft jawline and short dirty-blond hair, glasses making the brown eyes staring at her larger and more penetrating than she remembered.

She pulled her earbuds out. "Jace?"

"Yeah. I've only been standing at your desk for a solid thirty seconds." He leaned over to glance at her screen, which had up a document with all of Rodgers Talent Management's clients and connections. Her new Gold Partner wouldn't get her closer to landing the ever-elusive Leonard Nulty, but it did give her an in with a certain superhero and a Disney Channel darling. "I could've sworn you had porn on, you were so engrossed."

She rolled her eyes to keep the truth from completely showing on her face—the porn had been real and hot, and she'd been one of the stars. "As if I'd do that in my open-concept place of work."

"A guy can dream."

"Gross." Sarah glanced at the time on her computer and then back up at Jace. School was out, but she'd never seen him in the office before. He was strictly on an as-needed basis for events. "What are you doing here, anyway?"

"Aunt Mags needs me to move some boxes and rearrange a little furniture, and I'm pretty sure she's going to have me spend my weekend painting if I don't put my foot down."

Sarah tried to hide her smile because *Aunt Mags* had most certainly duped her nephew. "The storage room? She's been talking about cleaning that out for ages."

"How bad is it?"

"Is she paying you?"

"Oh god." He shot a look at the closed door a few feet behind her. "This is going to take more than one weekend, isn't it?"

"Hope you don't have any plans for Thanksgiving."

"She conned me."

"Yup." Sarah shrugged. "Have any friends you can bribe with pizza and beer?"

"Hi, friend. Want to help me clean out a dusty storage room? I'll spring for PBR."

"Sorry, but Miss Webb is accounted for." Brian stood on the other side of her desk, a drink carrier in one hand. "Hey, babe." He leaned across her desk to kiss her lightly on the lips. The kissing in greeting wasn't new, nor was his use of *babe*, but it *was* the first time the audience was more than Leigh. He walked over to Leigh's desk, giving Jace quite the wide berth, and handed her a coffee cup. "You're going to love this one."

Leigh laughed and took in the order coding on the side of the cup. "Toffee nut and cinnamon."

"Trust me—your taste buds are going to be in love." He handed Sarah the other cup. "Skinny vanilla latte as requested."

Sarah tried to ignore the fact that Jace's expression had turned to stone the second Brian entered the building. She'd never meant to lead him on. He'd made his own assumptions clear at the baseball game, and she'd given him no ammunition after the ogling. But still, he hadn't been expecting Brian to appear—that much was clear.

Brian held out the last drink to Jace. "Pumpkin spice latte?"

"No, I'm good." Jace held up a Gatorade bottle she hadn't noticed until that moment. He knocked on her desk twice. "I'd better get to work."

Once he was gone, Brian pulled a chair from the waiting area over and sat down on it backward, his elbows resting on the back. His fingers tapped a beat on his arms, and his feet bounced against the legs of the chair. "The MyHR second interview went really well."

The interview process was moving fast with this company. His first interview had only been two weeks earlier, and he'd just had a second one. That had to be good. She'd been avoiding asking after his job interviews since none of them left him in Philadelphia, and after his day in Manhattan the other week, she couldn't handle the pressure. *Wait and see* would have to work because being in the know was driving her bonkers.

But she put all her enthusiasm into her response. It wasn't his fault the job market was awful. "That's great!"

"Yeah. And my Myer interview is in the morning—it's not the path I thought I would take, but the more I look into it, the more it seems like it could be really interesting, and with Ethan backing me up and, you know, it being in Philly, it could be a good fit."

"And you still haven't asked MyHR if you have to be in St. Louis?"

He shook his head. "It hasn't come up explicitly, but Ethan seems to think the location of the position is flexible, and they've mentioned team members in other offices. But if it is only a St. Louis position, I don't want to knock myself out of the running—getting in with this company would be a huge win. If nothing else, an offer from them could be good leverage elsewhere."

"Right." The disappointment must have been evident in her voice because he reached across the desk and took her hand.

"But I did some LinkedIn stalking, and there are members of the IT team in Philadelphia. I might have my pick. The job posting wasn't specific."

"I'm happy for you, Bri."

He grinned and started running a finger up and down her forearm. "What time do you think you'll be home?"

She was home the same time every night but placated him and his nervous energy. "Six. I can stop and pick up the food on the way if you like."

He shook his head. "I'll get it. You just get home..." He leaned in as close to her as he could get from the other side of her desk. "And get naked. I don't want to waste a minute of our sister-free evening."

Apparently, she wasn't the only one with this morning's activities on repeat. Jess had left early for an overnight work retreat in Atlantic City. Sarah had forgotten all about it until the suitcase appeared in the living room and Jess had snuggled Chuck as if she was leaving for a month instead of a night.

Sarah ran a hand across Brian's facial hair. It was now officially a beard, and it was damn sexy. Her mind circled back to this morning, her body coming to life as she remembered the feel of that scratchy beard against her softest parts. "Only if you promise to do that thing I like."

Brian arched an eyebrow. "Which thing do you like?"

"Sorry to interrupt." Jace stood far enough away that he couldn't hear their conversation. He didn't look at all sorry to be interrupting.

She sat back in her chair and picked up her latte. "What's up?"

"Actually, Brian, do you think you could help me move something?"

Brian stood and pushed his sleeves up, baring his forearms. Sarah loved his forearms, all defined and flexed when braced around her head. *Damn*, she really needed to get her mind out of the gutter. He had her fantasizing constantly. Except they weren't fantasies—they were reality.

"Sure. Then I should get going anyway." He leaned down and kissed her chastely—she was at work after all. "Text me your answer. I'll see you at home."

Home. The word just seemed to roll out of him. And each time it did, her insides melted. She loved that their home was the same and that at the end of the day, she could go back to her apartment and find him there. Everything could change soon. He could end up in any number of cities. And they still had to find a way to tell Jess that didn't end up with the two of them out of a home. Not that confessing to Jess would be necessary if he took a job somewhere that wasn't Philly.

Tonight, she wouldn't worry about it. Tonight, they would be together. They wouldn't have to worry about presunrise alarms and being quiet. Tonight, all bets were off.

THE DOOR WAS AJAR WHEN she arrived at the apartment. A warm glow filtered into the hallway, along with the tantalizing scent of Italian food. Good Italian, too, not the jar stuff they kept in the pantry for when all they could afford was a box of pasta. At least tomato sauce had some health benefits. She pushed open the door and dropped her things on the rack. The apartment was illuminated by candlelight. The table was set for two, with bread and a salad that she recognized from their preferred pizzeria. A bouquet of pink chrysanthemums adorned the table. Her stomach fluttered. Mums were her favorite, and she'd been eyeing these bouquets for weeks at the street vendor by her job. Of course, Brian had noticed. She was starting to wonder if there was anything he didn't notice.

Sarah plucked the card from the bouquet—*Meet me in the bedroom.* If he was naked on her bed, she was seriously never going to let him live it down. And they were never going to make it to that fabulous dinner. After taking a last sniff of the flowers, she walked to her bedroom. Nerves rattled inside her as she got closer. He'd gone all out. There were candles everywhere, the living room was clean for the first time since they'd both arrived on Jess's doorstep, and even Chuck had a little bowtie around his neck.

Inside the bedroom, Brian sat on the bed in a full suit and tie. His beard was trimmed. Whatever he was planning, he'd lost his No-Shave-November bet with Ethan.

She stopped a foot in front of him. "Hi."

"Hi." He stood and closed the distance between them then pulled her into him. He kissed her softly but urgently, and she melted into him.

"What is this?" She tugged at his lapels.

"Two months ago today, we went to the gala. And that was the start of something I could never have expected."

"Your love of Hot Pockets?"

He smiled, a flush reddening his cheeks. "Among other things." He stepped back and gave her a clear view of the bed, where the dress she'd worn that night was laid out. "You in that dress is the most beautiful thing I've ever seen. And since balls aren't exactly things that happen on the regular in the real world, I thought perhaps we could host our own to commemorate the night that brought us here."

She nodded, not trusting her voice or herself. This was perhaps the sweetest thing anyone had ever done for her, and the most romantic. Brian was putting himself out there. He was leaning in. So she would too. With shaking fingers, she undid the first buttons of her blouse and then slipped out of her pants. She picked up the dress, still so magnificent, and stepped into it.

She unhooked her bra and turned to him the same way she had in the dressing room that day. "Will you zip me up?"

And then his fingers were warm against her skin, and each caress kindled a fire in her that could not be extinguished. He traced a line up her back as his other hand pulled the zipper together. His breath stirred her hair and then his lips found her shoulder. "You're so beautiful, Sarah."

She turned to him, bringing their mouths together, and this time, it wasn't soft but needing and wanting. It was a different kiss from any they had shared. It said everything they hadn't yet put into words. She felt more than she'd ever thought she could for this man. He stepped back after a moment and guided her into the candlelit living room. He fidgeted with his phone until the opening chords of a highly cheesy but perfect ballad came through the speakers.

He held his hand out to her. "Can I have this dance?"

She placed her hand in his, and then their bodies were together, aligned so perfectly. His heart beat a calm and steady pattern in his chest, one she'd memorized these last few weeks without even knowing it until this instant. "Did you really download this song?"

He laughed. "I'm streaming it in incognito mode."

"It's perfect."

As they swayed and kissed and swayed and kissed some more, she knew she could do this forever, whatever came next. None of her past relationships had ever felt completely right, and now she knew why. She could see it in the way Brian's hand skimmed her shoulder and his eyes drank her in as if the sight of her could sustain him. And the way he said her name like it was a prayer.

She held his face and kissed him, letting her tongue dance with his. His heartbeat picked up as her hands came up and loosened his tie. "Do you remember what I asked of you that night?"

He nodded, his breathing swifter than the moment before. Because they both felt it, this shift in their relationship from sex to something more.

She unbuttoned his shirt and slid her hand over his heart. "Take me home, Brian."

Chapter 38

Brian

Sun streamed through those polka dot curtains that did absolutely nothing to block light. They might as well have been translucent. But at the moment, he didn't care. The sun was up, and he was still in Sarah's bed. He didn't have to sneak out and come back with coffee as if he'd gotten up early to get coffee from the place down the street before he went to work at a coffee shop. He didn't have to stay holed up in the bedroom until the two of them left for work. And Sarah wasn't freaking out that Jess was going to somehow discover the truth. No, Sarah was passed out across his chest, her hair haloed around her, his shirt haphazardly buttoned over her chest. It was a perfect morning for being otherwise completely ordinary.

He kissed her forehead before pulling back the comforter. The bed really was too small to share, but he'd fit his limbs onto a full if it meant waking up next to her. His foot had barely hit the ground before she pulled him back onto the bed.

"Where are you going?" She wrapped herself around him like a koala, nuzzling into his neck and then kissing a line to his earlobe. "I'm cold."

Brian pulled the comforter up over their heads and slid down until he was face-to-face with her. "Better?"

"Not quite." She rolled onto him, pressing into his growing erection.

He slid a hand up her leg and under the hem of the shirt, stroking up over her hip and her gentle curves. She gasped against his lips as his thumb found her nipple. "Better?"

A giggle escaped her, and she pushed the comforter away from them. Sunlight blinded him, but he refused to move that hand. He cupped her breast, letting his fingers flick the pert nipple. With his other hand, he worked on the buttons of her shirt.

She laughed again and pulled his hand away from her. "Stop it."

He pillowed his hands behind his head. "You started it."

"I have to pee."

Brian watched her stand, the look of her in his shirt sending even more blood rushing to his groin. Through the open door, Chuck came in and jumped on the bed. He stared at Brian accusingly. As was his right. The poor cat had gotten used to being fed at five in the morning, and a quick look at his watch showed it to be already past seven thirty.

"Fine." He sat up and scooped Chuck into his arms—he'd clawed off his bowtie sometime during the night. "Let's go get some breakfast."

Twenty minutes later, Sarah entered the kitchen, dressed in a flowy blouse and a skirt, her hair falling in wet tendrils at her shoulders. He handed her a plate with an omelet and sat down with his own at the kitchen table. "Did you fall in?"

She rolled her eyes. "I just realized how late we slept in, so I figured I'd get in the shower."

"Good thing I wasn't waiting naked on the bed for you or anything."

"I went back into the bedroom to get clothes, but unfortunately, my new favorite toy was missing." She ran her foot across his thigh and forked a piece of egg.

Brian watched her mouth as her foot inched higher, blood rushing downward. "Think you found it."

She climbed onto his lap and pressed against his body. *Holy fuck.* She was going to be the death of him.

"Oh..." Her hands slipped under his boxers until she freed him from their constraints. She kissed him, slow and deep, her fingers clawing into his hair. "Good thing I'm not wearing any underwear."

Brian gripped her hips as she pulled a condom from some unknown pocket of her skirt and then fit herself onto him. His eyes closed as she moved with him, and pleasure overtook all sense. He'd been wrong. This morning wasn't perfectly ordinary. There was nothing ordinary about Sarah Webb and what she did to him.

He could imagine future mornings like this, if they shared more than a bed in the middle of the night. Morning sex and showers. Laughter and desire. Sarah's warm smile and her grouchy scowl that was equally cute. Naked Saturdays and movie marathons and a life together that was theirs and theirs alone. Ethan and Tasha would be regular visitors, and Sarah would have special themed glasses for his friends, and Jess would roll in, using her key of course. They'd pet sit for Chuck whenever his sister went to see Ryder. With the soft gurgle of the coffee pot behind him and hazelnut hinting the air, he could almost imagine they were already in that reality.

"Sarah." Her name was a whisper as he followed her over the edge.

She smiled at him, a mischievous and satisfied grin that made him want to start all over again. "Good morning."

By the time they got cleaned up—a trip to the shower diverting them for far too long— breakfast was a wash. Brian flipped her a granola bar and then pulled one of his aprons out of the dryer. He'd decided, somewhere between twirling her around the living room and her mounting him in the kitchen, to verbalize everything he'd tried to show her the night before. She was one hundred percent going to reject him, but at least he'd go down knowing he made the effort. No regrets.

"I've been thinking... why don't you come home with me for Thanksgiving?"

Sarah's hands stilled on the granola bar, and he held his breath. Thanksgiving wasn't Sarah's Hawkins holiday. She usually went home for that one, but he also knew that this year she'd intended to spend the day with Tyler's family, and it wasn't in her budget to make the trip home. Even though Jess wouldn't be there, she had already suggested that Sarah spend the holiday with their family, but Sarah had only shaken her head and said she'd figure something out. Except, to his knowledge, she hadn't made any plans.

Sarah glanced up at him. "How would that work exactly?"

"Well, we'd get in Betty and drive to my parents' house. Then we'd do all the same shit we normally do when you're in Fairford, except this time, Jess would be in Connecticut and there'd be sex involved."

"I meant," she said, rolling her eyes, "how would we explain why I was there without your sister?"

There was his opening. He clasped his hands behind his back and forced his gaze up from his feet. "You could come as my *girlfriend.*"

Her expression was unreadable, but she didn't laugh or run screaming from the room. He took that as a good sign. "Did you just ask me to be your girlfriend?"

"Are you saying yes?" he asked.

"Can I think about it?"

"The girlfriend part or the Thanksgiving part?"

She crossed the room and wrapped her arms around his waist, pulling his body to hers. "The Thanksgiving part."

"So instead of being your *fake* boyfriend, I'm now your *secret* boyfriend?"

"That would be correct."

Secrecy would only make things worse. They'd already gone too far to go back, and whenever it came out, it was going to backfire on them. He felt it in his bones. Yet he also knew he would be her secret for as long she required. "But we *will* tell my sister soon."

Sarah nodded but gnawed on her bottom lip, uncertainty coloring her expression. "I just need to figure out how."

"Just come to Thanksgiving." He held her face with both hands. "You know Mom wants you there. And it doesn't have to be a big deal."

"It *is* a big deal."

"I don't want to be your dirty little secret."

"But you're incredibly dirty," she said, her eyes twinkling, "though not so little."

He flushed. "I don't want to be your dirty *big* secret either."

"I know, and I get it, but Jess is my family. I owe her an explanation before I flaunt our relationship in her face at a family function. Okay?"

How could he argue with that? "Okay."

"I promise I'll think about Thanksgiving."

He kissed her forehead. At least she was considering it—that was more than he would have gotten a week ago and way more than he'd been expecting from this conversation. "Thank you. So…" He brought his lips down to hers. "Does that mean you'll come to Ethan's *as my girlfriend* tomorrow night?"

She flushed, the color making her only more beautiful. "Yes, anything you want."

He grinned and slid his hands down her curves, digging his fingers into the soft fabric covering her waist. "Oh, you're going to regret that offer."

She nipped at his bottom lip. "Bring it on, boyfriend."

Chapter 39

Sarah

"Oh, you're mine now, boyfriend." The word felt so natural in her mouth already. And it was addictive. She hadn't been able to stop saying it for the last twenty-four hours. She mashed a few more buttons on the controller, and Princess Peach swerved away from a banana peel.

Brian nudged her shoulder, causing her fingers to slip off the keys. "Not even close."

"Wanna bet?"

"Are you sure you want to do that? They don't seem to work in your favor."

"Don't they?"

She saw him smirk out of the corner of her eye. "Still not letting you win," he said.

She snuck a hand across his lap. "Are you sure?" The door swung open, and she snatched her hand back. On the screen, Peach ran into a bomb. "Dammit."

"Hey, guys." Jess hardly glanced at them as she kicked the door closed, a bag of groceries in her arms. Sarah inched farther away from Brian, tucking herself into the corner of the couch. "What are you doing?"

Brian held up his hands triumphantly as Toad crossed the finish line. "Kicking Sarah's ass in *Mario Kart*."

Jess rolled her eyes. "Like that's hard."

"Hey now! I'm sitting right here."

Jess eyed her, her lips curving into a frown. "Since when do you play video games?"

Sarah just barely refrained from looking at Brian. Instead, she stood up. Chuck promptly took her place on the couch, and damn, if she wasn't jealous of that cat. "I wanted to see what all the hype was about. Are there more bags?"

"Yes, actually. There's, like, no parking, so I'm down around the corner."

"I got them." Brian scratched Chuck's head before slipping into the sneakers he kept next to the couch. It *was* technically still his bedroom. He took the keys from his sister's open hand, and then he was gone.

Sarah fell back onto the couch. Jess still stood at the front of the room, arms crossed, brow furrowed, inspecting the situation. "Nice socks," she said finally.

The fuzzy pink socks would not be Sarah's undoing, especially since she'd been wearing them nonstop since he bought them for her. "It's cold in here."

"Uh-huh."

"What, Jess? Just spit it out."

"You and Brian seem awfully friendly since Halloween."

This, at least, she could answer truthfully. "Well, yeah. We had a really good talk when he volunteered to dress up as Superman for sick children. We worked out our differences. It makes living together a lot easier."

"True, and you did swear on your sorority letters not to date him." Jess laughed, but it wasn't her usual laugh. It wasn't even close to real.

This was an opening, and Sarah couldn't take it. Jess was fishing, and she'd brought up the promise. Even when she'd practically accused Sarah of sleeping with Brian, she hadn't mentioned that long-ago vow.

Her best friend turned to her, her expression back to neutral. "Want to get drunk and watch DCOMs tonight?"

This was why they were besties. Not everyone would think binge-watching Disney Channel Original Movies while drinking was an appropriate adult activity.

"Actually, I have a date," Sarah said.

Brian returned just then, and she silently cursed the cosmic gods for their timing. Someone must have been having a good laugh at this horrendous charade.

"Really?" Jess asked.

"Is this that guy I swiped right on for you the other day?" Brian called from the kitchen. Oh, he was lucky to be so far away because she could have smacked him.

"Biker isn't really my style."

He poked his head out from the kitchen. "But the porn 'stache..."

Sarah threw a pillow at him, but it didn't even come close, instead sending Chuck skidding out of the room. "I'm going to go change."

"Wait," Jess said, grabbing her arm. "Who is the date with?"

Sarah shrugged. "Some guy from Tinder without a porn 'stache."

"Well, you know the rules." Jess held out her hand. "Show me his picture and tell me his name and where you are going."

"Jess, it's fine. We're going to be in public."

"It's not *fine*."

"Seriously?" Sarah huffed out a breath. This was her own doing. She hated lying. And this was lying directly to her best friend's face. It wasn't skirting the truth or omitting it. "I'm going out with Jace."

"Your boss's nephew?"

"Yes."

"You think that's a good idea when you're rebounding?"

"I'm not on the rebound. Jeez, it's been over two months since Tyler."

"And you haven't dated anyone since then." Jess sat back and crossed her arms. "This is a bad idea."

There wasn't time for this, and she literally couldn't stomach another blatant lie. A movement from the front of the apartment caught her eye, and she watched Brian watch them. His expression was grim, but when he noticed her, he gave a smile and shook his head. Now was not the time. If Brian was agreeing with her, that was all she needed.

"Well, it's mine to make, so stop acting like you're my mother."

Brian stepped into the room, his hands clasped in front of him. "So, I have to head out, but are you two going to be okay?"

Jess looked like she wanted to strangle her brother. "Yes. Sarah knows the rules."

Sarah bit her tongue on a retort. While her bestie had a point, she'd also spent the whole summer breaking the rules with Ryder, and the agitation wafting off Jess was contagious. If she didn't get out of this conversation soon, Sarah was going to spill the beans, and the tension in the air didn't bode well for a positive outcome.

Brian held his hands up. "I guess I'll leave you two to it, then."

"Actually," Jess said, arms crossed, "since you and Sarah are all close now, maybe you can weigh in. Do *you* think she's on the rebound?"

Sarah's jaw dropped open, and her heart raced. What the hell was going on with her best friend tonight?

"No." Brian's voice was steady and certain, and if she'd had any doubts about her own feelings, they would have been diminished by that single word. "You are right that we're friends. And I have been around Tyler more than I'd like in my fake-boyfriend capacity, but I can pretty safely say they are in a good place. Chestnut here is ready to date. Even if it's that tool from the Phillies game."

Without even sparing her a glance, he picked up his wallet and cell phone from the table and left. She needed to get her shit together because that meant he was going to be waiting for her on the stoop. She hastily scrolled through her phone and opened up the first social app she found. Jace had started following her after the Phillies game, if she remembered correctly. She found him smiling, clad in the outfit from that game front and center. She handed the phone to her best friend with shaking hands. "This is Jace Clairmont. We're going to play mini golf in Franklin Square." Then she turned on her heel and slammed her bedroom door.

SARAH HAD GOTTEN TO see many sides of Brian over the last few months, but she'd never seen him with his friends. In college, they'd spent a lot of time avoiding him because one wrong look would start Jess off on a tirade. It had honestly been easy to swear a blood oath. Tonight, Brian was happy. There wasn't a woman to impress or a sister to avoid. There weren't job interviews to prep for. Brian was in his element with his people—and Sarah had become one of them.

"I guess Supe didn't tell you that *party* was code for helping Ethan pack up his apartment."

Sarah glanced over at Tasha, who was wearing the same outfit she'd worn in that Tinder photo what felt like ages ago. How quickly that idea had gone sideways, to Sarah's immense benefit. She adjusted a few game cases until the last one fit in the box. "He didn't, but this is nice."

"Nice because you can stare at him like that and no one cares?"

Of course, Tasha would know the story. Ethan probably did too. She'd spent all these years in Philly, and outside of Jess and her Wish Factory team, Sarah hadn't made many friends. She hadn't needed to. Jess filled that role perfectly. Hell, she was the whole reason Sarah had ended up in this city, far from anything she knew. But Brian had built a life here in just under three months. There was an ease about him as he stood with Ethan, packing kitchen plates and pint glasses in newspaper. He smiled often. His laughter was louder than it was at home.

"Nice because I want to know his world," Sarah said.

"You know, I told him, day one, that you were in love with him."

Sarah laughed. "I most certainly wasn't in love with him then."

"But you are now."

It wasn't a question, and Sarah didn't treat it like one. She could hear snippets of the guys' conversation—interview this, benefits that, salary, PTO, and on and on—so she knew Tasha could hear it as well. "It might not matter."

This woman, who probably knew more about the relationship than Sarah herself did, looked at her as if she was daft. And maybe she was. No one would say she was the smartest when it came to matters of the heart.

"It always matters," Tasha said.

"What are you two talking about?"

Both women straightened at Brian's voice.

"Oh, just making sure Sarah knows she can do way better," Tasha said.

Brian flipped Tasha off and then sat down in the armchair next to the couch, pulling Sarah onto his lap in the process. He kissed her softly. It was over too quickly, but they had an audience. "Hey, Chestnut."

She entwined their fingers, wishing she could kiss him again.

"You know, there's a bedroom over there if you two need a minute." Ethan plopped down into the spot Sarah had just vacated and immediately started perusing the box she'd meticulously packed. His girlfriend—also a new addition, according to Brian—squished in next to him.

"Or thirty seconds," Tasha chimed in, her words laced with amusement.

Brian picked a cheese ball out of the bowl and chucked it at Tasha's head. She caught it in her mouth. "Nice. You're getting better at that."

"Yeah, well, I don't like to waste food, and you're constantly throwing it at me."

"Stop making such asinine comments all the time, and I'll stop throwing food at you." He tossed another cheese ball. It bounced off her nose.

"Are you sure you want to start this with your girlfriend here?"

He held up his hands in surrender. "Fine, fine."

"Wuss." Ethan's easy retort and the natural flow between the three of them caused an ache in Sarah's chest. But maybe it meant he would stay.

"Hey, I like my thirty seconds of glory. And despite what you believe, cheese powder is not an aphrodisiac."

That was a challenge if there ever was one. And she wanted to take it. She didn't have to sneak a caress or hide a smile here. She could be as easy and natural as the three of them. "I don't know..." She picked up a cheese ball and rolled it against his lips. Brian's eyes widened and then closed as she slanted her mouth over his.

"She's good." Ethan said over the overwhelming white noise of the kiss.

"I think I'll take that bedroom now." Brian held up his hand as if calling someone. "Check!"

"It's yours." A look passed between Ethan and Brian that Sarah couldn't quite read, but then Ethan was feeding his girlfriend cheese balls and making suggestive comments, and Brian was making circles with his thumb on her palm, and she really did want to get that room. She leaned back into him. "Thank you for bringing me tonight."

"Thank you for coming."

"Anything for you, boyfriend."

"All right, you all officially suck." Tasha thrust two controllers at them and another two at Ethan. "Are we ready to play yet, or do you have more crap for us to pack?"

Ethan rolled his eyes. "We can play. I'll even let you pick."

"Keep in mind that finger masher here can only play the basics," Brian said, dropping two ten-dollar bills on top of the one Ethan had just placed on the table.

"I don't play at all," Ethan's girlfriend, Jenny, said. "But if you need a referee, I'm your woman."

Tasha looked between the members of the group and then dug through the games Sarah had just packed. She pulled out a white case with cover art that even Sarah could recognize—*Super Smash Brothers*.

Ethan whooped, and Brian fist pumped Tasha, who slapped a ten down on the pile and said, "It's going to be so much fun kicking your asses."

Chapter 40

Brian

Brian hadn't thought he could love Sarah any more than he already did. And he did love her—there was no denying that—but then she'd beaten them all at *Super Smash Brothers* with Jigglypuff, the worst freaking Pokémon in history. She'd smashed so many buttons that she'd unlocked things none of them ever knew about. As if they would play as that pink blob besides on a dare. She'd taunted them like a pro the entire game, a giant smile plastered on her face, even though he knew she didn't particularly like video games. Her triumph made the news that Brian was on a short list of applicants for the job at Myer even sweeter. Especially since the hiring managers were meeting to pick the candidate first thing Monday, and Ethan had been invited to weigh in. It was all the confirmation Brian needed. Hopefully, by Monday afternoon, he wouldn't have to negotiate terms with a St. Louis company to stay in Philadelphia or have to work alone in a rental office space while the rest of his company conquered upstate New York. He could be here. With his friends. With Sarah.

His alarmed buzzed for the second time, and Brian groaned. The last thing he wanted to do was leave her after the night they'd had and the love they'd made, but he was already pushing the limits of when Jess usually stumbled out of bed to pee—only one of the weird things he'd learned from sleeping on the living room floor. Even before the stealth alarms, he'd become conditioned to finishing his shower by 4:52 or not starting until 5:02. His sister was like a clockwork camel.

He kissed Sarah's forehead and then maneuvered out from under her arm. Waiting a minute for his eyes to adjust, he searched for a shirt as Sarah was currently wearing his. He'd only just saved his boxers from her grasp.

He pulled on his most recent Zumba tank top—this one with a prone T. rex and the words "T. rex hates plank"—and he slowly pulled open the door, bracing for the creak it usually admitted. The living room was bright. He blinked a few times and glanced down at his phone. No, the sun wouldn't rise for another hour at least. The lights were on. And his sister sat on the couch cross-legged, the television on mute or so low he could barely hear the episode of *Boy Meets World* she had on. She held a cup of coffee, and an empty plate with what looked like muffin crumbs on it sat on the coffee table. She'd been waiting. Which could only mean one thing. *Shit.*

He shut the bedroom door, steeling himself against what he knew was coming. "You're up early, sis."

"Lose your pajamas again, brother?"

Successfully pulling off another lie was unlikely. His sister had been up long enough to eat and make coffee. And they hadn't even bothered to set up the fake bed last night, too caught up in ripping each other's clothing off.

But he had to try. "Just getting my stuff ready for work."

"You're empty-handed, and it's Sunday. You work at seven on Sundays because of the public transportation schedules."

Fuckity fuck fuck. "What do you want me to say, Jess?"

"I want you to say that you're screwing my best friend and own it like a man instead of sneaking around in my eight-hundred-and-fifty-square-foot apartment as if I wouldn't notice."

"I'm not *screwing* Sarah."

She stood up and approached him, fury and something that looked a lot like hurt playing on her face. "Stop lying to me."

He motioned toward the kitchen, and by some small miracle, Jess crossed the short distance. Once there, she whirled on him. He held up his hands in surrender. "Fine, yes, I'm sleeping with Sarah. But it's not what you think. And I don't see how keeping that secret is any different from you not telling Sarah you were dating Ryder for three months."

"Because Ryder isn't your best friend. You promised me you'd stay away from my friends after Bella."

"Are you really calling back to some bullshit from high school? We're not teenagers doing stupid shit anymore."

She crossed her arms and fixed him with a glare. "We may not be teenagers, but you two are still doing stupid shit."

"I love her, Jess."

Her expression hardened, her lips curving into a sneer. "Why would I believe anything you say? I asked you point-blank if you were sleeping with Sarah, and you lied to my face."

"I wouldn't lie about something like this." He wrung his hands in front of him, meeting his sister's eyes, even though the betrayal he saw there hurt. "I'm in love with her."

"Up until two months ago, you hated her guts."

He ran a hand through his hair with a sigh and glanced back toward the bedroom, praying that Sarah couldn't hear any of this. "Two months ago, I didn't know her. Then you threw us together on a fake date, and things changed."

"Do you really think I didn't know what I interrupted the night of the gala or every other time you two were together? You went to freakin' Zumba with her. If there was ever a dead giveaway... I gave you every chance to tell me the truth, including tonight. I mean, how oblivious do you think I am? You two literally left at the exact same time the instant I got home. And yet you just kept lying."

In that moment, he hated his sister. He'd disliked her plenty over the years, but never before had he so loathed her or the fact that he might have to bend to her will. "I *love* her, Jess."

She shook her head, her eyes fixed on some spot on the floor. When she spoke, there was a catch in her voice. "All that stuff I said tonight about her rebounding—I meant it. Sarah is my *best friend*. I know when she's rebounding. I'm not going to let some tryst between the two of you blow up our friendship when she comes to her senses in a few months or you get a job offer across the country and leave her."

"You mean like you're planning on doing?" He could hear the cruelty in his voice, but he didn't care. His sister was being ridiculous. "Is this even about me and Sarah?"

Jess took a breath, and when she looked up at him again tears soaked her cheeks. "If you walk away now, I'll pretend I never knew."

The words hit him like a punch. He couldn't walk away from Sarah. Not now. "You have no right to ask that of me."

She stomped her foot, and Brian was reminded of his sister's stubborn streak. "I have every right. I will not lose Sarah because you couldn't keep it in your pants."

"I'm not going to walk away from the woman I love because you have some ridiculous insecurity."

Jess's lips flattened into a line, and she crossed her arms. "I'm going back to bed, and when I next come out here, I expect you to be well on your way to getting your shit out of my apartment."

BRIAN CRAWLED BACK into bed and pulled Sarah close as a storm raged inside him. His body shook, his hand trembling against the soft skin of Sarah's arm. All he'd wanted when he came to Philly was a reprieve from the soul-crushing truths of moving back in with his parents. A life, friendship, love—those were not part of the plan. But he'd gotten all of them, and now his own sister was threatening to take it away from him. Lavender and mint and the unique scent of Sarah surrounded him as he burrowed deeper into the blankets. Each breath filled him with all that she was, and each exhalation sliced like a goodbye he wasn't ready for. She wouldn't pick him. His sister might be scared to lose her best friend, but this wasn't high school or one of those rom-coms she so faithfully watched. Brian would tell Sarah the news, and Jess would put down her foot, and Sarah would leave him. There could never be any other outcome.

It was another hour before Sarah stirred. He should have already been on his way to the store. But he couldn't let his sister get to her first, and waking Sarah to deliver bad news would have been cruel—if he could, he would never let her leave this bedroom. So he'd done something he'd never done to Tasha—he called out sick.

"Hey, boyfriend." Sarah's eyes fluttered open, adjusting to the morning light. "What are you still doing in here?"

"It's okay. Jess thinks I left for work." He nuzzled into her neck, burying himself in her scent and closeness.

"But shouldn't you *be* at work?"

"I took the day off." He kissed her slowly and deeply. The taste of her lingered on his lips, and he wanted to remember it forever.

"You okay?"

"I will be if you kiss me again."

"Brian?"

He swallowed her question, pulling her into him until they shared the same breath. Piece by piece, they stripped off the few clothes they wore. He entered her gently, his lips never leaving hers as their bodies moved together. They spoke with caresses and kisses and more. Each movement bringing them closer. He watched her fall apart beneath him, her body tightening as she lost herself, and then he followed her down.

I love you. The thought broke him, and he pulled her tighter still.

"What is it?" she asked, cupping his face and searching his eyes.

"I love you." It was unfair, but if in another ten minutes it would all be gone, he needed to know he'd said it and meant it. He needed to know she'd heard his scream into the void. "I love you so much."

Tears brimmed under her eyelids, and her smile cracked. She ran a hand through his scratchy beard and kissed him so fiercely the process almost started again. But then she pulled back and locked eyes with him, tears dotting her cheeks. "I love you too."

Chapter 41

Sarah

"Please tell me what's going on." Sarah held both of Brian's hands in her own. Her breathing hitched. "Is it… Did you get the job in St. Louis?"

Brian shook his head, and her heart revived itself. She couldn't imagine what other reason he would have to have kissed her like that. Like she was his one and only hope. Like he was saying goodbye.

"Jess knows."

A chill washed over her at those two simple words. "She knows what exactly?"

He shrugged. "Everything? She was waiting for me at four thirty this morning. And you were right. She's not happy."

Not happy didn't seem quite as dire as Brian's tone indicated. She tried to keep her rising panic in check. "What did she say?"

"Maybe she just needs a minute." He brushed her hair behind her ear and gave her the saddest smile in the whole world. "I bet after a few days away with Ryder and a chance to sit with the news, she'll cool down."

"What did she say, Brian?" Her voice rose, all that panic rushing to the surface. There were few things that got her best friend truly angry, and *cool down* was not a phrase Sarah ever associated with her.

"She told me to end it or to get out." He took a breath, and she watched him bolster himself for his next ask. "Come home with me for Thanksgiving. Be my girlfriend. Fight for us. Because I love you, Sarah, and I will gladly crash on every friend's couch to be with you.

I will work double shifts and two jobs and whatever I have to do to get us a place of our own. Just say you're with me."

Defeat shadowed his features before he'd even finished the sentence. And she couldn't blame him. Sarah had made it more than clear exactly where her loyalties lay from the moment she'd stormed through the door and stolen Brian's bedroom. He was the interloper. And now she loved him. But how could she choose him when the other choice was losing her best friend? The answer was as easy as telling him she loved him. She was going to choose him anyway.

"I'm with you." She kissed his cheek.

Brian exhaled the longest breath, and it came out as half a laugh, half a cry. The sound broke her, and she brought her lips down on his and kissed him until they were both breathless. Then she stood up and pulled her ponytail tighter, readying herself for battle.

"Let me talk to her. Maybe it'll be better coming from me."

The words rang untrue even as she said them. If anything, Jess would probably be angrier with her because of that stupid promise. White noise settled in her mind, and she clasped her hands to stop them from shaking. In all their years of friendship, she and Jess had rarely fought—at least not about anything important. They supported each other and told the truth even when it hurt, but they also accepted each other's decisions, even ones that were an obvious mistake.

But Brian looked ready to crack, so she squared her shoulders and set her expression to anything except terrified. "I love you."

Brian's lips quirked in a sad imitation of a smile. "I know."

JESS WAS IN THE LIVING room, packing. The air mattress sat in a crumpled heap of deflated plastic on the ground. A garbage bag, filled to the brim, rested against the coffee table—the edge of a controller and the blue of Brian's comforter peeked out. Her best friend snapped open a second bag and attempted to shove the air mattress into it. She gave up halfway and threw it all back on the ground with a creative curse. Chuck hissed from the couch where he sat, pawing at the catnip-doused bowtie Brian had given him. Even the cat looked sad, as if he knew his friend was leaving. All signs pointed to Jess really kicking her brother out.

Sarah reached out and stilled Jess's hand before she yanked the game-system wires out of the wall. "Stop, Jessie."

Jess recoiled at Sarah's touch, and that hurt more than anything had in Sarah's entire life. "Don't you dare call me that."

The familiar pressure of unshed tears built up in her head, and she sat down, her face in her hands. The situation between the three of them was always going to end badly, but the reality was worse than she'd imagined. "It doesn't have to be like this."

"You're fucking my brother, so it does have to be like this." Jess straightened, kicking the bag she'd already packed. "I had one rule—one small thing I asked for. And then not only do you sleep with him, but you lie about it to my face."

"I'm not *fucking* him, and you know it." Sarah put all the confidence she could muster into that statement and channeled everything she felt for Brian into her next words. "Let's skip the bullshit—I'm in love with your brother. One hundred percent head-over-heels I-want-to-have-his-babies kind of love."

Jess stopped and looked at her, a bit of surprise cutting through the anger, but then she shook her head. "I've witnessed years of your mutual hatred of each other, and I find it really hard to believe that you two are suddenly madly in love. Lusting after each other, sure. But you don't love him."

"But I do. I tried not to." Sarah's voice cracked as she forced the words out. "I pushed him away and stayed at Maggie's. I wanted to keep my promise to you."

"Well, you failed spectacularly."

"You think I don't know that? You think I haven't spent the past few weeks trying to figure out how to tell you?" Sarah clasped her hands. "I know you had your reasons for making me agree to that promise—whatever they were—but we *love* each other, Jessie. Shouldn't that count for something?"

"It might have two months ago when I asked you if something happened with my brother. But you lied to me for weeks. You could've told me after the gala. I wouldn't have liked it, but at least you would've been honest with me. At least then I wouldn't wake up to go to the bathroom and be greeted by an empty air mattress and unmentionable sounds from your bedroom. I wouldn't have felt like a third wheel in my own apartment. But no—you both just kept lying and acting like I was so wrapped up in my own bubble that I wouldn't notice."

Sarah's body curled in on itself. Jess wasn't wrong. They had lied and snuck around and been careless with their secret. "Tell me what I can do to make this better."

Jess crossed her arms, and her face softened a fraction. "I don't know, but you can't have me as your best friend and him as your boyfriend."

"You're making me choose between you?"

"Yes. And if you pick him, there's no going back. You can't come crawling back to me when you realize you fell in 'love' with your rebound and none of it was real."

"Jessie." She hugged herself tight, holding back the tears. "It is real. It's the realest thing I've ever known."

Jess swiped a hand across her face and straightened. Her eyes were sad but unrelenting. "You can't have me as your best friend and him as your boyfriend."

"Fine." The words were barely audible over the sob that escaped her chest.

The tears she'd tried to hide spilled down her cheeks. Jess took a step toward her, and for a moment, Sarah thought she might take it all back. Instead, her best friend turned and walked out of their apartment.

The hole in Sarah's chest widened and widened until she wasn't sure she'd ever find her way back out. She held herself together, her fingers so tightly wrapped around her arms that her nails pricked her skin. Thirty more seconds. She'd give herself thirty more seconds to cry. The seconds ticked by as tears and whimpers and a deafening silence ripped her apart. *Twenty-eight... I love you... twenty-nine... I'm sorry... thirty...*

Chapter 42

Brian

Brian blinked back tears. Sound in this apartment traveled. His sister was making Sarah choose. He hadn't been able to hear Sarah's response, only the awful guttural noise that followed his sister's entreaty. But she wouldn't choose him, and if she did, she'd be giving up everything—her best friend, her home, her happiness. He couldn't be her happiness. In the end, she'd resent him. And what would happen if they lasted? Seeing Jess at every holiday would be death by a thousand paper cuts.

His phone buzzed on the bedside table, and he reached for it if only to avoid what he knew was coming. He stared at the screen, his stomach threatening to betray him. *Heard from my bro... offer should come in tomorrow.* A photo came in next—a picture of the team logos for the Cardinals and the Phillies with a lowercase *v* in the middle, stolen from any schedule on the internet. *So, who's it going to be?*

The door swung open, and there stood his dream girl, tear streaked and disheveled. Hardly breathing. He chucked his phone onto the bed and raced to her. She didn't return his embrace, only stood there, stoic and broken.

"It's okay, Chestnut."

She shook her head, more tears falling. "I can't do this."

"I understand."

"No." She grabbed him now, her eyes blazing. "I choose you. I love you, and I can't—"

"You have to."

"No." She sobbed, and he died a little inside at the sound—a sound he had caused, all because of that stupid kiss on those stupid stairs.

"I'm moving to St. Louis," he blurted in a panic. It was the only thing that he could think of to make this any easier.

"You're what?"

"Ethan just told me his brother said to expect an offer tomorrow. I haven't heard from the other company here." The lie cut at him as it came out, as his plans from a few hours earlier dissolved. "So I guess I'm moving to St. Louis."

Her eyes glazed over, and she loosened her grip on his arm. "Oh."

"Pick my sister and forget about me and all of this."

She shook her head. "I'll come with you."

"Sarah, I…" He couldn't finish. Her words had sucked all the life out of him. He knew what the offer must be costing her—not just his sister but also the life she'd literally been running away from for as long as he'd known her. He brought his lips to hers and kissed her—it tasted like Sarah and tears and goodbye and forever. He'd never thought to ask her to go with him. Never considered that it would be an option. Now it was, but he couldn't consider it.

She reached up and wiped tears off his cheek. "I'll come with you right now."

"I can't let you do that." He shook his head. "You said yourself that Jess is your family. I can't—"

A laugh, bitter and broken, cut through his sentence. "You Hawkinses. You don't get to tell me who I can love and what I can and cannot do. Jess is family, but I love you. If that means moving to St. Louis and risking my friendship with your sister, then I guess…" A sob splintered her words. "I guess that's what you do for love."

He shook his head and pushed her hand back down to her side. His heart shattered at the betrayal on her face as he stepped back from her. "No."

"No? You love me, but you don't want me to go with you?" Fresh tears spilled down her cheeks.

"I want to be wherever you are, Sarah. I love you in ways I didn't know were possible, but you can't lose Jess, and she can't lose you. Not over me."

"She'll get over it... eventually."

"Maybe. Maybe not. But even if she does, your friendship will never be the same. And I can't—I won't—do that to you." He cupped her face, running his thumb gently across her cheek. "Please, please just let me go."

She stared at him for another moment, and then she stepped out of the way. Anger flashed across her features, and she hugged herself, shaking her head. "I wish you had never kissed me that night."

"I'll never wish that." Without stopping to pick up any of his things, he walked through the open door.

Chapter 43

Sarah

Brian's face, devastated yet compassionate as he begged her to let him go, would haunt her for the rest of time. The memory of that last kiss would break her for eternity.

Sarah had been wrong. She wouldn't heal from this. Not in ten days or ten years. Brian would always and forever be the one that got away. And every day with her best friend would be a reminder of what she had to give up to keep Jess there. She rolled over in bed, her eyes dry and itchy from a day of crying.

But she had to go to work. Eight hours. She could pull herself together for eight hours today and tomorrow. Then she'd tuck herself back into bed for the long Thanksgiving holiday Maggie always gave them.

She hadn't even made it to the bathroom before she was crying again. Sometime the night before, Jess had finished packing Brian's things in the living room. They sat in a neat pile behind the couch. That didn't account for all the stuff in Sarah's—their—room. Brian was gone, and Jess was silent. None of this seemed like a win. It sucked all around. After showering in her own tears, she'd thought she couldn't possibly have more left, but when she saw the text from her mom, who was trying to schedule a video chat around what she assumed were Sarah's alternate Thanksgiving plans, she'd dry heaved. Her voice had cracked that morning in the coffee shop when she'd bought her full-priced non-Starbucks latte from a bored hipster named Greta. Some people would consider that a blessing, but Sarah preferred her coffee in a siren-themed cup. But she knew Brian would be manning the bar at Starbucks, and she wouldn't force herself on him. Not after she'd let him sacrifice everything. And he had. Nothing about him had looked happy when he said he was moving to St. Louis—if that was even true—or when he implored her to choose Jess or when she declared she wished he'd never kissed her. That was perhaps the biggest lie she'd ever told.

The office was buzzing when she arrived a few minutes after nine. Leigh and Maggie had their heads stuck into the former storage room, and she could hear Jace's booming laughter from inside. This was the last thing she needed. Keeping her head buried in answering emails and filing had been on her docket for the day—definitely not anything that required conversation, because the second she opened her mouth, she would cry. The tears were already there waiting for her at the sight of the backward chair at her desk. She'd never fixed it. He always readjusted it anyway. He used to, at least. Brian wouldn't be back in her office again.

"There you are!" Maggie's voice was light, her expression relaxed.

Thanksgiving was her favorite holiday. Each year, Maggie alternated traveling to one of her siblings' houses—including Jace's father—and hosting at her place. It was her year, and Leigh and Sarah already had guesses on record for just how early she'd close the office on Tuesday. Sarah was guessing noon. Leigh fully expected Maggie to send them home that night and not expect them back for a week—there were pies to be made and a turkey to brine after all.

"Morning," Sarah mumbled, sitting down at her desk. Her eyes took in the dark wood that was usually covered in paper. "Where's my stuff?"

"Over here, dear."

Dear? Maggie had never called her dear in her life. "I'm really not in the mood—"

Maggie pulled her out of her chair and tugged her toward the storage room... which had been transformed into an office. Sarah stepped into the room and picked up the name plate sitting on the desk. Sarah Webb, Senior Development Associate. That was her.

This is my *office?* Next to her name plate sat what she knew was called a tombstone, thanks to a certain season of *Suits.* Her first Gold Partner was etched there in glass.

"What's going on?" Sarah asked.

"You didn't really think I had Jace clean and paint the storage closet on a whim, did you?"

"Yes," she said, laughing. "I did!"

Jace grinned at her from behind her desk. "Totally sold it the other day, huh? Thought that boyfriend of yours was going to lose his mind when he walked in and I was inviting you to help out."

Tears spilled down her cheeks unbidden at that. Her relationship with Brian had been real for so many people. Months of real and true love that other people saw and respected and recognized. And now it was gone. She sat down at her new desk, only crying harder at the framed photo of her and Brian at the gala. Maggie must have pulled it from the gallery. It was one she'd never seen, with the two of them sitting on the Rocky Steps, laughing, a moment before he kissed her for the first time. They looked in love even then.

She heard Maggie shoo Jace and Leigh out, and then gentle hands were on her shoulders. "He got the job in New York?"

She'd forgotten she'd told Maggie about that, but of course, her boss would remember. "No... Jess found out."

"Ah."

"And now he's gone, and she's still not talking to me, and I'm going to be alone on Thanksgiving. I feel like I lost everything in one awful moment."

"Not everything." Maggie rubbed her back. "And you are certainly not going to be alone for Thanksgiving. You'll come to my house. There are so many Clairmonts no one will even notice you're not family."

"Thank you." She gestured around the office. "For all of it."

"This," Maggie said, mimicking her motion, "you earned all on your own. Now, wipe those tears. Today is a good day. And this office isn't today's only news. Jace, Leigh!" Once they were all stuffed into the office again, Maggie turned to Sarah and Leigh. "Part of the reason I knew it was time to get this space cleaned up was because we also have a new part-time staffer in Jace. He'll be acting as our Community Outreach Coordinator and building a partnership with his school district—starting with creating a mentorship program with some promising young students."

"Speaking of those students," he said, a blush rising up his cheeks, "I must get going. I only have a sub for my first two periods."

"One last thing," Maggie said, holding him in place. "Tyler called me last night, and they found Tessa a kidney. I was thinking, who better to kick off our mentor program?"

Sarah's eyes filled again, but this time they were happy tears. Tessa was going to be back to her healthy teenage self. She was going to get to keep designing, and she'd gotten offers for internships with more than one clothing company that she could now take. "I love it."

"Now..." Maggie stood and ushered them all out of the office. "Let's let Ms. Webb get settled in."

Sarah sat down at her desk after they'd all left, closing the door behind them. She picked up the picture of her and Brian, memorizing the contours of his face and the way their knees collided and the slight lean in. By any right, this photo shouldn't exist. But it did. Just like their relationship. She pulled up her last text thread with Brian on her phone. The last thing he'd sent her was a photo of him holding up a ridiculous shirt that had Yoda on it and the words, "Yoda one for me." Of course, he'd bought it. Her hands hovered over the keys, shaking with the desire to ask him to stay. To tell him she didn't want to live in a city he wasn't in even if they couldn't be together.

That path would only lead to more pain for both of them, but God, she wanted to ask him anyway—beg him not to leave her completely.

Sarah bit back a cry and shoved her phone into her desk drawer. It would get easier. It had to. Step one would be to focus on anything that wasn't her broken heart. She turned her attention to her inbox, where three emails from Tessa—each with more exclamation points in the subject line—awaited her.

Chapter 44

Sarah

Twelve o'clock it was. While Maggie was more than generous with their time off, she also had a nonprofit to run. So, with Leigh out of the office until next week, Sarah and her boss had spent a quiet morning in their respective offices before Maggie shoved Sarah out the door with a demand that she bring a dessert to Thanksgiving.

She'd stopped at the store to buy ingredients for her mom's famous chocolate pumpkin oat cookies. They had been a Thanksgiving staple since childhood, and she and her mom had tweaked it to perfection over the years. Not that she'd been home the last few Thanksgivings. The first one after moving to Philly, she hadn't had enough money to get home, and the last one she'd spent the day with Tyler at one of his coworkers' swanky parties. And this year... Well, she was starting to wish she'd planned to make the trip home. At least then she would have had a thousand miles to cry out her heartbreak.

Sarah was feeling *not terrible*—which meant she'd stopped crying every ninety seconds but had still woken up to wet cheeks and had a good sob in the bathroom when Tessa asked if Brian would come to their postholiday "hurray, I got a kidney" gathering. *Okay* was the goal for the moment. *Good* was a faraway land she hoped to one day visit again. She wasn't even thinking about *great* yet. Distraction was key, and a virtual baking session with her mom sounded perfect.

But when she pushed open the door to the apartment, something immediately felt wrong. She dropped the bags and kicked the door closed. A feeling of emptiness weighed heavy in the air. For so many weeks, Sarah, Brian, and Jess had been crowded into this space, their things and their lives overlapping even when they didn't want them to. In the living room, the pile of Brian's belongings Jess had stacked behind the couch was gone.

No. Sarah crossed to her room and threw the door open. Gone. There were no sneakers by the closet door or apron ties hanging out of her dresser. The jeans he always had slung over the chair she kept in the corner of the room were missing. She pushed at the sliding closet door until it clicked open. Brian was gone.

Despair smashed free of its shackles, broke its best friend—heartbreak—loose, and rallied its partner, anger. A sob racked her body, and she was soon drowning in her own tears. Sarah threw back the covers on the bed and tipped the mattress up. *Thank God.* The bundle of green remained. She pulled the Binghamton hoodie out of its hiding spot and cuddled it to her chest. She'd stuffed the sweatshirt there that morning after sleeping in it again. If Jess found it, she would probably burn it. Sarah hadn't meant to keep it from Brian, but she hadn't expected him to come for his things so quickly.

Leaving the sweatshirt on, Sarah returned to the entryway and picked up her bags. Once unloaded, she pulled the keyring of index card recipes off the fridge and flipped to the cookies. Her mother's familiar handwriting stared back at her. She propped her laptop up on the counter and clicked through to call her mom.

"Hey, honey." Her mother's voice was as musical as ever, her accent a bit heavier than Sarah was used to. This tended to happen when they hadn't spoken for a while and all Jeanine's conversations happened in town. But by the end of the call, she'd be back to the neutral American she'd pushed Sarah to speak her entire life.

"Hi, Mom."

"What is it, baby?" She touched the screen as if she could stroke Sarah's hair through it. "Is it Tyler? I know the holidays can be hard after a breakup. I wish you could've come home."

Something between a laugh and a cry fell out of Sarah's mouth. "It's not Tyler."

"Let it out." Her mother's eyes implored her to spill all the truths she'd kept hidden because of Jess—no, because of herself. *She* had been scared to put it out there because once it was out there, it was real. And if it was real, she could get hurt. "Come on—you can tell me."

And so she did. As Sarah measured and sifted and mixed, she told her mother everything. She cried over pumpkin puree and ate half a bag of chocolate chips. The story ended as she slipped the first tray of cookies into the oven. "I've never felt like that before, like I could love someone forever and never be bored, you know?"

"Yes, I know the feeling."

"Really?" Sarah asked. Her mom loved fast and hard. She'd seemed to flit from guy to guy for so much of Sarah's young-adult life.

"Yes, honey."

"Don't say it was Dad, because that is not going to give me any hope."

"It wasn't your father. If it was, we'd all have a very different story, don't you think?"

Sarah spun through the men in her mother's life, but none of them fit the bill. "Who?"

"When I was a bit younger than you, I met a wonderful, kind man. He used to say we fell in love over one cup of coffee. He asked me to marry him after only a month. I didn't say yes... at first. But life had other plans for me and him, and he was taken from this world far too soon."

"Mom." The word was soft and sad. Her mother had never spoken about life before her father, and Sarah hadn't asked. It hadn't been relevant. Or so she'd thought.

"But then I met your father, and we were happy for a time, and we had you." Jeanine wiped away the memory. "All that is to say, if you love this boy, make sure he knows it."

"I can't." Sarah's voice cracked on the words. "Jess is my best friend."

"If she's really your best friend, then she'll get over it and forgive you."

Sarah shook her head, wishing as hard as she'd ever wished that any part of her believed that to be possible. "You didn't see her."

"Then maybe you need a better best friend." Her mother sighed. "I know Jess has been like family to you, Sarahbear, and it might be hard to hear, but if you and Brian love each other like you say you do—well, I say that supersedes any promise you made to your friend, because if she can't see the pain she is causing and what you're giving up, then what kind of friend does that make her?"

"I can't lose her, Mom."

"And yet you were ready to go to St. Louis with Brian even though you've avoided coming home for *three years*." Her mom's eyes narrowed on the screen.

Maybe Sarah was a bit overdue for a trip home. St. Louis wasn't home, but it was close enough. She hadn't even wanted to be anywhere near the Midwest since she left, but she had offered to go with Brian.

"He asked me to let him go. He took his things. He's moving across the country."

"And *you* let him leave."

The timer dinged on the oven, and Sarah thanked all the cosmic-timing gods because she was about to burst into tears. Was her mom right? Had she let him go too easily? It hadn't felt easy—it had felt like ripping her heart out and stomping on it and then stitching it back into place with a dull needle. But she had let him leave. She'd allowed the sacrifice. *She'd* made him believe Jess was more important all along.

The front door opened as Sarah put the second tray of cookies in the oven. Jess poked her head into the kitchen. "Smells like Thanksgiving in here."

Those were the first words her best friend had spoken to her since Sunday morning. They were painfully normal and wholly inadequate. Sarah glanced from Jess to the screen where her mom had on her "I'm about to tell off your friend" face. She said a hasty goodbye and hit the red *X* before words could be said. If Jess noticed the quick farewell or the tearstains on Sarah's cheeks or the fact that Sarah still wore Brian's sweatshirt, she didn't let on.

"They still need to cool." Sarah barely bit out the words, keeping her eyes on the mess of measuring cups. Everything her mother had said ricocheted around her head, threatening to blow up this olive branch.

"I brought you something." Jess held up a Target bag.

She knew what it was before the spray bottles hit the counter. Sarah had a post-breakup routine, and Jess was a key player. It cost a lot to permanently dye her hair a shade of neon. First, she had to bleach it, and then she had to go back and color it. Before any appointments were made, she tried on the color with the temporary hair dyes. They were harsh enough that the color would show up for the length of one shower if she used a bottle or three.

"I was thinking," Jess said, picking up the purple-capped bottle, "this is one you haven't tried in a while."

Sarah shoveled the extra dough into the trash and squirted too much dish soap into the bowl. The bubbles quickly overflowed the rim, and she started scrubbing away the remains. "I don't think I want to dye my hair this time."

The thought alone made her stomach churn. She dyed her hair when she was done with a relationship. It was an easy and transient change that gave her a fresh start. But she wasn't *done*, and she didn't want a *fresh start*. No, wallowing was the way through this one. A good long wallow. And her chestnut-colored hair had to stay. A montage of all the times he'd called her that stupid nickname ran through her mind. The last one, so heartbroken and resigned, couldn't be the final time he called her that.

"Oh. Well..." Jess put the cans back in the bag. "Do you want to maybe order from that Indian place you like and watch a movie?"

Naan made everything better. That had been their motto for as long as they'd known each other. Rom-coms and naan had helped them through every single breakup. Sarah chanced a glance at her friend. Jess gave her the smallest of smiles.

Sarah gripped that olive branch with all her might. "What movie were you thinking?"

"You have to ask?"

She didn't. There was only one movie they watched after a breakup, because nothing quite cured a broken heart like Ryan Reynolds, Sandra Bullock, and Betty White. "I'll get the DVD." Sarah stopped halfway to her bedroom. "Jess?" Her friend turned, and something like hope shone in her eyes. "Order extra naan, please."

Chapter 45

Brian

He missed his air mattress. It was ten times better than this futon, and it certainly didn't have the threat of death by treadmill. But his sister had popped it in her rage-fueled trash bagging of his things—he wouldn't dignify what she'd done by calling it packing. He'd gone back Tuesday morning to get his stuff after watching Jess, and then Sarah, leave for work. Sarah had looked a mess despite being dressed for the office. According to Tasha, he looked just as bad, which was the only reason she had taken pity on him and switched around his shifts before the holiday. He'd driven to Fairford the day before to avoid the bulk of the holiday traffic, but at the moment, he was reconsidering that decision. Tasha's pullout couch and stand-still traffic would have been better than a night on this futon.

He rolled over and pulled the pink camisole out from under his pillow. It still smelled like her body wash. He hadn't planned on taking it, but then he'd seen the arm of his favorite hoodie sticking out from under her bed. If she wanted to keep a piece of him, then he could keep a piece of her. He remembered when he'd seen her in the camisole that first night. She'd been painting her nails a matching shade. And he'd hated her so freaking much. He wanted to hate her again. Hate had been so much easier.

But she'd said, "I'll come with you right now." And she'd meant it. Maybe only for that moment. Maybe she never would have made it to the gate, but in that room, faced with losing her best friend or him, she'd chosen him. And he'd walked away. It was the right thing to do. It was also possibly the most dickish thing he'd ever done because he'd cashed in on his love for her. Hurting someone to save them never worked. Even Brian had seen enough rom-coms to know that. But death by a thousand paper cuts—that was what their future would have been.

He balled up the satin and pushed it back into its hiding spot. Never leaving this futon seemed a great idea. Taking the day to nurse his wounds and consider his life choices was probably a good idea. But he had some decisions to make. True to Ethan's tip, MyHR had come through with an offer yesterday morning. Myer had called two hours later with a competitive offer. Both had given him until after the holiday to accept. And then there was Scott and Johnson. After everything that had happened, hiding in Fairford seemed almost as good as hiding in St. Louis. At least here he'd have his oldest friends. The cost of living was nothing compared to what it was in the city. He could buy a starter house in Fairford. He could rent and still save money to start over in a few years. But that wasn't how his hometown worked. By the time a few years passed, he'd have roots. He'd probably be married to someone he'd known since he was in diapers. He'd be happy. Maybe. Eventually. And still, all he wanted was to crawl back to Philadelphia and take it all back.

"Brian!" His mother's voice, followed by a knock, forced him out of his thoughts. The door opened as if he wasn't an adult who demanded privacy. "It's almost lunchtime. Really, what are you doing still in bed?"

"Enjoying my vacation time?"

"Nonsense. I need you to help me bring pies over to the senior center."

"Mom, seriously?"

"Oh, stop whining. Your friends will be there."

"Why would my friends be at the senior center?"

He knew the answer even as he asked the question. Because Corey had become the heart of this town, so of course he'd be serving pie to the elderly the day before Thanksgiving. His mother gave him a look that screamed for him to stop being an imbecile.

"Fine. Can I at least shower?" he asked.

"Obviously. You aren't going to impress your future boss if you walk in unshaven and in mesh shorts."

"He's not my future boss." He scratched at his beard, which was almost to the unruly point despite him having cleaned it up recently.

"Also, that thing on your face is not invited to Thanksgiving."

"It's for charity," he said teasingly. "It's No-Shave November."

With a huff, his mother left the room. She didn't close the door, and he heard the clacking of her shoes as she made her way back to the kitchen. But the sound stopped long before the kitchen at what he knew was the bottom of the stairs. He waited, coming to stand in the doorway.

Her voice echoed through the house. "Don't even think about wearing one of those graphic tees."

Less than thirty minutes later—which was a miracle, considering it took twenty minutes to get to the senior center from their house—he stood in what was essentially a gymnasium, putting slices of pie onto paper plates. He'd played many hours of recreation basketball on this floor. In fact, he knew how half the scuff marks had happened. He and his friends had all been campers, sitting crisscross applesauce, in here for years, and then they'd been teenagers at town-sponsored rec nights. Those had lasted all of three summers and then were canceled, probably thanks to the antics of him and his friends. Now the seniors had taken over. This gym was a step up from the bowels of the municipal building, he supposed.

"Smells like sophomore year, right?"

Brian looked up at the sound of Corey's voice. He stood across the table in a full suit—always the full suit, even for Fairford. Brian took his hand with a smile that actually felt genuine. "Smells like our whole lives."

"You get used to it."

That was what he was afraid of. He studied his friend, wondering what he'd be like as a boss. How would that change their dynamic? He wondered if he could stomach working *for* Corey. No matter how much Corey said the company was a family and a team and he hired people he trusted and knew and valued, Brian wouldn't be working with Corey or alongside him. He'd be working for him. Corey would pay his salary. That sounded like a great way to ruin a friendship.

Brian pointed to the pie holder behind him. "My mom said that's for you, Andi, and Emily."

"Oh man, did she make chocolate mousse or black-bottom banana cream?"

Brian's mother approached carrying an oversized Tupperware that looked like all the other pie containers. "Both, of course."

Corey grinned. "You are too kind, Mrs. Hawkins."

"Nonsense." His mother looked at Brian pointedly, conveying quite obviously her desire that he not mess this up. "I'll leave you two to chat."

"Subtle," Brian murmured as she walked away.

"Never a mom's specialty. You know, we're having a small Thanksgiving tonight with some of the Scott and Johnson family—you should come. I think you know everyone."

As if that wasn't a given in Fairford. "I'll think about it."

"No pressure, but at the very least, you'll get some of my mom's pumpkin bread."

Warmth spread through him at the memory. He hadn't had Mrs. Johnson's pumpkin bread since high school. It was a staple of any sports-related event—team dinner, award ceremony, homecoming, start of the season, end of the season. They'd had to run doubles because of it. Yet they still ate it every time. One time, Corey had even stolen a whole loaf, and they'd all eaten it straight out of the baking pan with sporks left over from camp. There were so many memories in this town. And they were good ones. He wasn't one of those kids who'd hated high school. High school had been good to him. But he couldn't be Brian Hawkins, former star shortstop of the Fairford baseball team, for his entire life. That wasn't who he was.

He wondered, not for the first time, how Corey could have borne it all these years.

"Bro! The gang's all here!" Dustin, another one of his oldest friends and now a teacher in town, walked up to the table. He gave Corey a hug and then brought Brian in for one too. "Couldn't stay away, huh?" He rubbed his chin in mock thought. "Fairford grows on you."

"Yeah," Brian said wryly, "like mold."

"I may not be a science teacher, but I do not think that is accurate."

He laughed and tried to ignore the happy look he could see on his mother's face from across the room. She was practically glowing. His phone buzzed on the table next to the pies, and a familiar and heartbreaking photo stared back at him—Sarah. No. He couldn't answer it. The phone buzzed again, and he refused to consider why she might be calling him. Brian might have begged her to let him go, but she'd still let him go. He couldn't go through that again.

"Who's the girl?" Dustin asked with a waggle of his eyebrows.

The room narrowed down to those pie plates. A weight settled on his chest. He wondered what he was doing with his life. He took a breath, but it caught in his throat. Brian's chest constricted further until finally, the call dropped.

"Do you think...?" He motioned toward the pie. "I need to get some air."

He didn't wait for an answer, just walked away as quickly as he could without bringing attention to himself. He flung open the doors and stepped outside. The brisk breeze hit him, and the pain in his chest lessened a little. He breathed in the clean air, so unlike the city air his lungs had grown used to. The car wasn't an option since his mom had the keys somewhere in that giant purse of hers. He laced his fingers behind his head and looked up the street. It was a tedious walk home, but he'd done it a thousand times.

Without checking to see if anyone had followed him, Brian started toward Main Street. He wanted to believe the walk would clear his head and ease his pain. But he knew better. This pain wasn't going away—certainly not today and quite possibly not ever.

Chapter 46

Brian

The familiar smells of Thanksgiving at the Hawkins house filled the air—turkey, cinnamon, honey, bacon. His mother, always the hostess even to her own children, never failed to cook a pancake breakfast while also prepping the dinner to be on the table by three. Theirs wasn't the big Thanksgiving that some families had—it was usually just the four of them. But this year, perhaps because Jess had bowed out, his mother had invited the extended family. It was the perfect opportunity for everyone to pressure Brian into making a decision about his next steps, with his uncles giving him meaningful shoulder squeezes and not so subtly shaking their heads, saying without saying that he should have been back on his feet by now. Well, if that had been what his mom had in mind, she was too late.

Brian had planned to walk straight home the day before and drown his sorrows in video games and maybe even ping Ethan for a joint viewing of *Star Wars: A New Hope*. But instead, he'd found himself wandering around town, visiting his old haunts, fighting against the pull this town had on everyone who grew up here. When he reached the high school, he sat on the bleachers for over an hour, running through every homecoming and game day and nights on the field long after the town was asleep. On that field, he'd had his first kiss freshman year, earned his varsity letters in baseball, watched a girl he could have loved walk away from him, and so much more. Every spot in this town held memories.

Brian had walked a path through his childhood and had decided his future. And then he'd told Corey. That had been his first stop after he finally stepped off the bleachers and headed back through town. Now he had to tell his mother, and then he had to tell *her*.

He wiped away the fog on the mirror and stared at the beard. The night before, he'd been sure he wanted to shave it off and start fresh first thing in the morning. Even though there were only two days left, in those hours between deciding his next move and going to bed, he'd wanted it gone. But now he could see why Sarah dyed her hair when the whim overtook her, creating temporary change. He looked like a different person. The beard brought out his eyes and made him look older. He ran a hand through it and then picked up his razor. He'd at least trim it. That would make his mom happy, and it *was* Thanksgiving. Maybe it would be good to start his new life with a new look. He could be whoever he wanted.

"There you are," his mother said when he entered the kitchen ten minutes later with a closely trimmed beard. She patted his cheek. "And there's that face I love."

He rolled his eyes. "You could still see my face before."

"Barely."

"Love you too, Mom."

She placed a short stack of pancakes and too many pieces of bacon in his spot at the kitchen table. "Happy Thanksgiving."

"Happy Thanksgiving." He poured himself a cup of coffee and then took a seat. The vanilla aroma of his coffee—his parents' flavor of choice—mixed with smells of breakfast to create the complete sensation of home. Today, he could appreciate it. "Where's Dad?"

"Out front, futzing with the scarecrows again."

"Can you call him in? I have something to tell you both."

His mom's eyes widened and then immediately sank to her feet. "It's St. Louis, then. I at least thought you'd stay in Philly with your sister."

"I don't think Jess wants me there."

His mom looked at him with discerning eyes, and it occurred to him only then that she might know the truth. "That may be, but it's your life. Sometimes that means making messy decisions."

Oh yes, she definitely knew. "Well, fortunately, I had an easy one available to me. New city, great job, a chance to start over."

"As long as that's what you want, dear." She turned her back on him and poured herself another coffee. "It's so quiet in this house without Sarah, don't you think?"

"Real subtle, Mom."

She shrugged and grinned into her coffee. "Moms don't have to be subtle. It's our right."

"Jess told you?"

"No. You did. Every time we talked, you were with her. When I'd video chat with Jess, I would hear you two laughing in the background. I have social media."

"Most of those photos were fake. To help her make her ex jealous."

"They may have been posed, but I don't believe they were *fake*."

He shifted in his seat and pushed his plate away from him, his stomach turning at his mother's words. "Well, I'm moving to St. Louis, so it doesn't really matter."

He pulled his phone out of his pocket as if an important message was coming in. He held it up, and his mom just rolled her eyes and watched him exit the room. The phone wasn't buzzing, but there was a notification on it. From Hannah. Thank God his mom hadn't seen that. She'd never shut up if she did. Like she'd said, it was her right to not be subtle, and she had many feelings about how his relationship with Hannah had ended.

He opened the text, already knowing what it must be about. One coffee shop visit did not put him back on Hannah's Thanksgiving text chain. *Happy Thanksgiving. This is Leonard's direct number. He's expecting her call.*

He stared at the ten digits that followed in a separate text. Hannah was trusting him with this number. She'd pulled a connection because he'd asked, and now Sarah would get to fulfill Chris G.'s wish.

Thank you, he typed back. The words felt inadequate.

He's happy to do it. There was a pause as the three dots appeared and then disappeared and appeared again. *Have a piece of your mom's rhubarb pie for me.*

He pocketed his phone and headed back to the kitchen, where his mother was flipping new pancakes. His father leaned against the counter near her, eating a sausage link. There was an ease about them—always had been—but he noticed it now in the way his dad leaned in and in the curve of his mom always toward him. There was a warmth in their eyes that was only for each other, a crooked half smile that Brian only ever saw on his dad when his mom was in the room. He could have loved Sarah like that. He probably already did if his mom had seen it in a few social media photos and thirty-second snatches of video.

Brian sat back down and pulled his plate toward him. He sipped his coffee, which was still blessedly hot. He would enjoy the day. He would endure the extended family and eat his weight in pie. And then tomorrow, he'd return to Philly to say a final goodbye to the love of his life.

Chapter 47

Sarah

It had been a good day. After she'd given in and called Brian yesterday, and he hadn't answered or called her back or even acknowledged her existence, she'd almost canceled her plans to go to Maggie's. But she'd rallied. It was his right not to talk to her. And what would she even have said if he answered? Nothing had changed. Except maybe her. But he was hurting, too, and it was her stupid promise to Jess—and his ridiculous act of what he probably thought was chivalry—that was keeping them apart. She'd still woken up in tears, as she had every day since he'd left, but then she'd powered through and gotten to Maggie's, and there hadn't been time for moping. The Clairmont clan was huge. Sarah wondered if Maggie kept that large house all for herself simply because she got to host a holiday every few years. It had been stuffed to the brim with guests, even spilling over into the backyard, where a tent and table and chairs had been set up. Maggie was seriously the best hostess ever. Even a day later, sitting alone watching *The Family Stone*, Sarah felt buoyed by the clutter of Maggie's family.

Thanksgiving night had always been reserved for movies. After too much turkey was eaten and the cookies were gone, Sarah would settle in for her own Thanksgiving tradition—a viewing of *The Family Stone*. Most years, she and Jess watched the movie together from their separate homes, texting through the whole movie about their holidays and their plans for Black Friday sales. She missed her friend. Even if Jess fully forgave her and things went back to normal, she was probably moving to California. And Ryder would now be her plus-one at holidays. Where would Sarah fit in?

With Brian. The thought came to her unbidden, and she squeezed her eyes shut. She wouldn't fit in, because she couldn't bear to sit across from him at holidays and not love him.

She dabbed at her eyes. But those tears weren't for him. No, this was the sad part of the movie, after all. She sniffled. *Dammit.* Stupid sad movies.

A key sounded in the door, and her heart leapt into her throat. Jess was gone through the weekend, which meant... Brian. She swallowed hard, forcing down the panic in her chest. If he walked in that door, she'd never be able to resist. She would literally jump into his arms and beg him to—

The door swung open, and Jess entered. Her hair was a mess and her expression frazzled. Sarah jumped to her feet for a different reason now.

"What happened?"

"I had to come back," Jess panted. "I... just the thought of you here all alone on Thanksgiving. I've been in traffic for hours, but I'm here." She held up a Popeye's bag. "It's the best I could do this late on the holiday."

Sarah laughed, a full-belly sound that filled the apartment. Tears sprang to her eyes. Happiness warred with devastation in her soul. Her very being didn't know what to do with this. The right sentiment. The wrong Hawkins.

"Where's Ryder?"

"I left him up there."

Sarah raised an eyebrow. "What did he say?"

"He handed me the keys, kissed me on the forehead, and told me to go be with my bestie."

"He's a keeper."

"I know."

The two words hit her hard. She might never be able to hear them again without thinking about *him*. "Well, I appreciate the fried chicken, but there's leftovers in the fridge. I mean, you knew I was going to Maggie's."

"Yes," Jess said, stripping off her coat and pulling Sarah down next to her on the couch, "but that's not family." Her best friend gave her a sad smile and a look that said she had more to say. Sarah waited, but nothing came. Jess just picked up the remote and motioned toward the scene frozen in place on the screen. "What part were you up to?"

Sarah glanced at her friend, who obviously already knew the answer to that question, but couldn't read her expression. Anger brewed in her gut at the all-too-familiar feeling. When had they started hiding things from each other—and why? She knew why she'd lied about Brian but not why Jess had made her make that promise in the first place. There were too many questions rolling around her mind, and her mother's retort that Jess was being a bad friend, not the other way around, compounded her anger because she was starting to believe it was true. Sarah had given up the man she loved, and Jess was still keeping secrets. Not to mention that Jess might very well be leaving to *follow her own heart* with a guy she'd kept secret for three months.

"Why did you make me promise not to date Brian?"

It came out more accusation than question, but she supposed that was the truth of the matter. Sarah *was* angry. She was terrified of losing everyone, but more than that, she was pissed that there'd ever needed to be a choice. Because there was no going back. There'd be no more holidays or family weekends or any of it. She couldn't bear it if he was there. And she couldn't bear it if he wasn't.

Jess didn't answer. She fidgeted with the remote and stared down at the Popeye's bag. Sarah wondered if her friend would really have the gall to not answer her. Part of Sarah wanted that to happen, because then she'd walk out that door and not look back. She'd find Brian, and that would be it.

As if sensing this shift in her, Jess grabbed her hand. "My freshmen year of high school, Brian started dating a good friend of mine. Not my best friend but one I'd known for most of my life. They were together for two years, and we got really close. I thought it was awesome—you know, that it made us like sisters. Except when he went off to college, they broke up. Junior year, I had to find a new lunch table. I stopped getting invited to things. I had my own friends, so I wasn't like a social pariah or anything. But basically, she got close to me to get to Brian, and then when she was done with him, she was done with me. I promised myself I wouldn't let that happen again, so when I went to the same college as him, I decided to be proactive."

Her explanation didn't make it better. Sarah would never have done that. And Jess, of all people, should know that. "I would never do that to you."

"You might." Jess's hand slipped from hers. "What if it didn't work out? You have never stayed friends with an ex. You could barely stand to be in the same room as Flynn when you broke up junior year. And look at you and Tyler. What would that mean for us?"

"If you don't know by now that our friendship can survive anything, me dating Brian or not is not going to be what breaks us apart."

"I came back for you," Jess said, her voice weak.

Sarah clicked off the television and stood up. "No, Jess, you're the reason I was here alone in the first place."

"You betrayed our friendship. Was I just supposed to let you spend the holiday with my family like that hadn't happened?"

"No. *You* betrayed our friendship. I might have lied about what was happening with Brian. But it was happening in the moment. It's not like I was actively dating someone for three months and going on trips with them in secret like you did with Ryder. What if something had happened to you or if he hadn't been a nice guy? I wouldn't even have known who you were dating."

Jess opened her mouth to respond, but Sarah plowed on. "When you first asked about Brian after the gala, I didn't even know what to say. I thought I had shut it down. But more than that, I never should have felt like I had to lie. You could've told me that story about that teenage witch ages ago or anytime in the last few weeks. Instead, you tried to trick me into telling you about Brian. And then you trapped him and, by extension, me. You kicked your own brother out of the house for *loving me*. You *broke* my heart. And why? Because you were scared I would love him more than you?"

"That's not fair."

"None of this is *fair*, Jess." She stalked away but stopped outside her bedroom door. "The saddest part is, it isn't even a competition. My love for you has nothing to do with loving him. They are two completely separate sides of my heart. And after everything he went through last year, he was finally starting to be happy again, and you took that away from him for no other reason than because you could. And that's on you, not me."

Sarah slammed the door behind her, shutting out whatever Jess might try to say, and then burst into tears.

Chapter 48

Sarah

Retail therapy had seemed the perfect option, and since the mall had been open most of the night for Black Friday sales, she'd been able to get out of the house early enough to not have to see Jess. She hadn't meant to get angry and storm off. Her friend had probably sat in hours of traffic to get to her yesterday. But if Jess hadn't trapped them into exposure, or if she'd had any empathy, that wouldn't have been necessary.

Sarah pushed open the car door and breathed in the fresh air. She'd spent the last thirty minutes bathed in cinnamon and sugar and pastry. She'd stuck the triple-bagged pastry in the back seat, but it hadn't helped. Jess didn't even deserve the damn thing, but Sarah had walked past and turned back around three times before she just bought the cinnamon roll. She'd gotten herself a pretzel glazed in fabulous amounts of salty butter, but even the tantalizing smell of Auntie Anne's had been drowned out by Cinnabon.

Sarah trudged up the stairs and knocked on the off chance that Jess was nearby before fumbling for the right key. All the plastic bags wrapped around her wrist really hurt her mobility. She'd just found the key when the door opened. Jess stood there in sweats and a cami, with her mascara smudged, bags under her eyes, and her auburn hair in a messy topknot. She looked worse than when Ryder had *not* asked her to move across the country.

"Let me help you." Jess grabbed all the bags and shoved them onto the counter in the kitchen as if they were groceries. Sarah started to protest, but Jess whipped around and held up her hands. "I have to tell you something."

Sarah was surprisingly willing to hear Jess out, but first, she wanted to make a cup of coffee and unpack her Black Friday presents to herself. "Can it wait?"

Jess shook her head and thrust an envelope at her. "This was on the table when I woke up this morning."

"Creepy."

"No, just..." She shoved the paper at her again. "It's addressed to you."

Creepier.

The envelope was small, one of those ones that her mom used when she wanted to send a thank-you note to someone in town. She flipped it over, immediately recognizing the scrawl. Brian had been here. Her fingers trembled as she lifted the flap and pulled the small card out. It had to be from his mother's collection—there were innocuous flowers painted on the front and no printed message inside. In his handwriting, it simply said *Leonard Nulty is expecting your call.*

She stared at the phone number. *How did he...?* No, she knew how. No wonder he'd been shady about the details of his trip to New York. Nothing like asking your ex-girlfriend to help out your new girlfriend. Tears filled her eyes. How much he must love her to do this. Her heart ached for him—for every moment that they were missing because of this bullshit. She loved him. All the way. And these six words and ten digits proved he felt the same way.

"I'm going to find your brother, and I'm going to tell him I love him." Sarah clasped her hands together to stop the shaking, but it didn't work. She gripped the back of one of the kitchen chairs instead. "And I'm going to be with him, hopefully, forever. If I don't do this, I'm going to regret it every day for the rest of my life. And if it ends in a year or three or ten, I'll be okay with that. Because I love him now, and that's enough. I should've said this to you the other day, but I'm saying it now. I'm sorry if my relationship with your brother hurts you, but I love him with my whole heart. You have to decide if that means we can still be friends. I hope we can, but right now, I choose me. And that means I choose him."

They stared at each other, the choice between them like a living thing. Jess's mouth quirked at the corner, and then she gave a curt nod. "Then let's go."

Sarah grinned and dragged Jess toward the door, stopping only long enough for her friend to slip on shoes and grab a jacket. The instant they climbed into the car, Sarah threw it into gear. She paused, her foot still on the brake. "Did you have something to tell me?"

"Brian told my parents he's moving to St. Louis. My mom called me yesterday morning. I'm sorry. I should've told you last night, but I didn't want to upset you, but then I did anyway. So yeah, I suck."

"Did your mom call before or after you left Ryder at the proverbial altar?"

Jess giggled, but it had a nervous undertone. "After."

Well, that was something at least. "I knew. I mean, he told me when... Well, I thought he was bluffing." She pulled out into traffic. "Did your mom say if he took the job yet? Like, officially?"

"No, just that he turned down the job in Fairford."

"Fuck." She thrust her phone at Jess. "Call him. We need to find him."

"He's not answering, but he wasn't, like, on his way to the airport. He still has to give his notice and find a place to live."

Sarah muttered another curse and then made a turn. She wasn't sure if Ethan had moved yet, but if Brian was in town, that was where he'd be. She'd have to risk it. If Ethan had moved, there was a one percent chance that Tasha was at home and not at Starbucks.

"Plus, it's a holiday," Jess said, and Sarah relaxed a hair's breadth. It was *sort of* a holiday. "It's not like he can take the job today."

If he hasn't already accepted. "There's this magical thing called email," she hissed, "and not all companies have today off."

"So, he'll rescind his acceptance."

"And do what?" Sarah barely kept her hands on the wheel as frustration bubbled out of her. "He can't turn down an awesome job to stay in Philly for me and work part-time as a barista! Do you know how long he's been looking for a job?"

"Yes."

Out of the corner of her eye, Sarah saw her bestie shrug. *Shrug!* She tightened her grip on the wheel. They'd find him. She'd spill all her emotional baggage at his feet. It would be fine. It *had* to be fine.

Jess put a hand over hers on the gear shift. "I bet he would do it anyway."

"You are not helping, Jessica!"

"Then what would you like me to say?"

She turned down another street, and there, finally, was Tasha and Ethan's building. She pulled up next to the line of parked cars and slammed Betty into park. "You stay here."

Without waiting for Jess to get into the driver's seat, Sarah jumped out of the car and sprinted into the building. She slammed her finger into the elevator button until it dinged, and the doors opened. Nervous energy coursed through her. Her hands shook at her sides, and her foot tapped along to the beat of the song playing in the background. Her stomach roiled.

"Come on," she mumbled as the elevator passed the fourth floor. She didn't even wait for the doors to fully open on the fifth floor before she took off, counting the rooms until 509 was in front of her. She hesitated for just a moment—there could be a poor unsuspecting stranger on the other side of the door. But she didn't think there was. It hadn't even been a week since game night. She knocked, fast and hard. Nothing. No padded footsteps, no video game sounds pinging behind the door, nothing.

She knocked again, leaning her forehead against the door. "Where are you?"

Sarah walked the two doors to what she hoped was Tasha's apartment. Ethan was probably spending his day sprucing up his new place, but Tasha was most certainly working, considering that Brian was supposed to be away the whole weekend, not wandering around Philly, using phone numbers as love letters. She knocked half-heartedly. The door swung open, and Tasha stood there in her pajamas, glasses hanging off the end of her nose—Sarah had forgotten it was still early since she'd been out shopping at five in the morning.

"Dear God. First him, now you?"

"He was here?"

"Yeah, like, an hour ago, I think? What time is it?" She glanced at her wrist, but there wasn't a watch there. "Gave me his two weeks' notice before eight on my day off."

Sarah's heart hitched. Official or not, he was setting up for a change. She swallowed. "Do you know where he is now?"

"If he's not next door, then I have no freaking idea." She pushed her glasses up higher on her nose. "He said something about wanting to say goodbye. I assumed he was going to you."

She wanted to push more, but she could see that Tasha was getting annoyed, and she didn't blame the woman. Tasha hadn't asked to be in the middle of this drama. "He left a note for me with... well, I guess, a parting gift." The panic in her voice rose with each word, and she couldn't quell it. "I can't let him leave. He has to know..."

Tasha put a comforting hand on her arm. "I really don't know where he is."

Sarah nodded and said her goodbyes. Slowly, she turned from the apartment, walked back to the elevator, and rode it down. She stepped out into the brisk morning air, the first of her fresh batch of tears falling. She had no idea where he might be. This had been her guess. He didn't have a favorite spot in the city that he'd mentioned. He always seemed most happy on the couch with Chuck.

Jess stood outside the exit, the keys to Betty clutched in her fist. Her eyes met Sarah's tear-filled ones, and she pulled Sarah in close. "I'm so sorry. This is all my fault."

"It really is," Sarah said, half laughing, half crying.

"It's just I told you I might be moving to California and then, like, not a week later, you were all chummy with my brother. I wasn't even gone yet, and you were replacing me."

"I could never replace you."

"But that's what it felt like. You just moved to the next available Hawkins. And you two were so obvious and happy, and Ryder was so far away. And then that night..." Jess wiped at her tears. "I found out while I was at my work retreat that I was passed on for a job in California. I wanted to tell you, but you two didn't have time for me. You didn't even miss me, and you were living in *my* apartment. I just lost my mind."

Sarah refrained—barely—from saying that it wasn't Jess's apartment but *their* apartment as she paid rent. "It's okay."

"No. It's not okay. I was cruel to the both of you, and now my brother is leaving another city because of another girl, and you might lose the love of your life."

"The love of my life." That was what he was. *Of all the people to say it first...*

"I was upset, not blind, Sarah. You two were about as subtle as Chuck when he wants to eat."

Sarah sighed. "I didn't mean to bite your toes."

"I know." Jess heaved a breath and ran a hand through her hair. "And I know if I had just told you the moment I knew what was happening with you two, none of this would've happened. And it's not an excuse, but I hate long distance. Like, fucking hate it. And I can't get a job, and oh my god, I sound like my brother."

"Move to California with or without a job. Go be with the love of *your* life."

"I might, but Ryder's also been interviewing back on the East Coast."

"He really does love you."

"Yes, he does. And Brian loves you. I didn't see it at first. Or I didn't want to see it. But he... He walked away so that you wouldn't have to choose. And you were right. I shouldn't have ever put you in that situation or thought I knew better than you what you felt in your heart. I didn't want to lose you, and then after all those things you said last night, I realized I lost you anyway." Jess sniffed, and Sarah could see the tears building behind her eyes. "We have to find my brother and fix this. Where do you think he is?"

She squeezed Jess's shoulder but couldn't find words. She couldn't absolve Jess of the pain she'd caused, but she wasn't going to hold it against her forever. There was clearly a lot for all three of them to work through. She turned her thoughts to Brian and where he might be. She thought of what she might do if she was leaving Philly—what spots she might visit to say a final goodbye. There were so many. But Brian wasn't saying goodbye to a city—he was saying goodbye to her. She tugged her phone out of Jess's coat pocket. No missed calls. No texts. She navigated to her recent calls and tried him again. The phone rang before a click signaled that someone had picked up.

"Brian?" she half yelled.

"Hey, Sarah, it's Ethan. Hold on. He's just in the middle of re-assembling my dining room table."

There was a shuffle, and then Brian's voice—rich and familiar and not the sad one she'd memorized from their last en-counter—filled the line. "Sorry I missed you before. I was dragging a couch up the stairs."

"Did you pivot?" The joke fell easily from her mouth as if she hadn't spent the last week crying over this man.

"Unfortunately, no. Hence the delay in returning your call." There was a pause, and she could hear him moving, most likely outside, based on the background clatter. "Listen, I—"

"I need to see you."

He stuttered something unintelligible before clearing his throat. "Is everything okay?"

"Just meet me at the Art Museum?"

"Sure. Give me a half hour or so. Where will you be?"

She clutched the phone tighter. He was coming. He was still here. There was still time. "You have to ask?"

"No," he said, his voice gruff. "I'll see you soon."

She hung up and turned to Jess. The smile died on her lips. Her friend was pale, tears still running down her cheeks. She stood just out of Sarah's reach.

"You're not coming with me."

Jess shook her head. "This is your moment. You chose him. You risked our friendship to choose him. He deserves to see that." She pointed down the street. "Betty's around this corner at the parking garage, third floor."

Without another word, Sarah took off down the street at a run.

Chapter 49

Brian

Five miles had never felt so long in his life. He'd walked that far through his hometown on Wednesday afternoon, and it had felt faster than this damn bus ride. The first thing he was doing when he got settled in St. Louis was buying a car. He was sick of public transportation. Perhaps it was a good thing he wasn't going back to New York—sentiments like that would get him kicked out of the city.

The Art Museum was finally in sight. His stomach hadn't stopped churning since he'd hung up with Sarah. "I need to see you," she'd said. He couldn't help but wonder why. And then his sister had texted him the most innocuous thing ever: *We should talk after...*

What the hell? He'd sent her back a series of exclamation points and question marks but hadn't received a reply. Brian mentally scrolled through all the times he and Sarah had been together. They'd been safe every time. So it couldn't be that. Right? It had barely been a month since Halloween, so it would have had to have been...

No, he was not going to go down that path. The bus would stop at the museum in a minute, and Sarah would tell him whatever she needed to tell him. And it would be fine. Whatever *it* was.

He stood, itching to be off this crowded bus. Shopping bags brushed at his ankles as he moved toward the front doors. Then finally, finally, the bus stopped, and the door swung open. He practically jumped the steps to get onto the street. He jogged toward the base of the Rocky Steps, searching between the loiterers for her familiar chestnut hair. Unless she'd already erased that tie between them and gone back to pink or blue or whatever color helped him vanish from her memory. He scanned the small crowd again, and his eyes alighted on her sitting on a stair, chin resting on her hands. She waved as he approached, the tiniest of smiles brightening her face. His whole body went warm and then cold and then warm again.

His heart raced toward an unachievable finish line as he closed the distance between them. "Hey, Chestnut."

She grabbed his hands and tugged him down next to her. The touch set his blood on fire. He winced but let her keep her hold on him. "Thank you for whatever you did to get me that phone number."

His heart slowed down a notch. The note. That made perfect sense. "It was nothing. I didn't even do anything."

"I know you must've pulled a connection you didn't want to pull. Don't deny it. It means a lot to me."

A flush crept up his cheeks, and he looked away. He took in the pedestrians and the city view and the beauty of it all, and his chest ached with the weight of a goodbye he didn't want. "Well, Chris G. deserves to get his wish even if his taste in music is lacking."

She squeezed his hands, her eyes wet. "Listen, you can't go to St. Louis."

He'd known the moment he told his mom about his decision that she would tell Jess. He'd hoped that despite his sister's anger, the information would work its way to Sarah. Not that it would be news to her, but now it was official. She deserved to know that even though he knew she wasn't going to protest. Not after she'd let him walk out of the apartment that morning. Yes, he had forced her hand, but she had let him leave. Still, he'd been counting on the two weeks' notice he'd given Tasha to give himself time to come up with a way to say goodbye—to avoid this desperate rush to the one spot he didn't want to be with *her*.

"I have to go. I can't stay here and not be with you. The weight of it is too much to bear," Brian said, opting for the total truth. There was no point hiding it—he was running.

"So don't."

"I just told you—"

"I love you, Brian. I want to be with you and only you for the rest of time. I want game nights and *Star Wars* marathons. I want Zumba Wednesdays and our own apartment and a little dog that you carry around in a man purse."

He grimaced. "Really? A dog?"

"What would you prefer?" she asked, the slightest edge of mock annoyance underscoring her words.

"An orange-and-white tabby named BB-8."

She rolled her eyes but smiled, all happiness and teeth, just like he'd hoped. "Fine, we'll get an orange-and-white tabby named BB-8. Just please, don't go to St. Louis."

"What about my sister?"

She shook her head. "Are you listening to me? I. Love. You. No one is going to stop me from being with you. It took some yelling, but your sister accepts that. Now, will you please stop being an idiot and just say you'll stay?"

He laughed through his tears. Another day, he'd get that story. But the details didn't matter. Sarah loved him. His world righted itself. The ache that had taken up residence in his whole body receded until there was only joy. He pushed to his feet and then extended his hand and pulled her up next to him.

"Tell you what..." He embraced her, leaning in so close her hair brushed across his face. "I'll race you for it."

A mischievous glint came to her eyes, and she surveyed the length of his body. Their eyes locked. *Damn*, he loved his woman. She looped a finger through his belt loop. "And what do I get if I win?"

He wrapped his arms around her, keeping her close while also feasting on the sight of her in all her teasing glory. He never thought he'd get to see that smile again. "Forever."

"And if I lose?" she asked, nipping at his bottom lip.

He held her face and brought his lips to hers. "Forever."

Epilogue
Sarah
Nine Months and Twenty-Four Days Later

"What are you doing?" Sarah leaned against the doorjamb of their bedroom, watching Brian's fingers fly over the keyboard. An orange-and-white fluffball sat on the back of his chair, its white paws kneading at his shoulder. "You are going to be covered in cat hair."

Brian held up the lint roller. "Just one more—"

"No." She crossed the room and stilled his hand. "The Wish Factory database can wait."

It hadn't taken long for Brian to become a Wish Factory volunteer after he'd decided to stay in Philadelphia. He moved into Ethan's old apartment, started his new job at Myer, and by Christmas was dressing up as an elf at the holiday party. After that, the last several months were a blur of changes, big and small. On Valentine's Day, Sarah officially moved all her stuff in. They adopted BB-8 on Brian's birthday in April. A month ago, Brian had stayed up all night helping her with the planning for this year's gala and decided Wish Factory needed a major systems overhaul. He'd spent too many hours glued to his computer since then. But he loved it, and she loved him—more every day. And here they were, running late, as had quickly become their MO.

"Yes, sorry, you're right." He picked up BB-8 and nuzzled him close before dropping him into the seat he'd just vacated. A run with the lint roller later, he held out his arms and twirled around. "How do I look?"

"Handsome as ever." It was true. Brian Hawkins in a suit was always a sight.

He kissed her, lingering too long as usual—hence the always-being-late part. "You look stunning."

"Thank you." She felt the blush creep up her neck as it did every time he complimented her. Which was often. Though she knew that this little black dress was his favorite. "You realize we don't have to dress up for the food tasting, right?"

"But it's also our anniversary."

She rolled her eyes. "It is not our anniversary."

"It's the anniversary of our first kiss. It counts."

They'd decided in a heated debate that they'd mark the start of their relationship as November 2—the night of the party they never attended. But still she'd woken up to breakfast in bed and a bouquet of mums that morning. "You're such a marshmallow."

"Only for you, Chestnut."

"Yeah, yeah." She tugged him toward the door. "We're really going to be late."

He laughed but—mercifully—grabbed his keys from the bowl by the door. Once outside, she stopped short at the black limousine sitting outside the building. It could have been for someone else, but the timing was too coincidental. And then the driver swung open the back door for her, tipping his hat at Brian.

"A limo, really? What are you going to do on our actual anniversary?"

He shrugged and followed her into the vehicle. "I'm sure I'll think of something."

Fifteen minutes later, they were not at the banquet hall. She stared up at the looming steps of the Art Museum. "We don't have time for this. The food tasting is at seven."

He grinned at her. "It's actually at eight."

What the…? "You and Maggie planned this."

"Why, yes, we did." He handed her a small bag that she hadn't noticed was already in the limo.

She peeked inside, only to find her sneakers. "We're seriously going to do this?"

"Afraid you'll lose?"

She narrowed her eyes, burning holes through the fine material of his suit. "Nope. I've been training."

Sarah followed him out to the edge of the stone steps, not caring that they both looked ridiculous in their fancy attire and running shoes. He was right—this moment meant something monumental to them. It was worthy of celebration. And in the dimming light of the day, the museum was almost as beautiful as it had been that night. Every moment was etched into her memory—his fingers in her hair, her hands on him, the searing heat of that kiss. And then, the second time they'd been here, more kissing, so different but equally heated. This was their spot. She lined herself up with the first step, running in place.

Brian pocketed his phone, where he'd probably been typing more code, and stepped up next to her. "On three?"

She grinned. "One."

"Two."

"Three." The number had barely fallen from her lips before she was sprinting up the stairs. She didn't stop to see where Brian was as she ran, the air rushing past her and her breathing the only sounds she could hear.

She crested the last step, victorious, and stopped dead in her tracks. Her eyes scanned the small group assembled there. Jess and Ryder. Her mom. The Hawkinses. Ethan and Tasha. Maggie, Leigh, Jace, and Tessa. Each group held up a sign, hand-painted and glittery. She read them, her heart pounding and not from the run up the steps. "I donut know what I would do without you." "I forking love you." "Yoda the one for me." "I love you a latte." "Words cannot espresso how much you mean to me."

Tears sprang to her eyes as she took in all their friends and family, here in one spot. Slowly, sound came back to her in the form of footsteps finishing their climb.

"Sarah?" Brian's voice was so close behind her.

She turned carefully, afraid and ecstatic and so full she thought she might burst. And there he was, on bended knee, his heart in his eyes. He smiled at her, big and toothy, and then pulled a small box out of his suit jacket. He took out the ring, a solitaire cut diamond set into the finest of bands, and held it up to her.

She sucked in a breath, her world narrowing down to Brian and that ring and a future she'd never planned for but wanted more than anything.

He took her hand, his eyes never straying from hers. "You okay?"

She nodded as more tears fell down her face, and a half cry, half laugh escaped her. "Yes, totally fine."

"Good." He grinned. "You changed my life, Sarah. You push me to be a better man every day. And each day I wake up grateful that you chose me. I love our life together, and one year ago today, that life started right here with a kiss that knocked the wind out of me. And a few months later, also standing here, I promised you forever. Today, I'm making good on that promise."

A cheer sounded behind them. And she laughed at the shouts of encouragement from the assembled crowd.

Brian brought the ring to the tip of her finger. "Sarah Marie Webb, will you marry me?"

Her heart exploded with joy at the simplest but most amazing of questions. Words failed her. So instead, she nodded emphatically as he slipped the ring over her knuckle and nestled it in place, where to no one's surprise, it fit perfectly.

She sucked in a breath, finding her voice. "Yes!" she exclaimed, the word wholly inadequate. "A thousand times yes."

Brian stood and pulled her into him, slanting his lips over hers in a far too public display. But she didn't care. That was what they did in this spot. More cheers and a lot of applause sounded behind them, and she felt a blush rise to her cheeks.

She cupped his face. "I love you."

He smiled warmly, and it was that smile that was only for her. He covered her hand with his own, his eyes locked on hers. "I know."

Acknowledgments

Writing this book was so much fun. It was the first book I wrote while knowing I'd have a published book in the world. I loved pulling Brian out of *When We're Thirty* and seeing what happened to him after Hannah walked away from him that day. I loved building an expanded universe where all my characters lived and breathed in the same real time.

I wouldn't have been able to write this book without the help and support of my critique partner, Erica Lucke Dean. Thank you for answering every message I sent and reading every word I wrote—even when they were horrible. Thank you to my beta readers—Anne, Janet, and Jennifer. Your feedback was invaluable. A big shout out to my fictionistas in the Ink Tank—your support and friendship over these last several years has been everything, and I can't imagine navigating the writing world without you.

A special thank you to my editors, Angie and Sarah. You are both amazing and make my stories the best they can be. To Lynn McNamee, thank you for your continued belief in my books and characters. I love being part of the Red Adept family.

And lastly to my family—Tim, Hailey, and Charlie—I couldn't do any of this without you. Thank you for always supporting my dreams and being my biggest fans.

About the Author

Casey Dembowski loves to write stories that focus on the intricacies of relationships–whether romantic, familial, or platonic. Her novels focus on the inner workings of women and how everything in their lives leads them to exactly where they are, whether they like it or not.

The first story Casey remembers writing was in the second grade, though it wasn't until she turned twelve that she started carrying a battered composition notebook everywhere she went. Since then, there hasn't been a time when she isn't writing.

Casey lives in New Jersey with her family. She has an MFA in Fiction from Adelphi University, and currently works in corporate marketing communications. In her (limited) spare time, she enjoys reading, baking, and watching her favorite television shows on repeat.

Read more at https://caseydembowski.com/.

About the Publisher

Dear Reader,

We hope you enjoyed this book. Please consider leaving a review on your favorite book site.

Visit https://RedAdeptPublishing.com to see our entire catalogue.

Check out our app for short stories, articles, and interviews. You'll also be notified of future releases and special sales.